# DRINKING WITH THE COOK

Also by Laura Furman

*The Glass House*

*The Shadow Line*

*Watch Time Fly*

*Tuxedo Park*

*Ordinary Paradise*

*Bookworms: Great Writers and Readers Celebrate Reading*

(with Elinore Standard)

# Drinking
## with
### the
# Cook

Laura Furman

WINEDALE PUBLISHING
Houston

Published by Winedale Publishing Co.

Published in the United States by Winedale Publishing Co., Houston
Distributed by the Texas A&M University Press Consortium

www.winedalebooks.com

Some of the stories in this collection appeared first in other publications:
"Sunny" and "Buddy" in *The New Yorker;* "Melville's House" and "Hagalund" in
*Southwest Review;* "Beautiful Baby" in *The Yale Review;* "What Would Buddha
Do?" under the title "Shards" in *The Threepenny Review;* "The Apprentice" in
*Ploughshares;* and "That Boy" in *The Sound of Writing,* Alan Cheuse and Carolyn
Marshall, eds. (New York: Anchor Books, 1991)

Library of Congress Cataloging-in-Publication Data

Furman, Laura, 1945-
Drinking with the Cook / Laura Furman.
p.   cm.
ISBN 0-9701525-2-3   (cloth : alk. paper)    ISBN 0-9701525-3-1   (pbk)

1. United States – Social life and customs – 20th century – Fiction.
I. Title
PS3556.U745 D7 2001
813'.54—dc21   00-069318

Manufactured in the United States of America
2 4 6 8 9 7 5 3
First Edition

Book design by Harriet Correll
Jacket design by D.J. Stout and Julie Savasky

*For Susan Crile*

*For early mornings at the farm*

# Contents

# DRINKING WITH THE COOK

*Drinking with the Cook*

The dark glass was kind and, as we drove, I watched the black woods through a pure image of myself. I saw only the outline of my features, shapely holes for nostrils and eyes.

"It's a point of pride with them," Don said, "eating what Randy shoots."

"What about my pride?"

"Push it to one side and eat the vegetables. She grows them. And freezes them. Or cans them. Or something. It all tastes good enough."

Don never liked to let on just how much he cared about food, considering it fussy in a man to dwell on the subject, though in private he was more than capable of going on and on about one cut of meat versus another or the quality of a vinegar he'd never met before.

We were passing between the river and the woods. Don guided his little truck over the roads that were still rutted from the previous winter's plows and drifts. It had been a dry spring and summer, and the fall was a darkening process, absent the rains that normally made the bright leaves glow, hang heavy, and drop. When winter came, the declensions would fill with snow and ice, and would we slide into the river?

"Who lives there?" I asked as we passed a trailer, a shack, a mansion in the Federal style, probably genuine, for that's when the district began.

"The man who cuts my wood," Don said, and, "A guy who killed his wife and another man," and, "They're from the city. I haven't seen them much this year. They'd better do something about that roof. But that's their business."

He turned onto a road parenthesized by birches. For a crazy second the truck danced on two wheels. I steadied the bottle of wine on my lap.

"This is their drive," he said. "It's too close to the river."

A light came on at the side porch, shattering the image of myself I'd been admiring. In the sudden glare I saw myself startled and afraid, no beauty and aging. Dogs barked madly. I couldn't tell how many.

A voice screamed, "Calm down, you dumb bastards! Shut up, you hounds!"

"The dogs are old and toothless," Don said.

I wouldn't get out of the truck until Don held out his hand for me.

"Here you are." The voice came again, close now, and a man appeared. Randy, our host, held himself so well that I wondered if he had studied ballet and held taut an imaginary string from his tailbone to the top of his head. Because of his carriage, he might have been young but I could see from his face that he was our age. "I thought Don was going to keep you in hiding."

"I've only been here two days."

I'd met some of Don's friends over the years, but we kept to ourselves on the odd weekends I visited. I had enough of people at work, and Don could have spent every night reading, then going to bed early. He was trained as a scientist and had pretty much ignored everything else until his forties when he started reading novels. He read methodically, one author's entire body of work at a time, sometimes chronologically, sometimes as he could find the books. There were advantages to the way he read, though he complained time and again that all the writers repeated themselves. Everybody repeated themselves, I assured him. Now that we lived together he'd see soon enough.

"We've been looking forward to meeting you at last," Randy said. "Don, I need to show you that saw."

I held up the bottle of wine. "I'll go inside," I said.

"Tribute. Excellent," said Randy. "Geraldine's in the kitchen." His tone made it clear: if Geraldine were there, all was right with the world. I imagined from that one phrase their marriage, their closeness, the long seasons together.

I knocked, then opened the porch door. The screening covered with sheets of plastic made a sucking sound. The plastic was covered with dead bugs and dried leaves and had obviously been up for years. The other seasons were just the before and after to the real weather here—winter.

A path led between stacks of newspapers and cartons filled with empty bottles and jars: wine, beer, whiskey, mayonnaise. The inner door was half glass and I watched Geraldine, her skin flushed, poking something in a steaming pot with a wooden spoon. She turned her head and, seeing me, set the top back on the pot carefully, came over, and let me in.

"You must be Peggy," she said.

"I knocked," I said. "I didn't mean to startle you."

"You didn't."

The warm kitchen air was being compromised by the damp porch, and I closed the door behind me.

She was my age but gaunt, aging by getting tauter. Her hair might once have been red but now was gray and white, longer than most women her age could carry off. Only a really confident woman would have dared to look as haggard as she did. I tried to recall which aged French actress she reminded me of, then realized she resembled only herself, another point to her beauty.

"The glasses are in that cabinet," she said. "The wine's not too bad tonight."

"I brought this," I said, and set the bottle on the table next to the jug. Acceptable wine may be found in jugs, but that jug wasn't one of them.

Geraldine gave the bottle her full attention.

"That didn't come from around here," she said.

"No. The moving van seemed so handy that I splurged and bought some cases."

"A woman after my own heart. The corkscrew's over there."

The elegance of her well-used utensils and hand-thrown pottery emerged, preening themselves next to the foreign bottle. I chose glasses with stems, poured a glass for her and a glass for me. Before I could drink, Geraldine raised her glass, proclaiming: "Welcome to the county."

Fun, I thought. I was new to living in the country and everyone seemed to be playing house.

The wine hit me hard, but was only a taste to Geraldine. She filled her glass and drank it down in a few swallows, then she sighed and refilled it. "It's really nice wine," she said. "I've forgotten. We drink anything." She turned to stir the pot. She was cooking one of their own rabbits, she told me, a dish that took days, soaking and soaking to make it tender.

"I was there once," I said, looking at the wine label with its engraving of a château. "It was on a tour." The smell of the meat cooking didn't make me sick, which was a relief. I looked around the kitchen.

Though there were piles everywhere of clothing waiting to be folded, magazines, cookbooks, unopened mail, it wasn't dirty.

"How nice to be here. Don's house looked so big before I moved my worldlies in. But my drapes fit! I had my living room drapes cut down and remade to fit his windows, and it worked. The seamstress said it was risky."

"You're really moving here?"

"I have moved here. Lock, stock, and barrel."

"And you sold your pretty place? View of the river? Don said it was a great apartment. I assumed from what Don said that you'd keep your place in the city. He said you'd be consulting."

"I sold it. I can consult from here. What a funny thing for Don to say. Perhaps you misunderstood."

"Maybe I did. And what other changes are you making? I liked the windows without curtains."

"Cozier this way," I said. "You'll have to come by. I'm rearranging everything for my furniture and books. And my watercolors. Beach scenes my great-aunt painted in Oregon. He's given me the little room above the kitchen for a study. It's very sweet and once I'm organized it will be just fine. I think my things multiplied in the moving boxes. My apartment was small, so I don't understand..."

I hadn't anticipated how ill-matched our possessions would look side by side. Even my engagement book from the Boston Museum looked odd next to his phone, and my birthday book, thicker than the local phone book. It was a birthday book I'd been keeping all my life and had birthdays recorded of relatives and of friends I hadn't heard from in years. There was a time when, as soon as I liked a person, I'd record the birthday in my book. I used to send out birthday cards nearly every day.

We poured another glass. Drinking was fun with Geraldine. In the city, I had a glass of wine when I got home from work and never anything during lunch. Here, the two of us could drink the bottle and start another, and the thought seemed exciting. Garden carrots, their greens drooping over the edge of the counter, waited to be washed and peeled. Potatoes with dried clumps of dirt were piled on a heavy brown platter. Green tomatoes ripened on newspapers all over the floor, for she was trying to cheat the first freeze. I sat in the visitor's chair, drinking with the cook, inside one of those houses whose distant lights you see from the road. Geraldine, adjusting the heat under the rabbit, was part of the room and the kitchen was part of a life that seemed eternal to me. We would be friends, I thought.

At dinner I talked too much, the way you do and are aware of it, aware of the others watching and nodding, waiting to interrupt.

"I left behind all my exercise equipment. There was room in the moving van, but I thought it was crazy to bring a Nordic Track to the country."

"There's plenty of fat people in the country," Don said.

"There's plenty of fat people everywhere," Randy echoed, and he ran his hand over his flat midsection.

"What is it when you pack? You look at the past and you look at the future. The only thing standing between you and a real stripped-down life is what you want. Desire." I paused to sip my wine, the last decent sip in the house. The dinner was taking a downturn that would become familiar, my wine to theirs.

"Geraldine and I haven't gone anywhere for years. You get a few animals, a garden…We used to subscribe to *Gourmet*." Randy laughed a little harshly. "Once, early on, I came back from teaching, and there was Geraldine in tears over some little place in Rome. But what can you eat there that you can't here?"

Truffles, I thought, baby artichokes and fresh *porcini*. The sound of a language you don't understand and a life that isn't yours. I liked the letters that readers sent in to *Gourmet*, well-educated letters thanking *Gourmet* for recommending a restaurant or an entire country. I imagined each letter writer and the letter writer's mate at a restaurant pictured in the magazine, and I imagined Don and me there too, discussing which wine to order, tasting what we'd never tasted before, something fragile and local that couldn't be had back home, then swapping drafts of our letter to the editor until it was perfect.

"Can't you find someone for your animals? A high-school kid?" I asked.

Maybe they hadn't tried very hard.

"We found out early," Randy said, "it doesn't do to pay others to take care of your own burdens."

"Expensive too," Don said.

"Yes. The older I get, the greater satisfaction I find in not spending money," Randy said. "We live on a steady diet of necessity, and it keeps us trim."

"Is that Thoreau?" Geraldine asked. "Or just being cheap?"

The three of them laughed as if this were an old joke. I remembered what Don had said about them now, that Geraldine had gone to an Ivy League college and met Randy when she was working in the gift shop of a museum and he was a graduate student. Like Don, he never finished his doctorate. Randy and Geraldine bought the place when they were in their twenties, with money inherited from a maiden aunt of Geraldine's. Their one child, a boy, was grown and gone.

"Well," I said, "now that I'm free, Don and I can go anywhere we want. Italy. England. Anywhere."

Don was looking at the fireplace and the pewter mugs lined up in order of size on the mantel. He hadn't changed since the boyhood photos I found the few times I'd searched his desk drawers for stamps: Don on a pony, Don on a bike, Don standing with an aunt or older cousin, someone he no longer could name. He was a stocky, blondish man with a slightly crooked nose whom women liked because they thought he was steady. His hair was graying, making his eyes look bluer. Last year grooves appeared in his cheeks. I wanted to take his arm and say, *Let's go home,* when I realized that he was completely at home and it was I who felt out of place.

Winter would not arrive for months, even if the Thanksgiving snow came on schedule, but the time was over for sitting on Don's porch in my nightgown and watching dawn over the valley. Don taught science at a boarding school about thirty minutes away. That was how he'd met Randy, who taught history there. Don had a Masters in biology, and they had him teaching everything but math and computer science. Nowadays my company was laying off Ph.D.'s by the bushel. I'd been there from the beginning and ended as second to the head of Marketing, but if I were starting now, they'd never hire me. Recently the new headmaster at Don's school had hired a young man with a Ph.D. to be the senior science teacher. I'd scrutinized Don for signs of resentment but found only relief. He had an easier job now, he told me, getting the students ready for someone better than he while opening their minds to science. He even enjoyed supervising long afternoon labs when he might have been home relaxing. Unlike many other teachers, he never tired of the inevitability of the school year or of the young students.

Don conceived of science as a shield, principles by which anyone might live better. One principle had to do with sticking with what could be proven. To him, love was an abstraction not to be defined or even much considered. To me, the atom was an abstraction, no matter what I knew about Los Alamos or Hiroshima.

On a November afternoon, weeks after the dinner at Randy and Geraldine's, I was still settling in to my study above the kitchen, trying to find a place in the tiny closet for my clothes that had to be on hangers. There weren't many closets in Don's house, and my clothes were all over on the little bed and desk. Don's few city clothes were all folded in his big chest of drawers, and I recognized the white shirts, hand-ironed, that had so touched me when he came to me for a city weekend. My clothes had to go somewhere or I'd never have a place to pay bills and write letters, or to stack my new books, all the art history and biography I'd listed for the past few years in a special section of my day runner. When I was offered early retirement the first thing I thought of was all the books I would read. Would a day be full enough if all I did was read and prepare a few meals, maybe force myself to take a walk? That was how I saw my life at Don's before I came. So far, I had not had a day to read because something always came up. I'd sent away to a wonderful garden bookstore around the corner from my former apartment, for a book on landscaping on paper. I was determined to draw the entire area around the house.

I had a box of files to put away that I hadn't been able to part with, though I'd rid myself of tons of bank statements and 1040s, paid bills, and a year's worth of catalogues I'd marked because I'd thought one item or another might make a good present. There was a time when I'd ordered Christmas presents in August when the catalogues had so much on sale, but now there were fewer people to buy for—my last living parent was dead, my brother clear across the country and we'd never been close. I'd long ago dropped the annual ritual of buying for my nieces and nephews, complete strangers to me now, for I knew only that they were around the same age as my daughter. I still sent her presents and received thank you notes on her monogrammed stationery. She'd married awfully young but then so had I. The last time I saw her was at her wedding where I was treated like a maiden cousin no one quite remembered and no one quite forgot. She was registered at Tiffany's. I gave her a silver serving fork. She was the sole beneficiary of my estate and in time would get much more.

I flew to her city with only a carry-on bag, arriving the morning of the wedding and pretending I had a plane out right after the reception, though I spent the night in a hotel near the airport. I didn't want to embarrass her or her father or stepmother, or, naturally, myself by demanding their company. The decision I made, to give her up, was final and I honored its finality by sending only a card and a conventional little present for her birthday, money for confirmation and graduation. No more and no less than a distant relative would. She was six months old when her father and I divorced. He wanted custody, and she was ten months old when he remarried. I trusted him to find someone quickly and he did, and it worked out. I had the life I wanted, my work and my independence, and, as things developed latterly, I also had Don.

I could have stayed in the city, I might even have found other work, but I couldn't face a whole other job. The thought of meeting a new set of people, learning the routines, the alliances, where I might fit, filled me with fatigue. My retirement package gave me enough to live nicely. I didn't want to stay in the city unemployed, inventing every day where I had been so occupied.

When we discussed my moving to the country, Don said, "If it's what you want. I wasn't planning on changing things, you know. I like them as they are. Of course, eventually, I suppose we would have had to come to some decision." And so he agreed by not disagreeing, the way he had for years when discussions of our future rose between us like early morning fog.

I heard someone downstairs. I looked out the window, and saw a beat-up Mercedes that had been repaired so many times that its body was like a patchwork quilt. I'd asked Don several times if there was someone who could build bookshelves for me, and maybe he had sent someone. But when I got down to the kitchen, the pantry door was open and I could hear glass jars clinking.

"Yoohoo!" I called out.

"Oh. Hello," Geraldine said. Her hair was pulled back with a faded yellow ribbon. I wondered if it was cut from the yellow ribbon

Randy had tied around a big maple for the MIAs or the soldiers in the Gulf. "I didn't think anyone was here. Just checking on Don's supplies."

Don's shelves were filled with glass jars in orderly rows of home-canned vegetables and fruits, jams and preserves. The jars were marked in an unfamiliar hand with the year. Now I guessed the hand was Geraldine's.

"Would you like a cup of tea?" I felt that I should offer hospitality and at the same time establish that it was my kitchen.

She checked the kitchen clock, which was shaped like a teapot, its face obscured by years of grease.

"Wine would be nice," Geraldine said.

There was a bottle open because, the night before, Don and I had a neighbor over and one thing led to another. There was plenty in the bottle but only ten bottles left to the supply I thought would last a year. We used up a whole bottle each time we went to Geraldine's for dinner and the one time they came to our house, four were gone. Randy was uncomfortable in Don's house and Geraldine had to drive home, though she wasn't much better off than he. "Randy's best at home," Don had said.

We settled down in the living room with the wine and two glasses and two ramekins of peanuts. The unexpected visitor and wine before five—wild freedom. Geraldine was in Don's chair. The way I had the living room, I could look up from my reading chair and see Don in his. Don read very slowly. Once in a while he turned back a few pages as if he'd forgotten what he was reading and had to start all over again.

"Before you came," Geraldine said, "I used to keep an eye on Don. You know. A man alone."

"And are you keeping up the service?" I asked. It was just as well that the bottle would be finished. You can get away with using turning wine in cooking but why do it? You can get away with so many things. "I didn't realize the supplies replenished themselves. The sorcerer's apprentice! I thought we'd finish what was there and then have our own. Once my gardens get going."

She shrugged. "Suit yourself. Don likes the stuff, and God knows I have an abundance."

"You're so accomplished, Geraldine. Where did you learn to do all that you do?"

"Books," she said. "The library. And pamphlets from Ball jars. Are you interested in canning?"

"No," I said. "I love fresh things. And you can get salt-free canned tomatoes already diced and peeled in the supermarket."

"But they're not your own."

"I don't feel possessive about tomatoes."

"Not a good summer for tomatoes," Geraldine said. "When you use up the jars in your pantry, that's all you'll get."

I waited for her to confide in me. Women always did at work. You are suspect if you're unmarried, and so I quickly told new women at work about being divorced and Don, and I knew they felt sorry for me because I had no family and saw Don on the weekend and not even every weekend because I liked my every other weekend at home, time to catch up, time to rest. Then they'd tell me their stories, more than I ever told them. Geraldine sipped her wine and looked out the front window.

"I'm cleaning up the yard," I said. "Little by little, to make a big herb garden in the spring. In Italy they have hedges of rosemary."

"This isn't Italy. Our winters are more severe."

"Oh, well," I said. "The most I can do before winter is dig the beds. It'll look practical, like a Victory Garden."

"Wise of you," she said, "to take things slowly."

Truth to tell, I was missing not only my few real friends but, even more, the kind of easy company I had at work. At night, Don had papers to mark and he'd had enough talking at school all day. I'd gone to church a few Sundays (without Don) but hadn't liked the look of anyone there.

"How's Randy?" I asked.

"He's perfecting his game. There's a bar in Schuylerville with a pool table. He spends his afternoons there."

"Doesn't he have classes?"

"Mornings," she said. "Randy says that teaching is the last civilized job in the world. It doesn't cramp his style during hunting season. Or pool season."

"We had someone like that. He worked when he wanted because he was so brilliant that he didn't need to spend all day like the rest of us." He'd been with the company since it started. Toward the end, even when other people were getting laid off, his position was secure. Was he still there, I wondered.

"And what did you do? Before you became a consultant."

"Marketing," I said, and then explained my job to her because most people don't understand what marketing is. Her eyes wandered. She took in the changes in the room. I'd repositioned the couch so that there was room for my favorite armchair by the reading light, and I'd added the drapes to the windows. During the day I kept the drapes pulled back but at night closed them or the black glass caught us in startled postures as we passed the evening reading, waiting for sleep. My framed family photographs mingled with Don's on the table by the telephone, and an oil portrait of my mother hung over the mantelpiece. Don liked the painting. I didn't remember my mother ever looking so young or soft mouthed, but I agreed that it did something for the room.

"What will you do," she asked, "now that you're here?"

She was sitting in Don's chair and the light behind her put her face in flattering shadow. When women age, it doesn't matter if they maintain their thigh firmness, glowing skin, cover their wrinkles.

What matters is how they've spent their time. Geraldine was not a woman at peace.

"Gardening. The house. When I worked, I spent my vacations with Don. Here. Now we'll travel."

"I see," she said. "I didn't know Don liked to go anywhere."

Geraldine had traveled in England before she was married, and she told me all about Cornwall, and Virginia Woolf's lighthouse and a little stone cottage she'd seen once on a hill, nothing left to it but walls. She'd been to Paris, too, and Rome and Florence. She'd skied in the French Alps and sunbathed on the Riviera. She said she didn't care to go back to Europe and that the Third World was out of the question because she disliked being made to feel rich. As for the United States, well, she'd been to California and it seemed wrong that a person should be able to go from mountain to beach so easily. She pointed out what a long drive it was to the Cape from where we lived. "That gives you time to make the transition," she said. The South was a total loss to Geraldine. Her mother's family was from Mississippi, not even the good part of Mississippi, and she had been dragged to a small, flat town every summer of her childhood. Geraldine never intended to go below the Mason-Dixon Line again. I wondered if the money she used to buy her house and land came from Mississippi.

I also wondered if I bored her which meant I probably did.

I opened the second bottle of wine without thinking about it, which is what drinking will do for you. Geraldine had another few glasses. She didn't drink for fun, one glass at a time, but like a woman at work. I'd seen her doctor a morning coffee with something to get her going. A sherry before lunch, wine with. It didn't matter how much she drank. Our conversation was the same. I held back and so did she.

She stayed so long that she just missed Don. From the kitchen window I saw their headlights pause, blend, then pass on the road.

. . .

It was nearly Christmas before I was used to the rhythm of my days at Don's. I became so acclimated to my country solitude that it was a chore to pull myself away from home to go into town to shop for food or whatever else we needed. Each morning crisp and clean, not heartbreaking the way spring is but touching. So much beauty and for what? To pass unobserved.

Don's house sat above the road in the brow of a hill. His driveway was a paved county road that dwindled a few yards past his house into a dirt lane, and I chose this ancient route for my morning walk. During a few winter visits Don and I had skied up into the woods, our tracks crossing the delicate trails made by rabbits and deer. The lane was deeply rutted by deer hunters' trucks from years gone by and the ruts were filled with leaves. I wanted to write a message on a leaf the way you put a message in a bottle and throw it to sea. A few times on my morning walk I heard other footsteps but found no one there. Once I looked up to see a cow at the edge of the trees where a neighbor's field began. She stared at me indifferently, chewing her cud.

It was on a morning walk that I decided it was time to plan our first trip. Don's school ended early in May. We might go to London where Don's cousin lived. She'd stayed with me once when she was on holiday and begged us every year in her Christmas card to return the favor. We would go to Kew Gardens, to Darwin's house, and we'd visit great houses with their gardens tended by knowledgeable gardeners for centuries. Somewhere we'd find seeds for my garden. We wouldn't stay long. When we returned, the patch of Earth I'd designated as a garden and seen so clearly on paper would look about as civilized as Ngorongoro Crater. In future years, I would hurry back from our travels for my garden, as hemmed in by domestic concerns as Randy and Geraldine.

I'd gotten as far as trying to decide on actual arrangements for air fare and accommodations, as the travel agent called hotels. Don's students were always restive right before vacation, worried by visions of the long Christmas break, and he was staying quite late at school a few times in the past weeks, stopping by Randy's pool hall for a glass of wine before coming home. I couldn't imagine what kind of wine there would be to drink there. (Don had a little liver damage from a bout with hepatitis in his twenties and he never drank hard liquor. Beer made him flatulent.) A few times I'd eaten dinner before he came home but I'd grown used to company at the evening meal, and my single dinner plate looked unappetizing.

One day I went to a town nearby and bought the biggest Christmas tree the grocery store had, to celebrate my first Christmas in the country. Don had always come to me for Christmas and I'd provided a tabletop tree for us, a clever one that folded back into its box at the New Year. I had trouble hoisting the tree into the trunk of my little car, and it was only because I hailed a passing neighbor that I was able to carry the tree into the house. As it was, I sprained my back trying to wrestle it onto the stand. But I wanted it up and ready for Don.

He came home late and I was lying on the couch, a heating pad beneath me. He looked around the living room, puzzled.

"Whatever made you get such a big tree?" he asked. "How did you get it in here?"

"I thought you'd be happy," I said. "It's our first Christmas—"

"We've been together lots of Christmases."

"Not here, Don."

"No. Not here." He looked down at the coffee table where I kept my travel folders, the articles clipped from magazines and my scribblings on yellow pads and the separate folders for side trips to Scotland and Wales.

"I wish you'd never sold your apartment. I liked Christmas in the city. In your apartment."

It had been a point of contention before I moved to the country, that Don didn't like to be away from his house and so spent less time with me than I would have liked. He spent only half of the Christmas break in the city, though once he was there we had such a good time that he regretted leaving. He didn't ask me to keep the apartment and it was ridiculous to think I could afford to maintain it just for an occasional weekend. He didn't say much, in fact, when he honored our agreement that I'd move to the country someday.

"Have you ever been to Cornwall?" I asked. "It looks wonderful. The little hills, the sea."

"I hope you don't think—" he began, then he stopped and started again. "I'm afraid we're about to have a misunderstanding. I don't intend to travel with you. I'm delighted for you if you want to go but I've never liked to travel and anyway—"

"I didn't know that," I said.

"I've told you often enough." Had he? I let the heat grow to be a little much on my back as I tried to recall. No. I couldn't remember him saying a word.

"But you've never really traveled," I said. "You've been to Europe twice, but it's generous to count the trip with your parents. Once, really, as an adult, and if it rained every day in Paris.... Paris is wonderful."

"Not to me," he said. "To you maybe. I don't like traveling. I don't like being away."

"You've never gotten far enough away, Don. If you let yourself go, you'd love it."

I dropped the subject and hid my folders and yellow pad from view before Don came home. The days grew shorter and colder. I took my morning walk at dawn to get the strongest light. It was long dark when Don came home and he ate in silence. No matter what I prepared for him, he ate it as if it were the same meal. Only the length of time it took to prepare the dishes varied.

One Sunday we were reading the Boston and New York papers that I'd driven to town to get from the little store that held them for me. It opened only at eight when I'd been up for hours. I'd thought of speaking to the woman about opening earlier.

Don said, "Look. You go. There's no reason why we have to do everything together."

"Go where?"

He made an impatient sound. "On your trips. You don't have to wait for school to be over. Go now."

"I suppose that once I settle in, I won't want to leave either."

"You're free to go during the school year."

"I heard what you said, Don. I need to think, that's all. I didn't imagine traveling alone. I imagined traveling with you. It's so much richer, the experience of traveling if someone else is along. Traveling alone—I might not mind the sightseeing so much as eating dinner alone."

"I am not leaving home and going to places I don't care to be just to keep you company at dinner."

"If I traveled during the school year it would be just like the old days, wouldn't it," I said, "when I didn't live here and we didn't see each other all that often."

"We saw each other plenty. Those were good times. Don't paint them as insufficient just to make the present superior. I liked our old times."

"I did too," I hastened to assure him.

We should have said more but Don and I were never big talkers. We'd met and fallen together easily. Our life together continued almost on its own, and that was the way we liked it. Often during the day I would invent a new discussion with Don, putting forth new persuasions, but I could just as easily reply as he would. He didn't want to go. He didn't want to go with me, and I didn't want to hear him say that again.

Though I have no graphic training, I'd worked until I had Don's place on graph paper, maples, hydrangeas, and lilacs, slopes and rises marked, the driveway, the road into the woods, the wooden fence falling down in front of the barn that was really no more than a glorified garage. Now I could begin to plan my beds. A white bed, I thought, like Vita Sackville-West's, near the porch so that we could sit on accommodating summer evenings and observe the flowers reflected in the moonlight. I could imagine myself there but not Don. Maybe when I was sitting on the porch, he would be in the room behind me, reading, or maybe he would be looking at the drapes that covered his windows, though by the time the flower beds were fully established, I hoped Don would take the drapes for granted. I drew the herb garden in winter, spiky miniature shrubs peeking through the snow. I wanted to set up a drafting table to display my industry and skill but to whom? No one ever came upstairs except Don and he never entered my little study. It was my domain entirely, and in the end I gave up the idea of a drafting table because there was no room for one unless I moved out the single bed, narrower than a normal bed, one I'd had made up from posts I'd found at a yard sale one summer weekend. When I had insomnia I moved to my study so that I wouldn't disturb him. Mornings after a sleepless night, I stayed in the little bed until he left for school and then I went to his big bed and slept until I could sleep no more. My fear was that someone would call on me unexpectedly, as Geraldine had that one time, and catch me in bed when the rest of the world was at work, but it never happened. I wished there was a way to bank fear and draw on it only when necessary.

I spread my wings that first winter. Afternoons I took drives, learning roads that I hadn't traveled before. Often my tires were the only tracks in the snow. Farm dogs waited by their mailboxes, watching to see if I would slow down. I could tell from the way some driveways were never plowed that the houses were empty, and once in a while I stopped on a deserted road and studied an empty house. There was something about the landscape that promised or threatened permanence, as if once there you would not be able to leave, but people did, summer people, the man who murdered his wife; even the man who cut wood for Don's fireplace went to Florida each year after his last delivery in November. One house in particular was unusual for the area because it was painted pink. I had Don's bird-watching binoculars with me on my drives, and through them the siding looked bisque or tan. The windows were uncurtained, and looked hollow as if inside there were endless space. Without magnification the abandoned house was as pink as something out of scorned Mississippi. Most of the houses in the area were white with dark green shutters and doors, though some had red doors. The pink house looked more cozy than most, and I thought myself into it, a widow who lived alone and looked at travel folders a kind travel agent sent her and who would have loved to travel but couldn't afford it. Except one trip she was saving toward, to Ireland, which her forebears had left to come to America. My forebears were from somewhere in Latvia and I had no desire to see it. On one drive I got the idea to go to Kyoto and see the cherry trees in bloom. I would plan my arrival in the old capital in time for the full moon. The cherry trees might look like the snow when the setting sun spread and colored it an icy pink.

Often on my drives, I thought of the past, as if it waited for me still, as if I might turn up a newly plowed lane and find my work life, the old friends, and the occupied hours that tired me for my quiet hours at home. As I viewed the pristine, orderly landscapes of farms, patches of woods, clear fields, I was also seeing my apartment; inch by inch I explored each familiar drawer and closet. Once again I slept in my own bed and lay on my own couch with my view of the city sky, for I could see even that as I drove.

One afternoon I passed through Schuylerville. I'd driven through the town before—the highway winds past the school, sharply around a corner, another turn and then across the Hudson and out of town—but I'd never more than noted the bar. This time I stopped. The dusty clapboard seemed more like ribbon than wood, winding up and down across the bowing front wall of the building. Neon beer signs winked in the windows, and the place looked so dark inside I wondered if it were closed. When I stepped inside I saw that there were three or four men in the place, including Randy, who looked like a whippet among tough mutts. He was at the pool table under a light, pool cue in hand, studying a shot. At the table beside him was a half-empty mug of beer. He would nurse the beer through the afternoon to keep his entertainment cheap. A book was open on the table, face down, and I wondered why he chose to drink and read here rather than his home. He turned around and his face looked different to me, softer and younger. With the sunlight behind me, he couldn't make out who it was and I didn't want him to speak to me or to think that I'd come there to find him. In that moment I saw him fully, like a character in one of the Russian novels Don was reading: the impotent hunter. I pulled the door shut behind me. I was on my way to the dentist in Saratoga and couldn't be late.

Following a whim one afternoon I ended up at Geraldine's. We were having dinner together the next night and I thought we might discuss the menu—something Randy shot, something she grew, something I bought—and I was cold. My feet stayed cold despite the sufficient heat in my car. I was hoping that if I made a little more effort, Geraldine and I might be better friends.

Her truck was there. The dogs were shut up in the barn. I knocked at the kitchen door and when there was no answer went around to the front door, but I had no luck there either. I tried the door. It was unlocked. She wasn't in the kitchen. I followed the narrow, curving stair up to the second floor; I'd been up there before during dinner parties to use the bathroom. Past Randy and Geraldine's room was the guest bedroom, which had been their daughter's. Two dolls slumped on top of a bookcase, and pink and white half-curtains hung on the windows. The room smelled of wine; two crystal glasses of red on the bedside stand, and one of my bottles, half empty, like the old test of pessimist and optimist. Geraldine lay in the girlish bed, beneath a pink and white quilt. The pattern was tulips. Her bare shoulders showed above the quilt. I wondered if there was a cat in the room, but it was Geraldine's snoring. Above the gingham curtains, the sky was a patchy blue above the white hills, and from her child's bed she might watch an afternoon pass by the window. I was terrified that she would awaken, for how would I explain my presence? Or she might open her eyes and not see me at all. I tiptoed downstairs, closed the door behind me carefully, and drove away. It was snowing like dust, and my tire tracks, I saw in the rearview mirror, were covered over immediately. When I got home, Don was there, home early for once.

Over dinner, I tried to describe the scene at Geraldine's and how odd it was.

"She should get out more," I said. "Maybe the long winters have really harmed her."

He didn't reply, but when we went into the living room after dinner to read, he said, "Worry about your own behavior, for God's sake. What were you doing there in the first place?"

I settled in my chair and tried to decide what to tell him.

The Christmas tree was in back of Don's chair. We could never get the tree right; during the day it leaned to the left. Don fixed it each night, grumbling, but it looked rich to me. The white lights looked like stars when the room was dark; we had no ornaments but lights, though I'd brought mine with me. Christmas is for children.

The light on his chair glared on him, making his hair seem thin and of an indeterminate color. I smelled chalk dust and wine.

As I talked, trying to explain, the tree fell on Don, or rather leaned over him so that it touched his shoulder. The tree was guy-wired by its lights and it didn't do any harm, but Don jumped up and threw his book to the floor, and shouted, "Goddamit! Why did you buy such a big tree? We can barely turn around as it is with all your furniture. How could you buy such a big tree?"

"You could have stopped me," I said, "if you'd been with me. You could have advised me or shared your thoughts with me. Your wisdom. But you're gone from morning to night."

"And you! Spying on my friends! Critical! You don't belong here!"

Don was pulling his armchair away from the tree, tugging on the wires to disconnect the lights. I saw that he meant to strip the tree and I rushed forward to stop him. But I tripped. He didn't try to catch me but sidestepped and it was I who brought down the tree. A light bulb poked my eye, and for a second there was blazing light and pain. I was trapped in the tree. He didn't reach a hand out to help me, and I struggled until I was free. Without stopping for a jacket or boots, I rushed outside in my fleece slippers and only a cardigan. I started down the road, slipping on the ice beneath the snow, half out of breath and waiting for Don to follow. But he didn't. When I was past our neighbors' house I looked back. I buttoned the last button on my sweater and waited.

The lights of Don's house and our neighbors' lights were yellow but the stars that were visible through the dusting snow were a dead white, so far away that they offered no comfort, and the road stretched in two directions, no tracks to be seen, no movement at all. There wasn't a cow in a field, a dog on the loose.

Don was mistaken if he thought I would leave quietly. I would never leave. I could wait him out and Geraldine too until there was a friendship or something that looked like one.

More than once when I lived in the city, I'd had calls from people who'd been let go when the company scaled down. They wanted to have lunch. It was an uncomfortable affair, lunch with someone who was wondering why the company had kept you. They're uncomfortable enough taken out of context, these office friendships tailor-made for a time and a place. So the next time there was a call, I said that I was going on vacation or had a busy week, and after a while they caught on. I wasn't friendly with the new people. There wasn't time to build friendships with them, the daily contact for decades. I didn't have decades left. When my time came I was spared explaining to those who would stay in the world I knew, spared saying that I'd always wanted to live in the country.

The cold came up through the fleece slippers sooner than I would have thought, and reached my ankles. It took quite a while to make my way up to the house, careful as I had to be.

*What Would Buddha Do?*

For years, Gina and Ellis ate no meat. They'd given up to-
bacco and marijuana, surely cheeseburgers wouldn't hold them in
thrall. It was hard at first, but meat became for Gina a memory like
smoke. There were a hundred reasons not to eat meat and only habit
holding them to it. Gina's sister Margaret said, "I always ask myself,
'What would Buddha do?' Would Buddha slaughter an innocent
when the world's full of squash and carrots?"

One evening in the fall, Ellis came home from work and told Gina
that he'd had lunch at a barbecue place off Twenty-ninth and
Guadalupe.

"Organic brisket," he said.

"But they have red beans and rice. Salads." He'd told her once that
beef smelled like wet dog to him.

"Come on, Gina. It doesn't mean you have to."

"You're right. It's your body."

"Things change," he said.

These days when he drove to Austin, Ellis dressed in a T-shirt and jeans, not the dress shirt, bow tie, and ironed khakis he'd worn when he owned his company. Ellis was a large man, square shouldered and strong. His knees were shot from football, he couldn't straighten the pinkie on his right hand, and his middle finger looked like someone had run over it with a truck. His cheekbones were high as an Eskimo's from his Russian grandfather, and his forehead hooded his small blue eyes. When Ellis came home from work, he looked patient, as if he'd been waiting all day for his reward and could wait longer still. Some days Gina was sure that she was enough.

Gina no longer knew what she looked like. When she caught a glimpse of herself in the window of the HEB, she looked odd—hair sticking up, lipstick thrown on crooked. In the mirror at home she was herself, reddish hair and brown eyes, sharp chin and long nose, her lips like a ripe bud—but older, somewhere between herself and her mother.

Sometimes during the day, Gina forgot about Ellis, as if he were dead or gone, even while she was doing his laundry, shopping for food he would like for dinner and cooking that meal—until he returned from work, and she realized he was what she had been missing, that all day she had been distracted and automatic without him. The feeling was like a firefly, a moment of illumination, a surprise to her after all was said and done. Still, before she closed her eyes, Gina dreaded sleep as if it might replicate the day she'd spent alone.

They lived in a three-story brick house on the edge of town. Their white cat roamed free, bringing home an occasional mouse or squirrel. While it wasn't living out in the country, it wasn't being in Austin with another house jammed up against yours. There were neighbors a quarter mile to the east, the Lozano family, with people coming and going and a Doberman and a toy poodle chained to a dog house in the dirt yard. To the west, the Presbyterian minister's house was close enough for Gina to hear the minister's wife playing ragtime piano in the middle of the afternoon.

The high school was across the road and during football season Gina and Ellis sat on the balcony outside their bedroom drinking beer and listening to the band and the crowd noises from the white-lit oblong. Far above the football field was the wide sky. On a clear autumn night the lights of the town were not bright enough to obscure the stars.

Their whole paradise included their house with the broad front porch, the giant pecan trees out front, along with an acre that backed onto a flat cotton field stretching as far as the eye could see. Except for the one week before harvest when the farmer sprayed his cotton with defoliant, it was perfect. In the no-man's land between their yard and the cotton field, the farmer turned his tractor, digging curved ruts that grew wildflowers and thistles. Gina had considered trying to tame it but Ellis persuaded her to be content with the evil of the day; they had enough work in their own yard.

They established peach, apple, and pear trees, and one wild plum whose white blooms were the early sign of spring. In their lawn, they discovered circular beds outlined in stone and filled with light soil, unlike the gumbo of the lawn and the cotton field. Once they uncovered the stone circles, they used them for their food gardens; working from the house and moving toward the cotton fields, herbs and lettuce, greens, tomatoes, eggplant, summer squash, sunflowers for the birds, potatoes, butternut and acorn squash, carrots, broccoli in the spring and fall. They tried to plant only what they would eat. Plenty meant enough, not waste, Gina believed. She dreaded the excess that came with each harvest.

Any day she expected Ellis to announce, *I've got the job, honey, let's pack up and move.* There was no work for Ellis in their town, some in Austin, but across the country in Vermont a small specialized company might offer Ellis what he needed. For now he worked part-time for a pair of brothers he knew in graduate school.

The Texas homestead law had saved their house and car when they went bankrupt, but they needed more cash than Ellis could make. When they lived in Austin, Gina taught fourth grade, and she had assumed that, if she wanted to, she could teach again—"Teaching's a good job in bad times," her father always said—but with all the bankruptcies, businesses closing and downsizing, teachers hung on to their jobs, and there were no vacancies in the school system. Part of the idea of moving to the courthouse town thirty miles east of Austin, was for Gina to stop teaching. Until they lost the business, she'd been able to stay home. She'd worked on the house until she felt that she'd touched every inch of it. She didn't want to go back to teaching anyway. She liked living in the town but she didn't want to see the children grow more like their parents as the years rolled along until one day she would find them with little children clinging to them in the HEB or clerking in the hardware store or fixing lawnmowers, jobs they would keep all their lives.

Gina put an ad in the weekly newspaper: *College graduate will clean your house.* Within a week she had all her days filled except the one she reserved for cleaning her own house. She had been cleaning houses for the year since the bankruptcy and found advantages to it. She was paid in cash and lived a cash life, separating her earnings into different envelopes with their purpose written in her clear schoolteacher's writing. She closed her checking account. Her Visa had gone in the bankruptcy. She felt sure that this was a new start with many advantages. She didn't have to dress up to go to work. It was a clear-cut task—dirty to start, clean to finish. The only thing she disliked was a house with too much dusting, talkative customers, and pets. Gina and Ellis kept their white cat outside. She figured that when she felt more indispensable she'd clean only petless houses and tell the people they had to be gone while she cleaned.

Ellis didn't like anything about it: the ad, the work, the fact that if they hadn't gone bankrupt she would never have been cleaning other people's houses. He remembered his parents tales of the Depression, of people being evicted from their homes, sitting stunned on the sidewalk with a few possessions, tales of neighbors and strangers staring at the evicted family, knowing it could be themselves any time. Even with all sorts of people going under (ex-governors, savings bank presidents), Ellis couldn't shake his shame. They'd gone bankrupt in a huge auditorium filled with other people who'd failed. Instead of a stern judge delineating the error of their ways, a mild-looking man stood in front of the assembled, asked if everyone's papers were correct, declared the hundreds in the room bankrupt, and left the stage. For a moment no one moved or spoke and then there was a great movement toward the exits. Ellis was at first enraged, then he laughed at himself and said that was just more of the same, expecting a big personal scene, as if his troubles were unique.

"Don't you love the house?" she'd asked Ellis one night when it seemed that finally they were back on solid ground. It was a hot night and the window unit in their bedroom groaned rhythmically. Soon they'd hinge the shutters closed. In the cold and dark they might be anywhere.

"Remember how it was when we found it?"

The family that lived in the house before them raised five children there. The last boy had gone crazy—or something—and lit his bedroom on fire. No one had lived in the house for five years before Ellis and Gina took it on.

"I remember the fire smell," Ellis said. "I still smell it sometimes when it rains."

"We changed all that," Gina said. "When I'm here alone in the afternoons, I feel the way the house sits, everything lined up and peaceful."

"It's a house. They lived here. We're living here now. Someone's going to be here when we go. Jesus, Gina, I can't stay here the rest of my life to keep the house happy."

"I'm not asking you to."

"And you can't clean houses the rest of your life."

"No. I don't suppose I could keep up the pace."

He didn't fear leaving the house, the town, the state. He didn't take the same pride she did in the fact that the house—once an eyesore—was reborn. Margaret said it was because Ellis was a man.

In the town where Gina and Margaret grew up—not so different from the one Gina and Ellis lived in now—there were nine churches. Their parents didn't go to church for reasons of their own, never made clear to the girls. From the time she was eight, Margaret wandered on Sunday mornings from one church to another until she chose one for that day. No one objected. Margaret stood in the back of the church listening quietly and she learned not to let the door make any noise as she left. A few people called on her at home, a Baptist, a member of the Church of Christ, to try to persuade her to join, but Margaret wandered until she was ready to choose. She settled on the Methodists, though she decided later that Christianity didn't suit her. Gina thought Margaret liked the wandering and the power the choosing gave her.

Gina and Ellis didn't go to church. They believed that you should do no harm to others and do good when an opportunity appeared even if it was inconvenient. Ellis didn't believe in a life after death. Gina wasn't sure. When she was with Ellis, the hereafter didn't seem important. Alone, she sometimes felt drawn to the idea of a reunion with the dead or to the comfort of floating for eternity in a dark state of neither living nor dying, like the moments between sleep and waking. Mostly she wondered at the richness of the world and of the fate that landed some people on a mountainside in Tibet and others in a town in Central Texas, one with her body, another with brown skin. Unlike Margaret, Gina didn't need to know the reason or even believe there was one.

Margaret lived now in Colorado, and the Buddhist group or sect she belonged to had taught her how to set up her own altar, how to pray, when to pray, and told her it was all right to pray for what she wanted. Ellis found this odd since he thought the goal of Buddhism was to achieve detachment and not to want, but he didn't question Margaret about it. Margaret sent Gina a picture of herself at a Pioneer Day picnic. The sect wanted to fit in and had built a float for the parade. Dressed as a pioneer lady, sunbonnet and all, Margaret looked like the old photographs of their father's side of the family, small, skinny, round-faced, and open-eyed, as if she'd never before seen a thing to match what was before her.

A few weeks after Ellis had his barbecue sandwich and Gina tasted fried chicken at a picnic, the crickets appeared.

The crickets covered the limestone walls of the county courthouse and the brick of the lawyers' offices in a mass. Only the windows of the stores around the courthouse square remained unblemished.

It was unwise to walk barefoot in their house and rare for Gina or Ellis to open a closet without hearing the scurry of stiffly jointed legs. They found crickets in the pantry and in the folds of their clothes. Gina cleaned until the house smelled of bleach, ammonia, and other deadly chemicals, but she still sensed the presence of the crickets.

"We've got to do something," she said. Ellis was home from work, settled at the kitchen table, watching her cook dinner. "These things give me the heebie-jeebies."

"Maybe now's as good a time as any," he said. "I've been thinking—"

"Okay," she said.

Lots of people left Texas every year, some of them thrilled to see the last of it. She waited for his announcement.

"Let's not back into this thing and pretend it isn't happening."

"Okay."

"I was talking to a fellow out near Maxwell. He'll sell us a pair of turkeys and a chicken for next to nothing. We'll put chicken wire around the whole back garden and the birds could eat every cricket that dared come around. Protect our perimeter."

"Then what? We eat the turkeys?"

"If we're going to eat meat," he said, "let's be responsible. Let's be conscious."

"Why the chicken?"

Ellis looked out the window as if he couldn't bear to tell her.

"Turkeys are too dumb to figure out how to eat by themselves."

"Oh, go on."

She followed his gaze. Outside, the sunflowers were blazing protectively around the tomatoes.

"That's what this fellow says. What do you think? Organic turkey for Thanksgiving."

"We won't feed them all that junk other turkeys eat," she said. "Once the crickets are out of their system. Maybe they like squash."

"If they're so dumb they need a chicken to teach them how to eat, I'll bet they love squash."

If Ellis was talking about Thanksgiving, there would be another three months without a move.

By next cleaning day, the turkeys and the chicken were installed in the back garden, penned in with chicken wire on stout oak branches and penned out of the stone garden beds by the same means. The turkeys did eat the crickets they could reach, and Gina and Ellis considered letting them loose a few hours a day so they could expand their territory while Gina was there to watch them. The female didn't gobble but the male did, and through the open upstairs window, he sounded like the continuo on a church organ.

Gina was throwing things away: work boots that were eaten up and moldy inside, Tupperware bought at a garage sale that smelled funny no matter what she did. She'd flown through the downstairs coat closet, half the kitchen shelves, and was on to the dresser in the second-floor guest room where she kept extra sets of sheets and pillowcases. She wanted only one of everything and wanted that to be perfect.

At the back of the bottom drawer was a bright yellow plastic bag. She squeezed it: tissue paper and something else. Gina opened the bag and unrolled the paper bundle. Solid against the wrinkled paper lay fragments of pottery, too many to count.

They'd been in New Mexico one summer before things went bad with the business, visiting Margaret and her boyfriend who drove them a few miles west of Santa Fe. In a dry arroyo they found a river of shards. Ted had brought them there to astonish them with the desert bloom of ancient pottery and a petroglyph of a horse on a ledge that rose above them. The sun, the thin air, the freedom of not being at home, and Gina and Ellis hunted like children after Easter eggs, calling out when they found another shard, stuffing their shirt pockets until they hung low.

It wasn't until later that it occurred to Gina that Margaret and Ted might have been appalled at their greed. By then they were back in Texas. By the time she thought of packing up the shards and mailing them back, it was too late. Margaret counted her downfall from their visit. After they left, she broke up with Ted and lost her job in the jewelry store that pretended to be a gallery. When she couldn't find another job and couldn't afford the rent on her pottery studio, Margaret moved to Durango where she had a friend. The site, if it could be considered one, was corrupted by their thievery and Ted's dumping them back there wouldn't rectify the situation. The Anasazi had made the pottery and it had been broken in their time and after, and now it was all that was left of them. Thanks to Gina and Ellis, there was even less evidence of what they'd been.

The phone rang and Gina ran downstairs to answer it.

"You sound out of breath." It was Margaret.

"I was cleaning upstairs."

"I had to move out of my friend's studio."

"What happened with your friend?"

"She just suddenly decided she needed to be alone. I mean, after begging me to move in. I always considered it was temporary. Until I got on my feet. But it's such a drag to have to pack everything up again. How's Ellis? Any news?"

"No news is good news."

"Don't you want him to get the job?"

"What difference does it make what I want?"

"Vermont's gorgeous."

"It might never happen. Hey. We got some turkeys."

"What for?"

"To be responsible. Ellis wanted the turkey for Thanksgiving. Are you coming?"

"Are you and Ellis eating meat?" Margaret asked.

"Don't worry about it," Gina said.

"Gina? Did Mom have high blood pressure?"

Margaret's voice sounded thinner and more childlike.

"Do you feel sick?"

"It's the silent killer," Margaret said.

"I don't think she had high blood pressure."

"It's hereditary, you know."

"We'll ask Daddy next time he shows up, but I don't think so. Are you coming for Thanksgiving?" She could feel herself about to tell

Margaret not to eat salt, to go get her blood pressure checked, but she stopped herself. It irritated Margaret when she fussed.

"My car wouldn't make it. Even if I could get the extra time off."

Gina considered offering to pay the bus fare. She'd given Margaret money for her taxes in August, and she hadn't told Ellis.

"I'd better get off the phone," Margaret said. "I just wanted to ask about Mom."

When Gina returned to the guest room, she rolled the shards into the tissue paper and put the roll back into the bag. To the turkey's music, she zipped the bag into a suitcase in the back of the guest room closet, refolded the sheets and put them back into the dresser, postponing all decisions for another day.

They named the turkeys, something they never thought they'd do.

"How will we eat something we've named?" Gina asked.

"Farmers do it all the time," Ellis said.

Abbott and Costello. Pyramus and Thisbe. Paolo and Francesca. Finally, Mavis after Ellis's favorite aunt who lived by herself way out west in Marfa, and Maxwell for the turkeys' home town. The chicken they called the Professor. The three birds lived amicably, sharing the corn and water provided by Ellis and Gina and the crickets sent to them, Gina wondered, by Buddha? If Buddha was in the business of approval and disapproval, he might not think much of their Thanksgiving plans but he might like the little community of birds and her service to it. When she scattered corn or brought fresh water, she noticed the color and complexity of their feathers and complimented Mavis on her wattle. The Professor was self-confident with the turkeys who were so much larger than she. The cat sometimes lay in the sun nearby to show that he was not intimidated by any of them.

It was no good thinking of the future. Snow might be falling in Vermont and darkness descending. Better to weed under the fall tomatoes, better to live in the present and not think of anything at all. Buddha would like this moment in the garden, so silent that the songbirds, the wind, the occasional cluck or gobble were the only sounds, as if Gina were not there. The big picture was anxiety. The future didn't exist, there was only this moment, pulling up a strand of Johnson grass that was trying to reach the fall tomatoes.

When Margaret was eleven and Gina fifteen, their mother died, and something stopped in Margaret, Gina knew. Before their mother died—not from high blood pressure—Margaret had been a cheerful girl who wanted to be an actress but she became shy, and lost her taste for clowning.

When Gina went to Austin for college, Margaret came to visit her every few weeks. When Gina and Ellis married, Margaret lived with them for a year so she could get adjusted to being away from home, and, since college, had come to them at Christmas and for part of the summer. Their father lived in the same town where Gina and Margaret had grown up, but he spent his time at elder hostels all over the world, sending them postcards from each new place, calling when he returned home.

Last Christmas, Margaret had come on a Greyhound and studied an Italian cookbook the whole trip. The first course at Christmas was stuffed squid sautéed in garlic and olive oil. Ellis wasn't sure he liked squid, but Margaret watched him eat every bite. She hovered, Gina thought, shedding the beam of her full attention on him as if he were a child who needed special encouragement. After her sister left, Gina realized that Margaret had treated their father with the same fearful attentiveness.

The number three was so strong—any three was her, Margaret, and their father, and any time there was three it was right after their mother's death, when no dulling by time and experience had taken place.

On Thursday Gina cleaned for Mrs. Perez at Plum Creek, a five-thousand square-foot house with floor to cathedral-ceiling windows, a collection of glass animals displayed on mirrored shelves, and a glass-enclosed Jacuzzi in the master bedroom. Dusting the fragile figurines was nerve-wracking, and the hard water made scrubbing the shower frustrating. In her heart Gina blamed Mrs. Perez and her love of shining surfaces.

As Gina and Ellis later figured it, while Gina was at Mrs. Perez's, the neighbors' Doberman got loose and headed for their yard. He vaulted the garden fence easily, and by the time Mr. Lozano came home from work and began looking for his dog, the damage was done. Maxwell was dead and partly eaten. Mavis was wounded.

Ellis had come home from work early, so it was Ellis who made the decision to save Mavis.

The vet gave Mavis a big shot of antibiotics and told Ellis, "You can kiss your organic Thanksgiving goodbye."

When Gina got home late from Plum Creek, Ellis said, "We need to bring her in next Friday. It's touch and go. She might lose her leg."

The vet's bill was more than Gina had made that day.

"Ellis. She's a turkey. We were going to eat her."

"I wouldn't eat her now," he said, "and neither would you after you take her to the vet's."

"This whole turkey thing wasn't my idea and I'm not working a day a week in Mrs. Perez's torture chamber to save a turkey's life."

"This was an emergency. It won't be so much next time. You would have done the same thing—Mavis was pathetic. The chicken's disappeared."

"The brains in the outfit," Gina said and went outside to inspect the damage. It was nearly dark out in the yard. October was half gone. Only Mavis was left among the wire circles. She lifted her head when Gina approached and her wattle shook. There was no sign that Maxwell had ever been there. Gina thought of the emptiness of a mountainside after vultures had eaten a corpse left by unsentimental Buddhists.

Margaret called one morning.

"Prime time," Gina said. "Are you in the money?"

"No."

"What's wrong?" Gina felt cautious, due at work in a half-hour, her day planned up.

"I just wanted someone to talk to. Someone nice."

Gina pulled up a stool from the kitchen counter and settled near the phone. "Has anything happened?"

"No. Nothing happens, that's the thing. You put one foot in front of the other and before you know it you're dead."

"I guess that's one way to describe life. Have you thought anymore about Thanksgiving?"

"Not exactly. Something else. I was thinking...my lease is up in two weeks. My job's the pits. I hate the stuff I sell. I feel like a thief every time I ring up a sale. And the incense and that music. I think I'm allergic to incense. I asked the owner not to burn it while I was working but he said the incense was part of the shop just like the window and the counters. I was thinking it might be time for a change. I could stay in your second-best guest room. Tell Ellis he won't even know I'm there."

Just before they went bust, they'd finished off the third floor, making it into one big room and a storage closet. Ellis had been thinking of the room as a home office but it had become a catch-all for a four-poster bed and some wooden trunks Gina had bought in flusher times.

"What about the Buddhists?"

"There's Buddhists in Austin. It's a world-wide religion, not just in Colorado. Listen, Gina—"

Money was coming.

"Do you have money for the bus?" Gina asked, to save time. *You're a patsy,* Ellis always said. *She's my sister,* Gina said, *don't you understand?*

"I'll pay it back. I swear. I'll help you clean. If we work together, we can take on more customers."

"We can?"

"Sure. We'll do the jobs in half the time, working together. So we can double the customers."

"Margaret, this is a small town. I can't take on extra people and drop them when you decide to move to Hawaii."

"Think it over," Margaret said, sounding cheerful once more. "I'm making you a great offer."

"Thanks," Gina said, "I'll think about it."


All through the long day of cleaning two houses full of children's toys and cats, Gina thought about pulling up the tomatoes and putting an end to her fall garden. The greens would last all winter, more or less, but the tomato vines were buggy, and with the days growing shorter and the temperature cooling, the hard green tomatoes would never ripen. Gina would pick them and lay them on newspapers until they were ready. Ellis hadn't mentioned moving lately. Maybe they were in for a peaceful time. He didn't like family all that much, hers or his, but this time he might not mind Margaret if she came. Sometimes it was enough for Margaret to say she was coming and then she found something to do where she was. There might be a call from her soon, guilty but excited about whatever it was she'd found to keep her in her own life a little longer.

Gina was more tired than usual that evening, driving home into the setting sun. She put the car in the garage and went around back where the sun was coating the stone beds. Native morning glories grew from tractor ruts in the no-man's land between their lawn and the cotton field, and twined through the chicken wire fences. The forgiving light made things look better than they were. Mavis raised her head. The turkey was doing much better and could hobble around the garden.

Ellis was in the kitchen, just returned from the vet.

He sat at the scrubbed oak table, looking out the window at the darkening field and at Mavis. The cat was out watching the sunset but didn't bother with the turkey, either because he was used to her or because she smelled of the vet's office. Mavis had been given a clean bill of health.

"The vet said we could eat her for Thanksgiving or anytime we wanted, but that we'd probably better wait until the antibiotics are gone. A couple of weeks."

"I'm afraid we're going to have to buy a turkey, Ellis. Or just skip it. I can't eat Mavis."

"Neither can I."

"I guess we have another pet."

"The vet offered to take her off our hands."

"I'll bet he did."

"And the cat."

"Why would we want to give him our cat?"

"I got some news today, Gina. That company in Vermont called. The guy who interviewed me."

In Gina's limited experience of job-seeking, you didn't get a phone call unless they were ready to hire you but she wanted Ellis to have the pleasure of telling the whole story.

"What did he say?" she asked.

"The position they thought I'd want has come open. They said they'd pay all moving and relocation expenses. Take care of the house while it's on the market."

"Do we have to sell it?"

"They're not paying me enough to keep two houses going, Gina. It's not IBM, it's just a small company. They're generous as it is. I didn't expect any help moving. I figured we'd be driving a U-Haul."

"So the vet will eat Mavis and kill the cat. "

"Gina."

"Margaret's coming for Thanksgiving. Things aren't working out in Colorado. She says she's allergic—"

"When?"

"Soon. She's letting me know. It could be any day. I invited her for Thanksgiving but she wants to settle here for a while and I figured that would be good for her. She wants to go into business with me cleaning houses."

He looked at her, engaging her eyes, and said, "Let's don't start this, Gina. We're leaving. This is a chance for me."

"But we don't know anyone there."

"We'll make friends."

It wasn't friends, it wasn't even leaving Texas, none of that was keeping her from being happy for Ellis and happy that they had a new chance.

"That's not it," she said.

"They want me there the week after Thanksgiving," he said.

"That's awfully soon. That's too soon for me to—"

"I know. I'll go first," he said.

"I'll stay here and pack," she said.

"The moving company will pack. That's what they're getting paid for."

"I need to get everything ready."

"Let's not take a lot," Ellis said. "I don't want anything really. Not so much as we have."

"There you go. That's what I have to do. Sort through. Decide."

What about Margaret? she wanted to ask. What about Thanksgiving? She felt the back of her throat start to swell but she breathed deep to make sure she didn't cry.

"I'll miss you," she said.

"Don't make it too long," Ellis said. "There's plenty to do when we get there."

A few days before Thanksgiving, Ellis laid his suit out on the bed and his three dress shirts. Gina picked out a few ties and he returned them to the closet and selected different ones. He'd never liked the bow ties Gina's father had given him when he retired. Ellis selected a down vest he wore on trips to Colorado and his fly fishing outfit.

"Can you fish in the snow?" she asked.

"I suppose the streams don't freeze," he said, but he looked a little doubtful.

Three pairs of blue jeans, a sweatshirt and a sweater, underpants and socks, running shoes and hiking boots, his suit, a few pairs of running shorts, khakis, and a sports jacket. While Ellis was packing, Gina watched, wordless, on the bed, her back propped up by pillows. When she tried to get up, she found that her muscles didn't respond. She struggled with the effort of a swimmer against the current. Ellis looked at her and said, "If you have something else to do—I appreciate your help but..." She had been staring at him. "That's all I want," he said.

"I'll pack the rest for the movers."

"I don't know," Ellis said. "I never cared much about clothes and I can't really see any pleasure in searching for more clothes but I have this itch to burn these things, just take them out back and burn them."

Though she'd only recently had plans to jettison all imperfections—shredded sheets, burned pots, clothes that didn't fit—she looked sharply at him to see if he was kidding. She couldn't tell.

"Why can't you come with me, Gina?"

"Margaret's coming. I can't leave the minute she gets here."

"I'm doing it."

"You're not her sister." Gina was his wife, though Ellis would never stake claim to her with the word. "I'll get there soon enough," she said. "Just let me get her settled."

"Settled where? This house is going to be empty soon. On the market."

"It would look better with someone still living here," Gina said. "Everyone says so."

"Not if it's Margaret. She'll scare the buyers away. She'll decide she can't be bothered getting out when buyers—"

"There's no buyers anyway. It'll take forever to sell a house this size with what we've put into it. The house on Cibolo Street—"

"I'm taking the truck over to Dick's this afternoon," Ellis said. "He said he might be interested in buying it."

"Why don't you drive it up there?"

"I'll get another vehicle. I need to see what they're driving in Vermont."

"I'm probably lucky you want to bring me," she said.

He looked at her with his hooded blue eyes seriously enough that she worried until he smiled and said, "Don't linger."

On the drive into the city, Gina inspected the fields: the cotton was finished and the sorghum gone but for stubs in the dirt. It was a waiting time of year when the heat of summer clung to the air, reluctant to part. Nearer the city, the landscape changed, no longer agricultural but rural trash: fields covered with tires and metal shacks set there for mysterious purposes, a collection of wooden houses that she thought was either a brothel or housing for field workers, and the odd, new houses built right by the highway that said dream house all over them except for their proximity to four lanes of traffic.

At the downtown bus stop, Gina stayed in the car, listening to the radio. She liked public radio most of the time but the music irritated her today and she kept trying one station and another until she ran out and turned off the radio and the car. She rolled down the window. She liked the sleepiness of downtown Austin, the low modest buildings on this end of Congress Avenue.

She watched the worn-out people leaving and entering the terminal, their jeans and wide-brimmed hats, their scuffed boots, the shorts on the thick blondes, the stolid Mexican woman and her skinny son, and the old woman with her tightly curled hair-do, and she couldn't imagine how different people would look coming off a bus in Vermont. Granite farmers? Gaunt spinsters?

Her first sight of Margaret dizzied her and sent her into the time immediately after their mother's death when she and Margaret fended for themselves that first summer. Their father was at work and often out for dinner. The girls took care of themselves. It was the time of the final letdown. No more drama about their mother's possibilities and the ups and downs of her progress toward death. There was nothing left to wait for now but they waited still as if even that link were worth preserving. Gina could only recollect their mother's face by looking at Margaret, except when she saw her in dreams. But there was someone else in Margaret's face, Gina herself, and when Gina caught direct reflections of an expression or a way of holding her chin, a strong feeling, stomach-turning and tearful, came over her.

She got out of the car and waved to Margaret who was looking up and down, everywhere but at Gina.

"Hey!" Gina called. "Over here!" then crossed the street to help Margaret with her suitcases and bundles and her portfolio.

"Whoosh. It's so hot here," Margaret said.

"Is it snowing yet in Durango?"

"No. But you have to wear a jacket all the time. They have real seasons in Colorado," which left Gina wondering if Margaret was sorry she'd come.

44

Margaret was full of news about a man she'd met on the bus who was a Buddhist, though not her kind of Buddhist.

"Will you see him again?" Gina asked. She was pulling away, trying to get across Congress Avenue.

"He's going to San Antonio," Margaret said.

"That's not the end of the earth," Gina said. She made her move and they drove smoothly south across the Colorado River.

"It was just nice to talk to him, Gina. I don't need to see him again. You're always trying to fix me up."

When they were almost clear of the city, Margaret said, "Look! A shopping center's going in."

"Look closer," Gina said. The back wall stood and the brick side walls. It was enough to call up an image of the whole: a grocery store in the middle, smaller shops fanning away. Spray painted emblems danced across the walls. "Some Dallas developers started to build it and either ran out of money or the company went belly-up. There was a For Sale sign for a long time but someone knocked it down. It doesn't matter. No one's going to buy it."

"I'm never taking the bus again," Margaret said. "I'm thinking—I've been a lot of places. I'll stay here for a while. See what this life's like. I sold all my clay stuff. I'm finished with that."

Gina looked quickly at her sister but Margaret was looking out the window.

"Ellis got the job," Gina said, waiting for Margaret to exclaim on his good fortune, but she said, "Oh, yeah?"

"The one in Vermont," Gina said. "So we'll be moving soon."

"When?"

Now Gina had her attention.

"He's leaving right after Thanksgiving. I don't know when I'm going. I need to put the house on the market. There's a lot more to moving than I thought. We've been in our house so long I've filled up all the closets and the attic, every nook and cranny and I need to clean out—"

Margaret's attention was back on the road. Only if Gina had said she was leaving tomorrow, no, only if Gina had said Margaret had to leave tomorrow would there have been sustained interest.

"Maybe you can help me," Gina said, a little sharply.

"Sure," Margaret said. "Once I settle in."

Over supper that night, they told Margaret the saga of Maxwell and Mavis.

"Well, if that doesn't show there's karma I don't know what does," Margaret said.

Ellis asked, "The turkeys? Us?"

"Everything living," Margaret said.

"Everything wants to replicate, Margaret, and that's all there is. It's pure Darwinism, not karma. Units of energy wanting to continue, life becoming itself again, flaws and perfection. The soul is a construct, Margaret, a story people tell themselves to feel big in the face of all this self-replicating life. As if each of us has a karma greater than DNA. As if each soul had an itinerary."

"We're saying the same thing," said Margaret, "in different words. There is something larger than ourselves. We come from it. We return to it."

"We are not saying the same thing," Ellis said. "Everything is not the same."

Gina waited for Margaret's reply. Margaret breathed evenly. Gina counted: inhale one, exhale two three. Once when Gina visited Margaret in San Francisco, they'd quarreled and Margaret held her breath. During the long seconds Gina realized that she feared for Margaret, and daily had a moment of fantasy that seemed like prescience. Sometimes Margaret died, felled by the same internal curse as their mother but decades younger; sometimes she suffered an exaggeration of life and wandered the streets, moving anchorless and penniless from place to place. In these visions Gina could do nothing to help her sister.

"I'd be happy to cook Thanksgiving," Margaret said.

"We can all cook it together," Gina said.

"I can handle it," Margaret said. Margaret had once assisted an Italian master chef at his demonstrations when she lived in Philadelphia and had dated a sushi chef in San Francisco though Gina had never tried her homemade sushi.

"I need to work up until the last minute," Ellis said. "The brothers asked."

"That's okay," Gina said. "Do you want to invite the brothers?"

"They'll be with their families," he said.

"We'll do something simple," Gina said. "And the cranberry-orange stuff. Parker House rolls?"

"Simple," Ellis said in a warning tone as if Gina always complicated things, and as she cleared the table she wondered if she did.

Margaret made the third floor her own in no time. She draped pieces of lace over the lampshades and hung a red silk robe from the closet door as a decoration. She placed scraps of ancient Peruvian weavings on the bedside table and the top of the dresser. She piled her collection of miniature books on the dresser next to clumps of fake pearls and shiny rhinestone bracelets. She filled the room. Even the powder spilling from the leopard-print box was distinctly her own. Gina felt that Margaret was more there, in the house, in the town, than she was herself.

In the end, Gina handed Thanksgiving over to Margaret. All her ladies wanted her to clean their houses with extra special care for the holiday so she couldn't cancel anyone. It was a relief to tell Margaret to cook whatever she wanted and to hand over the envelope of extra cash she had accumulated for the occasion.

On the evening before Thanksgiving, Gina came home exhausted. Mrs. Perez had asked her to switch days so she could be there while Gina cleaned the enormous windows. Usually Mrs. Perez hired two high-school boys but this year she wanted Gina high up on the ladder. Mrs. Perez told her about a nephew gone wrong and said, "You missed a spot. No. Over there." Gina thought Ellis was right. She couldn't clean houses forever.

Back home, she went straight to her bedroom and lay down on the hastily made bed. Margaret was in the kitchen, fixing dinner.

Gina too had wanted her house to be perfect but now she was too tired to do a thing. It was only the three of them after all. She had been assessing closets and drawers but had emptied only a few. Her trunk and backseat were full of bundles to contribute to Mrs. Lozano's church. The house gave no sign that soon she would be gone. Possessions, cleaning, mending, redistributing. Was this to be her life? It was too easy to blame living in this town, its smallness, its ordinariness, for her feeling of living a small, ordinary life. It would be the same anywhere and she wondered why she was leaving.

Thanksgiving was squash-based and delicious, Gina and Margaret thought. Gina worried that even her sister's skill wouldn't make the meal palatable for Ellis but he ate with a good appetite down to Gina's pecan pie from tiny sweet native pecans she'd gathered from their own trees.

The lace curtains that hung from the tall windows covered the stained glass window but allowed its color in. They did well against the golden walls. The dining room was the only room in the house with color on the walls. The rest were a dull white that changed with the light to pale gray or even blue. Through the double door opening into the living room Gina could see the serenity of their brilliant

Caucasian rug, the couch she'd reupholstered in linen the color of butter, the easy chair in pale yellow, the big rocker with its creaky rush seat and back. She had meant to install doors between the rooms. She had found the place for the hinges, faint indentations in the years of paint, but for all her searching the town's antique and junk stores, she'd never found the doors. She imagined the original pair sold and hauled off to Dallas, where they gave a condo a more substantial look. The next person in their house might sell off the stained-glass window and the glass-fronted, glass-knobbed kitchen cabinets.

Ellis thanked Margaret politely after dessert. He helped clear the table. When he'd washed the big things, the pots and pans, the serving utensils, Margaret and Gina told him they'd take over and he retreated to the bedroom, where he watched football and whatever else he could find, switching from channel to channel. Once Gina had taken this as a sign that he was disturbed; she'd thought he was seeking as he roamed. Now she believed he liked the randomness of the roaming.

That night, Ellis and Gina stood on the balcony outside their bedroom and looked over the darkened football field and the lights from the houses. The bleachers caught a glint from the streetlights. Ellis hugged her to him to keep her warm.

"Won't you miss all this?" Gina asked.

"I don't know yet. The only thing I know I'll miss is you."

"It may take a long time for me to pack. We've rooted into this house. And you know no one wants to rent in this town. Not to cover the mortgage."

"Don't dawdle here, Gina. Get the place on the market. The movers will pack everything and the company's paying. This is a different deal than we've ever had before. Get yourself on a plane."

"I thought I'd drive."

"Give Margaret your car," he said.

"But if it made it there, we wouldn't have to spend the money on a new car—"

"Gina. Just let it go. I know I'm sticking you with a lot to do but please just do it. We'll have enough money."

"But what am I going to do about Margaret? She's broke and doesn't have anywhere to go. I can't just leave her."

He let his arms drop and turned away.

"I'm going to sleep," he said. "Are you coming?"

She didn't stay alone on the balcony longer than a minute. Without him the streetlights looked tired and the space over the football field empty.

The day Ellis left, Margaret put an ad in the local paper and, with the last of her money, paid for it to run for three weeks: *Two College Graduates Will Clean Your House.*

"I'm not sure this is honest," Gina said. "I mean, I'm supposed to be gone in three weeks and then what are you going to do? Where will you live? I need to put this house on the market. Empty."

"It'll work out." Margaret looked flushed and happy from her walk to the newspaper office near the square. "I just love this town. You can walk anywhere. You don't *need* a car."

Once when Margaret was trying to live in San Francisco, she sent Gina a birthday present of Chinese slippers, dark blue satin with embroidered hummingbirds drinking from a lily on one, on the other a pagoda and a bridge with three figures holding lanterns. The shoes were different sizes. Only the left one fit Gina, the hummingbirds. She'd shown them to Ellis because she thought them so pretty and he said, "That's Margaret all over." Margaret hadn't been able to find a match, she later wrote Gina, but she could afford them so she hadn't been able to resist.

Without Ellis, time lurched. Gina saw the numbers change on her digital bedside clock and by habit she marked off the days on the Nature Conservancy calendar in the kitchen (December, the Alaskan White Fox), but her sense of minutes, days, season was altered. On warm days it might be summer. She was living in a house with her sister Margaret as if she'd never met Ellis and never married. They were sisters, waiting for their father to come home from work. What would they have for dinner? In the grocery store, the hardware store, the cashiers asked how Ellis was doing so far away, but here in the house it was as if he never existed. When Gina said she missed Ellis or wondered what Ellis would think about something or when she quoted something funny or smart he said, Margaret smiled in a mysteriously smug way as if she knew more than Gina. She looked away as if Gina were embarrassing her.

Taking the garbage out or mowing the lawn, Ellis's chores, Gina thought about him as if he were a troubling memory, like the dead before they settle into simplicity, into being forgotten. She should take down the screens, she thought, hose them down and brush them. She should wash the windows. She should go to the realtor on the square and put the house on the market, set a date for departure, call the moving company, but each day Gina found a reason not to make the phone calls or walk to the square. Often it was six before she even remembered what she'd intended to do.

After dinner, the sisters walked, going to the courthouse square and window shopping one time around before heading home. The biggest store had once been a women's clothing store that sold expensive clothing, attracting women from San Marcos and Austin. Now it was a Hallmark card shop. The old hardware store sold antiques. Its oak drawers and woodwork reaching high to the pressed-tin ceiling had been sold to a Houston interior decorator and the walls now sported crude shelving. A video store had taken up residency in the men's hat store. The clothing store had been faithful to seasons that had little to do with Texas: red and yellow paper leaves in the windows in autumn, fake snow in winter, more faithful even than Hallmark.

Margaret talked during their walks about the places she'd lived and about some of the things that had gone wrong in them, telling Gina stories that frightened her though she never showed this to Margaret. Gina responded as she always did, finding reasons why things had gone wrong and how, if Margaret happened to be in the same situation again, she might curve matters another way. Gina had learned never to criticize Margaret directly; she didn't take well to it and anyway what did Gina's opinion matter? There were plenty of people, Gina supposed, in Margaret's acquaintance who could tell Margaret that she had done nothing with her life, didn't get along with people, had lost opportunities and squandered her talents. Gina had seen Margaret shed friends and lovers who contradicted her, enough so that Gina modified all criticism into understanding. She listened to herself sympathizing and agreeing until she gobbled like Maxwell.

It was peaceful being with Margaret, one of the quietest times they'd ever had, but Gina found that she could talk with her sister about less and less. Not Ellis, not leaving, not the clutching she felt in her chest at the thought of the house sold and changed, not her boredom with cleaning other people's houses, not much but her delight in the mild Central Texas winter with its occasional blistering northers.

After their walks they brewed cups of chamomile tea with honey and repaired to their bedrooms. As she fell asleep, Gina could hear the sound of Margaret's radio playing oldies.

On a clear December morning, a week before Christmas, Gina tackled her bedroom. She had made her way through the kitchen, dining room, extra bedroom, living room, and library, taking away the possessions she'd part with, leaving what she wished to keep. Gina cleaned the chosen things carefully and returned them to their places or found new and better spots so that the house, as she moved through, gave the appearance of a redecorated place rather than one about to be abandoned. She did this, she told herself, for Margaret's sake. Margaret, for her part, ignored Gina's activities, as if she had more weighty things to think about, not helping, not even bothering to scavenge in the growing piles of boxes and pieces of furniture on the porch.

As Gina tried on clothes and said goodbye to skirts she'd out-grown and dresses she'd never wear unless she took up elemen-tary-school teaching again, she asked herself the same questions she had on her long journey through the house. How could she tell Mar-garet to leave? What would happen to her if Gina cut her loose? Gina couldn't see living without Ellis, but how could she leave? These questions no longer tormented Gina as they had. Maybe if you asked the same questions over and over again, they began to mutate on their own into answers.

When her own bedroom had been cleared out, Gina started on the second-floor guest room. On the floor of the closet she saw that Ellis had left a pile of discarded shirts and books. She breathed in deeply because for just a split second she wanted to throw everything un-seen and untouched into a big garbage bag, and haul it downstairs and outside, but she forced calm on herself. She had come this far do-ing things patiently and methodically. It would reflect badly on the whole process if she gave in now to impatience and carelessness. What would the house think? She investigated the pile piece by piece, agreeing with Ellis that these things should go into the great river of discards that held the world together, until she discovered the yellow plastic bag she'd stuck in the big suitcase months earlier.

She looked around the room as if Ellis might be lying on the bed and reading the paper, so she could tell him to take care of this for her, plus the house and the turkey and the cat and Margaret, but Ellis wasn't there. She went to the window and listened for him or another human sound, hearing the soft breeze across the cotton field. On these clear gentle days, not winter and not summer, the prevailing southeast wind brought the Gulf of Mexico to her. For a moment she believed she was on the beach, watching the big flat water, waiting for Ellis to join her at the end of the world.

She picked up the bag and walked downstairs, her footsteps thunderous in the empty house, through the dining room and the living room, the big kitchen, through the laundry room and out to the garden, all the way to the end of their yard.

The cotton was long harvested but the field wasn't yet plowed. There was cotton on twigs and cotton on the ground, left behind by the harvester, too little for anyone to worry about, and it sat, wet when it rained, drying when the day was fine, and occasionally, as now, shining in the sun like snow. Mavis was nearby and so was the cat who lounged belly up, waiting for attention. Soon it would be Mavis's time to leave for the vet, and the cat's too. The vet had a soft heart and the cat at least might live a long life.

The garden was over. Only the native morning-glories persisted, clinging to the solar system of wobbly chicken-wire fencing. The no man's land was full of weeds, dying wildflowers, thistles, little hills left behind by the tractor. Gina opened the plastic bag and reached in, ripping the rolled-up tissue paper until she pulled out a shard. On its cool surface was a jagged line that might once have meant lightning or departure. She raised her arm in back of her like a quarterback. How much better she would feel if she could return the shard to the earth whence it came. The shard would land in the ruts, be plowed under or smashed when the farmer came to plow. She could throw them all, one by one, then throw the bag away. No one would know that she and Ellis had snatched the shards from where they should be lying.

But the pieces of baked and painted clay persisting so quietly were evidence of the people who made them, their sign that they had been on earth. If anyone did find the shards—too many miles east, too far south—it would confuse all knowledge of those long-gone people.

It was a dilemma, and she wished Ellis were there to help her. He would have an easy, logical solution, something she'd never have thought of herself, and she would do what he said and ponder it later.

She couldn't ask Margaret, upstairs in the third-floor bedroom, lying on the four-poster and dreaming of her next place. She would not be sympathetic. The shards would remind her of her own troubles and she would blame Gina for the memory.

Gina looked out at the cotton field, closer to wisdom, and thought, *What would Buddha do?*

*Wonderful Gesture*

When Mary said that she didn't want the weekend to end, Olivia said, "Then you should stay," and Mary glanced around the Sunday breakfast table at the other guests whose names she had barely conquered. Not one turned or tilted an ear to listen. She and Olivia might have been alone with the chandelier that held real candles and the mural of peasants working in a rice paddy, the Great Wall in the background. It was Indian summer and a few more days in the house above the lake seemed like the most Mary could want from life.

"The house is empty all week," Olivia said. "Tomorrow the housekeeper comes but after that you'll have the place to yourself, unless—"

"Unless what?"

"It's too much to ask. Especially at the last minute. I'm being a brat. Patrick will say so."

"No," Mary said. "Really. Is there anything I can do for you here? If I stay." Mary assumed the favor would be to let in the plumber or the rug cleaner. All weekend Olivia had been complaining about the water pressure and a stain in the vast pale rug in the living room. It looked like a shadow to Mary, but Olivia blamed the spot on a drunken guest from the previous weekend. Patrick blamed it on Miss Jemima, the cat. Patrick didn't drink but Olivia enjoyed red wine until she spoke like an oracle, her eyes half-closed.

"It's Miss Jemima," Olivia said. "We're expected in Westchester for dinner tonight, and it's all very do-able except for her. I don't know why anyone has a dinner party on Sunday night."

Mary didn't wait for the request. Colin, Mary's ex-husband, Olivia's stepbrother, had objected to the way Olivia expected others to anticipate her needs, but others did so often that Mary admired Olivia for getting her way.

"So you'd like me to keep the cat here all week?" Mary guessed. "Until you come back? On Friday? Saturday?"

"Anytime," Olivia said. "Bring her in anytime and leave her with the doorman. You needn't call ahead. She's no trouble at all. Well, you have to feed her once a day. There's food in the pantry, all on one shelf, very neat. It's organic so it doesn't smell disgusting. Patrick! Patrick, the most wonderful coincidence. Mary wants to stay and keep Jemima for us."

Patrick pulled his attention from an elderly cousin of Olivia's, and directed his tired blue eyes to Mary. For an odd second Mary was sure that Patrick was pleased that she was keeping the cat, not because of the dinner in Westchester—Mary had the feeling that Patrick didn't care where he ate dinner or in whose company—but as though he'd won a bet with Olivia.

"I'm so grateful," Mary said, but he'd already looked away and her cheeks grew hot.

Olivia left Jemima's plaid blanket and a traveling cage in the curved alcove by the front door. Fluffy, blue-eyed Jemima roamed free in the car when Olivia and Patrick traveled to and from the city, but Olivia suggested the cage since Jemima had never been in Mary's car before. The cage looked small to Mary but what did she know about cats? Her family had been dog people. For years after she moved north, Mary had envied dog walkers in the park, but the idea of a dog of her own locked alone in her one-room apartment all day bothered her, so she did without. When she and Colin married, they'd intended to get a dog but couldn't agree on the breed, and now it was too late.

Once all the guests and Olivia and Patrick finally left, it was evening and blessedly quiet. Mary made the rounds, checking doors and windows. She found Jemima on the sunroom couch, nestled in a ring of light from a large white-and-blue china lamp. The cat looked up when Mary approached and squeezed her eyes together in a double wink of recognition, then shook herself off, leaped from the couch, and disappeared, leaving a cloud of ash-blond fur suspended in the air.

Remaining after the others had gone was Mary's attempt to prolong the pleasure she'd felt all weekend in the surroundings, minus the discomfort she felt with Olivia and the other guests. Mary was sure it was the last time she'd be invited to the country house, for Olivia would not keep up with the ex-wife of a stepbrother. Colin hadn't liked Olivia all that much and Olivia didn't like Colin, but that didn't matter, they were connected by family and Mary was disconnected forever.

Between jobs, newly divorced, Mary had no one waiting for her in the city. Later in the week, she might have an interview but she wasn't really interested in the job or any job. If she found a job, she would stay in New York, which seemed as complicated as leaving. She was pretty sure that Olivia, in her way, knew everything about the tiny settlement Mary had gotten, and what a fool she was to let Colin get away with it. Mary thought she must look pretty dumb, exactly the hick she'd always seemed to Colin's family and friends, but the law of community property made it clear that Colin's money, inherited before the marriage, was his. They'd sold the apartment they lived in for their five years of marriage, and split the profit. He moved to the East Side, to a new building with a garage and a view of the East River. She'd found a sublet on West End Avenue. He gave her, from kindness, the old car they'd been meaning to replace. It was parked now outside of Olivia's stone mansion above the little manmade lake, a VW Bug she would have been ashamed of driving if she were back in Texas, but one of the few things she liked about the East was that cars mattered less, a good thing because Mary couldn't afford anything else.

In the morning, while the housekeeper worked, Mary took Olivia's bicycle for a spin. It had more gears than she was used to and she ended up pushing it to the highest point around, a rocky area where the year before Olivia had a catered picnic, the last time she'd invited Mary to stay. The lunch Mary brought with her hung from the handlebars in a string bag that often collided with the front wheel.

Colin was connected in all the ways Mary wasn't, not only to Olivia's other weekend guests but to all the people and places in the world that intimidated and beckoned, including *pensione* in Venice and stone mansions in Scotland. Mary and Colin played up their obvious differences—his worldliness, her gullibility, his bland Waspiness, her sweet Irish-German face—far beyond their small truth. She knew how bored Colin was with her before he told her. He bored her a little too but she took it as part of their fondness, not understanding that he was lonely with her and needed someone more like himself.

She laid out her picnic next to her on the bumpy rock, leftovers from the weekend. Mary bit into a piece of quiche. The crust fell apart on her lips, savory prosciutto cutting the rich custard. Then the last slice of a pizza one of the guests had made, a strict rosemary and black pepper. Mary had included all the remaining cheese straws in her picnic, but they didn't flake as they had two days before.

The food was generous. The house was generous too, the large rooms, the expansive view over the lake and the hills, the armchairs waiting for you to sink into them with a book, a lamp by every chair and a small table to hold your drink and cheese straws. How generous Patrick and Olivia were too, letting her stay here, trusting her with their property, their home. She was the stingy one, counting helpings, counting drinks, counting money, counting kisses.

She had been dreaming in Olivia's house of the town in Central Texas where she'd grown up and the bungalow where her mother still lived. Mary and Colin had spent Christmas there the first year of their marriage and with his mother the second. Mary had expected them to return to Texas the third year and had dreaded it, but fortunately she got the flu, and the fourth year his mother died. They were divorced before the fifth Christmas had a chance to pin them down.

On Sunday afternoons in her childhood, Mary's parents put her and her brother in the back seat and they drove somewhere: to San Antonio to see her mother's people, to Fentress to pick peaches, to Goliad to the mission and the Presidio. Once a year they went up to Lake Whitney to visit her uncle who had been an early hippie and cultivated wine grapes and grew his own food. That too was a man-made lake but you could fit Olivia's lake, her house, the other big houses, and the nearby village in it, sink them, and never know the difference.

Mary watched the lake, smelling winter in the air. Her brother, now a lawyer in Dallas, said she was a natural-born victim when she told him the terms of her divorce. It was Colin's money from Colin's family, she'd told him, not hers to take, either in the eyes of the law or in her own sense of what was right. She was a fool, he said. Her mother, widowed, wrote her weekly, asking what she was planning to do now. Mary knew that if she returned to Texas she'd be as much a fish out of water as she was here.

Mary swallowed the last of her morning coffee with the last bite of homemade shortbread (her contribution to the weekend). She walked home, the empty string bag threatening to tangle itself in the front wheel. She would have ridden, but she was afraid of going too fast downhill and crashing Olivia's bike.

The first night, she'd fallen into a deep unbroken sleep. Tonight she heard the wind in the trees and the click of the dryer as her sweatsuit tumbled two floors below in the basement. She strained to make a rhythmic song of the clicking round and the whirling leaves when there was a crash and she sat up in bed, her heart trying to break from her chest. Mary lifted the flashlight from her bedside, hefting it in her hand like a weapon, and slipped on her loafers. She waited for the intruder. There was a rustle outside her door and the most subtle change of light. Mary flung the door open. In the dim light of the hall, she saw Jemima. A Chinese vase that had stood on an inlaid table was in pieces on the floor. Ming? Tang? Ching? Oh, the awful cat had broken Olivia's beautiful vase. What a nuisance Jemima was. No wonder Olivia and Patrick treated her like a piece of luggage to be delivered when convenient. Amazing that they put up with her as they did. Jemima, at the door of Mary's room, licked her front right paw and looked up sweetly. The cat knows exactly where I'm sleeping, Mary thought, and she wanted me to know it. She wants me to know we're both here. No, the wonder was that the cat didn't break more, poor thing.

In the morning Mary didn't feel quite right. She had planned to go to the town library to read a little local history, and then to the market to replenish the dwindling supplies (for she was determined to leave the place well stocked and had it in mind to buy cream, milk, butter, and English muffins so that Olivia would know she was a grateful guest). There was an antique store in the town, and Mary wanted to find a little something to set on top of the thank-you note that she'd leave on the kitchen counter before the coffee machine. *"Your house was a refuge and a help—"*but that sounded too desperate. She sneezed in the cool of her room. She would do well to spend the day in bed. Here it was harmless to stay in the high bed at eye level with the window. She might be on duty, guarding the lake.

Now that she was unemployed it had become more important than ever not to stay in bed, even for an extra hour, and so she sometimes rushed to finish her morning chores, then stood in a cleaned apartment, bed made, coffee pot washed and on the drainer, with nowhere to go and nothing to do at ten in the morning. She forced herself from her apartment, to the newspaper stand to search the want ads. When she was married, she'd worked to be honorable and not live off Colin's income. She had never found a job she wanted to keep, and even though she'd resolved not to expect satisfaction, the people she worked with grated on her so that each time she was fired, her first reaction was relief.

Still in her silk robe and flannel gown, Mary toured the bookshelves in the library. Half the shelves were of no interest, filled with matched sets, albeit Jane Austen, the Brontës, James Fenimore Cooper, Lord Byron. She wondered if the Cooper held its place in better company because its leather was a pretty green. On the highest shelf were crisp hardback mysteries, all from the past two years, three of them by authors Mary liked. She never bought hardcovers unless she was sure it was a book that would last forever, and murder mysteries were combustibles, though in fact she kept them forever and reread them as soon as she'd forgotten the plot.

Mary climbed on a wooden footstool to reach the shelf and, eye to eye with the frantic typography of the jackets, selected the three she wanted. The space they left revealed a small white box, which she also withdrew from the shelf. Mary set the books on the table before the couch and opened the package of delicate chocolate and pecan turtles, her favorite. Every Christmas until she died, Mary's great-aunt in New Orleans had sent her turtles. The chocolates looked fairly fresh. Fresh enough to eat. For an instant, Mary felt fonder of Olivia, at the thought of her hiding the chocolates. It didn't seem like Patrick at all, though so many people were in and out of the house, it might have been anyone. In any case, Mary would eat the chocolates and replace them, and then whoever it was—Olivia or Patrick or another guest—would find the new chocolates and wonder how they got there.

Armed with the mysteries and the sweets, she took to her bed, and for the rest of the day she didn't stir except to forage in the pantry for lunch. The sound of the can opener on fancy Italian tuna attracted the cat, who looked as though she were having the same kind of day as Mary. Jemima's organic food looked predigested and, as Olivia had promised, it didn't smell. Nor did it interest Jemima as much as the tuna, so Mary ended up splitting the tiny can with the cat. She kept the last of the smoked salmon pasta for herself, and the roast-beef finger sandwiches that were deliciously squashed and left over. White bread, Olivia had remarked, was becoming an endangered species.

It grew colder as the day wore on, and Mary half wanted the cat to appear to warm the bed. By late afternoon, Mary was interrupting her reading to tell herself to go for a walk, get her blood circulating, get some air, but she held out until it was almost dark. Then, still in her nightgown and robe, she crept downstairs, flicking on light switches as she went, and took a bottle of white wine from the refrigerator. She was not opening up a new bottle. She'd missed her chance that day to go to town—the stores closed in an hour—but maybe in the morning, first thing in the morning, she'd shop and replace everything she'd eaten so that when she left no one would know she had been there. Olivia might say that: *No one would know you'd been there, Mary, didn't you eat anything? Just a little drink?*

The pine library had been cozy, crowded even, with the guests and Olivia and Patrick. She had wished for less noise and now wished for more. The cat was wound into a tight sleeping ball on the window seat, behind her a pot of chrysanthemums that smelled sharp and rotten in the chill air. Mary didn't know how to open the flue and the housekeeper had left the fireplace so pristine that she didn't dare to try.

In the near-darkness, she made her way outside, opening the little-used door to what Olivia called the rose terrace. The wine tasted sharp but by the third sip the oak conquered the leftover chocolate in her mouth. She thought she could taste the hazelnut Patrick claimed was in the wine but it might have been pecan from the turtles. She knew nothing about wine. She knew nothing about food. Her head was full of people she was already forgetting from the mystery she'd finished.

It took place in an English village where everyone knew everyone else and all the houses had names. The detective was a woman doctor whom Mary wished to consult. She would tell her a few things, broken phrases, then the doctor would understand completely and tell Mary that what she needed was complete rest and relaxation. In the book, the doctor was able to tell when the victim was killed and how she was strangled, though no one believed her but Mary. The murder was simple. Had the murderer confessed at once, it would have been universally acknowledged as an accident. The solution was complicated and had to do with temperature, wind chill, rigor mortis, and the dripping of an old-fashioned icebox.

Mary stumbled. The hem of her nightgown was wet from the

grass and the cat was caught in her robe. Jemima looked annoyed and struggled to disentangle her claws.

"Well, who told you to grab me?" Mary asked. She reached down to help the cat and the last drops of wine baptized Jemima's head. The cat snarled and retreated into the house. Only then did Mary realize that she'd never seen the cat outside before. Jemima might have run away and then what chaos. What a lucky girl Mary was, what a lucky glass of wine. She looked for the sunset. Sunsets here could be spectacular, but this one wasn't. It was only the cold yellow sun abandoning her for the rocky hills. A breeze came up her leg and chilled her to the kneecaps. Her nightgown was wet and punctured, and so was her robe, the only one she had with her.

On the way upstairs Mary refilled her glass to the brim. She carried it carefully up the stairs and set it on the hall table, picking her way over the broken Chinese vase.

She'd never been in Olivia and Patrick's bedroom before. It was large, making its way around a corner of the house so that its windows overlooked the lake. The bed was a four-poster, skirted in ruffles that matched the three sets of pillows waiting, plumped in green linen, for the return of their mistress. There were two dressers, tall and cherry; the drawers held Patrick's country garb, his golf shirts and white t-shirts, plaid flannel shirts, chinos and dungarees, all neatly folded. For whose inspection, Mary wondered, for the drawers gave the impression not just of neatness but of a kind of bragging pride and contempt for the messiness of ordinary drawers.

In the bigger closet was Olivia's country wardrobe, hanging by use, fabric, and weight, and by color, or rather tone for the range was gray to bone. Olivia's tweed jackets nestled together as if in a trance at their own beauty. Built-in drawers lined with scented and flowered paper held Olivia's underwear and nightgowns. Mary couldn't borrow a robe from this immaculate receptacle. She could never replace it where she'd found it in its exact condition. It was beyond her powers. She felt the cat's presence behind her. All she needed was for the cat to curl up on a cashmere sweater and refuse to leave. "Out of my way," she said. "Shoo." It was a good thing the cat couldn't report to Olivia that Mary had been in here. Jemima stared at Mary, then turned and flew upwards, settling herself on the bed, in the middle of the fawn mohair cover.

Mary ate a late supper standing up in the kitchen, slicing off ham and cheese, rolling the slices and filling the tubes with honey mustard that she dribbled on her wet and tattered robe and didn't care. She refilled her glass until there was nothing left in the bottle and she could no longer remember how full the bottle had been or if she had drunk the whole thing herself. She had to replace it or Olivia would notice the bottle gone and she would talk about it.

Mary woke in the night to count the drops of water that fell from the faucet in the bathroom. Beneath Olivia's potpourris and the sandalwood necklaces she hung on hooks and doorknobs, the house asserted an empty, damp smell, and in the dark might be any house.

One Christmas weekend long before, Mary's family had packed a box of food, one suitcase for each of them, and schoolwork that wouldn't be looked at until the trip home, and they'd arrived at the Lake Whitney cabin by lunchtime Saturday. Mary's uncle had gone to his wife's family in Oklahoma for the holiday.

Mary and her brother were in the back seat of the Chevrolet and ready for the fried chicken her mother had made that morning at home. Mary was first out of the car, and she ran to the key hidden under the steps, threw open the front door, and slid inside, landing on her bottom. The downstairs area that served as kitchen, living room, and dining room was wet, and her feet had slipped from under her on the slick floor. The walls, papered by past owners with silver ferns on a gray background, were buckling with moisture, ferns rippling as though it were raining. It was a scene of ruin. They had come for shelter to find a disaster. Her brother stopped short in the doorway, her mother and father piled behind him.

"So the weather reached this far south," her father said.

It had been unusually cold that week, pipes bursting all over North Texas, and even here the pipes had frozen, expanded, and burst. The family heard the gentle hiss of hot water spraying into the chilly air.

The family carried out the ruined furniture and set it on the front lawn as if they were holding a yard sale. In the bottom drawer of a chest, Mary found a nest of baby mice curled together. She hoped they were sleeping. She'd seen mice just like this, pink and white, in a candy catalogue from a fancy store in Dallas, but these weren't marzipan mice. They were dead, and she felt responsible, as if there were something she should have or could have done. Mary forced herself to pick up the drawer and she plodded out to a little grove of cedars, and there she emptied the drawer of the dead mice, kicking leaves and rocks over the little bodies.

At dawn, Mary made coffee and brought it back up to bed where she finished the third mystery, an English police procedural with boring details that soothed her headache. She could read it and think at the same time, and by the time she'd finished the book she had a complete shopping list.

Mary dressed in the same clothes she'd worn for Sunday breakfast. She had three other outfits in her suitcase, for she'd always been a nervous packer, but for a ride the few miles into the village and back, worn clothes would do.

Since the market was closed from twelve to one, she drove straight to the antique store. She thought she was alone, but a "Hello" rose from the back of the shop, and she had to squint into the darkness to make out a tiny man swiveling ever so slightly in a high-backed desk chair. There was a desk beside him, so covered with objects that it was clearly never used for business. "Hello," she said, "I'm just looking." "Don't mind me," he replied, and swiveled his back to her. A gesture of trust, she thought, to show that he didn't think she'd steal anything.

Mary browsed the glass cases of medals, campaign buttons, and costume jewelry, and spotted a rhinestone cat pin, perfect for Olivia but nothing in it for Patrick. Besides, it was seventeen dollars, ridiculous.

She moved on to a round table laden with dishes and bowls, and there she saw a Chinese vase identical to the one Jemima had broken. Had there been a pair? If she gave it to Olivia and Patrick, there was the danger that they wouldn't believe that it was the cat who had broken their vase. The gesture had the smell of guilt to it, and—once she'd looked at the price—of overcompensation. No, she would gather the pieces and leave them for Olivia and Patrick; of course, they'd know someone who repaired china. She went back to the cases, returned to the table, roamed along the walls, gazing at class photos from Canadian boarding schools in the Twenties, then settled for a teacup with no saucer from Occupied Japan. A sleeping pearlescent blue cat graced the cup. She paid exact change to the man, who wrapped the cup in newspaper. When she was back in the car she regretted her purchase, for its one virtue was that she could afford it. What would Olivia or Patrick do with one teacup and no matching saucer? The rhinestone pin would have denoted a carefree heart.

She spent the last of her weekend money in the grocery store, buying expensive cashews and handmade chocolates, replacing the milk, eggs, bread, even buying a new jar of mustard that had not only honey in it but tarragon (she hoped they liked tarragon), and a bottle of white wine that was far better than the one she'd drunk but the store didn't carry that one.

Back at the house, she carried the bags into the kitchen one by one, carefully closing the door each time in or out. If she were to leave now she could get to the city before rush hour, drop the poor cat with the doorman, and be in her apartment by the evening news.

Hurriedly, she unpacked the groceries, and set the little cup, it didn't look too bad after all, on the kitchen counter on top of her note: *Lovely time, lovely house, Mary,* and washed the dishes and the glasses that she'd used, leaving them to dry themselves. Upstairs, she swept the pieces of the vase into a grocery bag and left it too in the kitchen, scrawling *Jemima didn't care for it* with a black marker she found by the phone. She made the bed and pulled the drapes together. Next weekend someone else would have guard duty and good luck with it. The bedroom was dark as night and she almost missed the three books on the bedside table. These she swooped up and brought to the pine library, along with the new chocolates. Before she put the little white box on the shelf, Mary ate one of the truffles. She would send Olivia and Patrick a dozen Oregon pears, if she could find the catalogue or remember the name of the place. Someone from out of town had once sent them to Colin after a weekend visit and she'd thought it was a wonderful gesture.

The last chore was the cat. While Mary was unpacking the groceries, Jemima had settled by the door to the basement in a position of polite expectation of lunch, but Mary was determined to delay feeding until she needed to put her hands on the cat. Now Mary stood in the kitchen door opening a can of cat food away from her so the noise would resound through the empty house. She waited with the oozing thing in front of her but Jemima didn't come. Mary opened a second can, reasoning that she could wrap it well and leave it in the refrigerator, but the cat stayed invisible. Mary washed her hands and began to search. A dog would never be devious or ungrateful.

Jemima was not in Olivia and Patrick's bedroom, not under the bed or in the closet or hiding behind the drapes. She was dead center on Mary's bed, a halo of hair around her.

"Time to go, kitten-face," Mary said. For the first time since they'd been in the house together, Mary advanced on Jemima. The cat flew past Mary and out the door. By the time Mary was in the upstairs hall she couldn't tell if the cat had run downstairs or into one of the open bedrooms. Mary searched Patrick and Olivia's room again, closing the door behind her, and did the same for the other rooms until she was in a darker hall. I am not a patient person, she thought, but a cat is patient.

Mary checked the sunroom, library, living room, dining room, and kitchen, then descended to the laundry, a large area with a modern washer and dryer and the equipment the household had used eighty years before.

The cat was perched on a drying rack that was raised up to the ceiling. So clever, she'd thought when Colin demonstrated the rack to her. They had laughed together in delight at the idea of hoisting laundry so high. Jemima stared down intently. Mary stared back. There was nothing to do anymore, no way to lower the rack without possibly harming the cat. She could have cried. Olivia must have gone through this every time she left for the city, this little game of cat and mouse, but now who was the cat and who the mouse? Olivia must have a trick, Mary thought, for she wouldn't tolerate being delayed by Jemima, although perhaps the trick had already been played on Mary.

She considered the basement, which was a lot nicer than some apartments she'd looked at, and saw a big table, for folding, probably. She climbed up on it to be comfortable while she outwaited the cat, but she lay down and then fell asleep, and when she woke, her back hurt in a terrible way. She climbed off the table awkwardly. Jemima's place on the drying rack was empty. The afternoon was almost gone. Because of the cat she would be stuck in rush hour or get home late and have to park the car in the dark and rush to her apartment without shopping for food. She would have to explain the cat to the doorman, for surely Patrick and Olivia would be out for the night, and she didn't want to see them even if they were decent enough to invite her up for a drink and a sandwich. Her time was eaten by others, her life given to others. She had no one to blame but herself, but still it made her head hurt behind her eyes to think of it.

Jemima was in the alcove by the front door, sitting on top of the wicker carrier.

"Ready to go?" Mary asked.

At the sound of Mary's voice, the cat raised her head yawned, and resettled herself.

Without taking her eyes off Jemima, Mary reached for the plaid traveling blanket and in one quick gesture dropped the blanket over the cat and held the bundle—cat and blanket—to her with all her strength. She could feel the cat's strong body struggling in a tidal wave of anger and hear the growls of fury. Mary's feet slipped on the hooked rug on the slick floor, and she staggered, then regained her balance. Mary was shifting the bundle, trying to figure out how to let go without being clawed or bitten, when the cat gave a ferocious twist against Mary's arms and then was still. Jemima had given up. It was the end of the game whose rules Mary would never master.

"Okay," Mary said, "let's get out of here."

She moved the carrier with her foot so that, still clutching the cat and the blanket in her arm, she could open its little door. Trying not to notice how roughly, she stuffed the cat into the cage, withdrew the blanket, and shut the door. The limp cat did not protest. Maybe Jemima too was ready to go back to the city, maybe this was another thing Mary didn't know. There was a scratch on Mary's arm, and she pushed her hair back from her face. She couldn't wait to be back in her rented apartment, be it ever so humble. Jemima, flopped in the cage, looked harmless really, just a pet.

Mary made one last tour of the house, closing doors and opening them, remembering how the housekeeper had left them. She smoothed Olivia and Patrick's bed and her own, settling the rugs she'd disturbed while looking for Jemima. The basement was easy. No one would know she'd been down there. Only in the alcove was there any sign of a struggle. She put the carrier outside by the car, then went back into the house for the foyer rug. She shook it outside, then returned it to the house, patting it until it lay as placidly as the rest of the house. Mary shook out the blanket also, watching the hairs fall like snow, and folded it neatly. She put it in the car, along with her suitcase and handbag.

The last thing in the car was the cat. Mary said, "Train's leaving the station," and set the heavy carrier carefully on the back seat of the VW. She closed the front door of the house and double locked it, just as Olivia had instructed.

*A*nnoyance in the room, his daughter's voice, a hum, and the heat of the fire. David shifted, trying not to look foolish the way people do when they awaken, and said, "A car?"

"Yes, Daddy," she said, patience obvious in her voice. "I told you. The road was iced over and it was snowing. So there was a coating. Like grease on soup."

Becky sat in the mustard-colored armchair telling her story while Magda listened from the turquoise chair by the kitchen door, her head bowed over the magazine in her lap. Magda's white hair was gathered at the nape of her neck in a bun.

"Dick was driving really slowly. Sue was in front. She always rode with her arm braced against the dashboard."

"That's dangerous for the driver. Irresponsible interference," David said.

"She had her reasons."

He waited to learn what they were.

Becky had been visiting for a week, and they had fallen into an after-dinner routine: Becky washed her dishes and her son's (he was asleep by this time); Magda washed hers and the cooking pots, and asked David each night to do his solitary plate and cutlery. She stood and watched him as he washed, ready to help if he needed it but determined that he should contribute as he always had to the household work. He remembered her standing by their daughters in the same way. Such were Magda's principles that she had determined in advance how many plates and glasses she was willing to sacrifice to her daughters' training.

Then they sat in the living room before the stone fireplace that was discolored from a leak in the roof that would not be fixed.

He poked at the fire and a log turned to ash, giving up its colors, yellow, red, like the autumn that threatened the summer. One year—was he imagining it?—they'd burned a dead apple tree and the burning branches gave a glow, pink as a rose. They'd given the ash to a potter friend of Magda's—name lost—who'd used it in a glaze. In their first days of living in the country, they'd taken self-conscious joy in knowing locals: potters and weavers, farmers and auto mechanics.

"We came up behind this old Bonneville that was going really slowly, and Dick stepped on the brake. Our car swerved, but he handled it, and we stopped."

"Does this story have a point? The suspense is killing me." Magda, turning the pages of the *New Republic,* sounded as if nothing would ever kill her. When they moved to the country almost forty years before, she'd given up her job on a woman's magazine—nothing so highbrow as the *New Republic*—and lately David wondered if she regretted it. She had considered working freelance, commuting a few days a week, then cast her lot utterly with him, although at the time he saw himself as the hero, carrying her as a heavier burden than before; the unemployed wife, the children, the house and land, all on his shoulders, all dependent on his job of work.

"The Bonneville hit some black ice, skidded and disappeared, so we followed its tracks across the highway. There were all kinds of saplings and huge trees, pines, big maples, but the car missed them all. It just landed in an open space like the trees had grown around it."

"Well, that's luck you can't count on," David said.

"I believe that's the nature of luck," Magda said.

"There wasn't a sound coming from the car so I thought…But this woman was just sitting, and her kids were in the back seat, a baby and a toddler. They weren't even crying. No one was wearing a seatbelt. The kids must have flown around in the car. It was a miracle and all the woman could say was that her old man was going to kill her."

His daughter had driven with her son all the way across the country in a little Japanese sedan with a bumper sticker: *Immortal—and you?*

"That's an unbelievable story," David said. "How could the car not hit anything?"

"Trust me," Becky said. She looked like her son for a moment, dark-eyed and dark-haired, cheeks red from the easy circulation of youthful blood. "I was there."

"I object to that locution," he said, and he pulled his wool shirt tighter around him. "It cuts off all conversation. 'Trust me'—as if that were the end of it. I trust you, but to do what?"

"Anyone for the candy garden?" Magda asked.

"Ryan was trying to get into the candy garden today," Becky said.

"No, he wasn't. He was playing with the brass handles on the sideboard. He doesn't know about the candy garden. We respect your wishes."

"Which you've made abundantly clear," David said. Becky was up on her high horse about the little boy eating sugar, so the three of them waited until Ryan was asleep to open the cabinet where they'd always kept candy. Becky loved the candy garden when she was little, eating its goodies like a champ.

David had in mind chocolate mints wrapped in cellophane. Before Becky came, he'd laid in a supply. He pushed up from his chair and, as he stepped on the turquoise area rug, he staggered in place. Magda breathed in sharply. Becky sprang from her chair. But he was fine, recovering his balance and standing as straight as he could at his age. Across the room on his own pins, he retrieved the crumpled bag of mints from the cabinet and journeyed back to his seat by the fire, glad to lower himself once more into the warm place. How dramatic his life was with the two women waiting for him to die.

Since the surgery he'd loved candy and ice cream more than ever. Comfort food, his younger daughter pronounced, as smug as if she'd split the atom. That daughter avoided candy in regard for her figure. He was beyond such concerns, a hunched-over little man who had to search in the mirror for his eyes to recognize himself.

He reached for the poker close to hand and gave the biggest log a push. A small puff of tired smoke appeared and disappeared.

Could a car fly? Odd things happened. He himself had two relatives who had disappeared off the face of the earth.

One was his cousin Sherman Kaufman, a gangster of small magnitude. Sherman's disappearance produced sorrow in the family, regret for a misspent life, and plenty of gossip, but no one was surprised.

The other was Milton Rosenberg, a lovely young man married to David's favorite cousin. His disappearance was less seamless than Sherman's, for Milton returned once to visit his wife and son in Brooklyn, a year or so after he'd stepped out one evening for cigarettes. Over the years he'd been sighted in Philadelphia where a branch of the family lived. Maybe he'd planned to return eventually and lost his way. Sherman was probably murdered or he'd found it useful to become someone else somewhere else. Milton might simply have cracked: not had the guts to stick it out.

"Mints?" he asked, offering the crumpled bag to Magda, who didn't like mints, and to his daughter, who did.

I didn't disappear, David thought. Whatever else anyone will say about me, I didn't disappear.

The next morning there was rain, and Becky went to town for the paper.

Magda tried to entertain Ryan by cutting out pictures from a magazine and showing them to the child. She insisted that her daughters had loved to watch her do this for hours, and didn't seem to notice that Ryan wanted the dangerous scissors for himself. "No, no," she said, as if that settled it. She cut out a woman in a strapless ball gown, a silver car, a red truck, and a black and white cow identical to the Holsteins in their neighbors' fields.

First the boy tried to eat the limp paper figures with their poisonous ink, then he reached for the scissors time and again until, frustrated, he collapsed in tears and David had to take him for a walk. David wore his hunting cap all the time now, for his bald head was cold indoors and out. He reached for his warm jacket and a scarf. Magda helped Ryan down the slick wet steps while David wrestled open the big umbrella to shelter them both.

They patrolled the perimeter of the house and David showed the boy the sights: "Chair. Hose. Leaf. That green is the lawn. The yellow stuff I should get rid of. Dandelions." The boy pointed to tiny mushrooms growing from the morning's rain and David said sternly, "Don't eat those. Ever," and reached down creakily to cover the boy's hand. "No."

The boy pointed: "Woods. Deer go night night in woods."

"That's correct, sir," David said. "One hundred percent. Deer go night night in the woods."

The night Ryan and his mother arrived, a deer had leaped across the driveway, a flash in the headlights, and since then Ryan had been campaigning for its reappearance. Soon he would be putting sentences together and telling pointless stories like his mother, but that would be in another place, far from David, who would never hear them. Maybe. Never say never.

"Deer," the boy said. He looked Irish, like his father. Between the luck of the Irish and the luck of the Jews, the boy would need all the help he could get.

David followed the boy back up the rise to the yellow cottage. When they bought the place he'd removed the shutters with heart cut-outs, but the house remained stubbornly picturesque, and long ago David had given up trying to make it into a house he might admire.

Inside again, coats off, wet shoes lined up by the door, they settled back on the couch and David instructed the boy to get a book to read. Ryan returned with two.

"Which first?" David asked and the boy handed over *Tootle*, a tedious tale of an engine who did badly in school because he wouldn't stay on the track. Instead Tootle took off into a bright green meadow to make a daisy chain and play with butterflies and dragonflies, dragging his coal car behind him.

David gazed at the drawing of Tootle's classroom, the roundhouse where he and the other young engines were taught the important rules, the first of which was to stay on the tracks, and it brought David back to the long hallway just outside his office door, the door with his name engraved on a plate. He breathed in once again its air of submission: A day's work ahead, a week's, a month's, a lifetime of working days. Put one foot in front of the other and you rise, though not too far. Far enough to earn more or less what you want: to move out of the city for the sake of the girls and commute the roads to Albany each day and pay the way for the girls to go to college and have weddings and a million crises in between. Each day when he left the yellow house and drove to Albany, he shed himself until, outside the door to his office, he was another person, a civil servant. It was honorable work. He tried to help people and in that way prided himself on his difference from at least some he worked with who worked for the good of the department only. He had risen as far as his ambition would hoist him and then he'd settled in for the long run.

On the drive back at the end of a working day, David made the transition from streets to highway to country roads, the driveway. David waited for the moment when—seeing a deer or other thrilling evidence that an accidental and beautiful life went on all day without him—he became himself once again.

Tootle's grinning teachers had an idea: Put stop signs up all over the flowered meadow. Instead of undulating like a snake, Tootle halted, started, halted again, until he learned his lesson and became the best little engine of them all at staying on the tracks.

"More," said the boy, "more."

The second book was all action and strong color, firemen with pudgy cheeks and big noses who looked as if they were truly axing the burning column, were really hauling a heavy ladder up the smoldering staircase.

The boy laid his pointer finger on the page to stop David from turning. David studied the gray smudges of smoke, the red helmets, the firemen in yellow coats, and he heard Becky asking, "Where's the camera?" for he was asleep with the boy waiting for him to turn the page.

At the sight of Becky the boy burst into tears, and she swooped down to recapture her treasure.

"The paper," David said, trying to stand and wake up at the same time.

"I got it." It was tucked under her arm in a death grip.

"Loosen your arm."

"I'm holding the baby," she said, but she relaxed and he slid it away from her.

They had breakfast out on the screened-in porch, Magda's pride and joy, marginally less gloomy than the living room, affording a better view of the rain. When Becky left, he and Magda could return to their slow watching of the days. She liked napping on the porch no matter what the weather. She claimed she didn't feel the cold as he did.

On the front page was an article about doings in the Ukraine, now called simply Ukraine, where they had all come from. At thirteen his father set out alone and pulled the rest to America with his hard labor, his will, and his luck, for surely there were plenty of boys who crossed the ocean and disappeared into the new continent, never to see their families again.

The only move David had made was to this country district with its diminishing number of dairy farms and increasing cultural establishments and luxury inns replacing estates, and he'd known it all his life, from holidays in moldy cabins with his parents, to summer camp, and weekends of listening to music with Magda before the children. In a way, he had been here all his life.

Past the news, David settled in to the Obituary page. The big stories were the death of an ancient Russian dancer and an early aviator, plus a man who had invented a method for dehydrating oatmeal. Today it was all octogenarians or better—no taking of the young or those in their prime. He scanned the death notices for familiar names. He never tired of this. He found someone he thought he knew who turned out to be a Catholic priest not of his acquaintance. Then he found his old friend's name, Nathaniel, and it really was he.

He'd loved the guy. The wives were pals and sometimes did their marketing together along Bleecker Street. More often than not of an evening the two couples strolled together to their favorite bar or a tiled Italian *caffe* where they sat drinking hot bitter coffee among the old men in black suits.

His feeling on finding his friend among the dead was the same he'd had on learning that Nathaniel was leaving for a wonderful job in San Francisco: loss, of course, and envy, but something else—the sharp nastiness of being surprised and excluded by someone he thought he knew backwards and forwards. How long had Nathaniel known about the job, applied for it, wanted it, and never said a word?

He'd thought all his friends were dead who could make him feel loss, much less envy.

"You'll never guess who's dead," David said, and told them.

Magda put down the Home section. "It doesn't seem right. You remember him, Becky. He was around all the time when you were little."

"I think I remember him."

"It seems so sad, all the way across the country—of course, by now he made a life there. June came from California. Remember, David? We used to call her California June? It was natural for her to want to be with her family, especially when they were about to have their first child. And the job! No one could have resisted that job. Now I see this like the hand in front of my face but then I couldn't understand why they'd break up the old gang. Then we moved up here and we all lost touch. How many children did they end up with?"

David consulted the notice. "Two sons, residing in Sonoma and Los Angeles, and June's still alive."

"I was so fond of her," Magda said. "I'll have to write to her. If I can find her address."

Becky said, "My friend Bert died this winter."

"Do I remember him?" David asked.

"You never met him. AIDS. When he was weak at the end, he was completely up front about dying. I didn't know what to say. Even to ask 'How are you?' It felt terrible to tell him what I was doing—the baby or plans. I never realized that we talk about the future all the time. He was so generous. It was like he forgave us—"

Becky had her eyes on him as if she were trying to convey a message but what was it? That she found it hard to talk to him about her future plans? Well, he'd grown used to that, living with Magda. When he wanted to get his one good sports jacket taken in, she'd asked, *Why spend the money?* but she'd been a good sport and taken him to her dressmaker. David felt a swift dislike for the dead man and for the scene which he saw like the old deathbed lithograph that used to hang in the drugstore; gaslight glowing over the bed, the dying man a lump underneath sheets and blankets. The important figures were the doctor and the hand-wringing witnesses. The dying man was a bit player, necessary but obscured.

"So," he said, folding the newspaper.

"So what time are we leaving?" Becky asked.

"Leaving?"

"Daddy, you and Ryan and I are going on an adventure."

"What kind of an adventure?"

"You know. We talked about it last night. We're going to Melville's house."

"The one in Pittsfield?" It was a place he'd never been. David hadn't read anything by Melville in decades. In college he'd taken a course with Melville's biographer and he remembered the large hall and light streaming in through windows that reached the ceiling, the dark figure of the professor, swaying as he lectured.

"I went there once with some visitor who took a great interest in Melville," Magda said. She might have read Melville in her college days, though then he was not the staple he'd become. Now she read books about local history and English mysteries set in country districts like their own. "All the furnishings looked like they'd come from yard sales. Is it really Melville's house?"

"He wrote *Moby Dick* there, for God's sake. We talked about this last night and you knew all about it, Daddy."

He turned his attention back to the paper for there was no need to take that tone, and he reminded himself of Becky when she was a little girl, her feelings hurt so easily and so often. If he didn't mollify her in time, she'd stay stony for hours. Now he forced his eyes up from the headlines to speak to Becky but she was gone. She and the baby and Magda had left the porch and he was alone with the sound of the rain.

"Don't forget the numbers," Magda said. She was patting her fingers on his back as they walked down the sloping lawn to Becky's car. The rain was abating now, a fine drizzle that clouded his glasses.

"Rest, Mom. Take advantage of the quiet while we're gone," Becky said. It sounded as if she'd said this before and he could imagine the women plotting out Magda's afternoon holiday from him.

"Hand," Ryan said, reaching up. He wore a blue slicker and matching hat, and his sneakers were brightly-colored, red, yellow, and green. Once he had their hands, he drooped his body forward to inspect the ground for rocks and bugs.

"Is this all right, Daddy?" Becky asked.

They swung the boy between them. He was heavy for David but not too heavy.

"Will you remember the numbers," she asked when they reached the car, "or should I?"

"I'll remember them," David said.

He sat strapped in the front passenger seat. The little boy was in back of David, enthroned in his car seat.

"If you get tired," Magda said, "come straight home."

"Being tired never killed anyone," he said.

They waited while Becky went up to the house and returned with a load of laundry she'd washed by hand that wouldn't dry so there must be a side trip to the laundromat after Melville's house.

"It always takes longer to get places around here than I remember," Becky said when they were underway at last, Magda a disappearing speck in the side view mirror. "I love seeing things but I always want to rush home."

"When you were little, you'd ask every mile how many more miles."

"All kids do that, Daddy."

"Your sister never did."

A mile from home, they neared a dairy farm, its big barn right by the road and the doors wide open. Twice daily, the herd of Holsteins lumbered patiently from their boulder-strewn meadow to the barn. The road was littered with manure which summer people complained about for it dirtied their cars and made the road slick. David and Magda had often been in the small gray house across the road from the barn, had sat in the kitchen drinking weak coffee with rich milk, breathing in the scent of cigarette smoke, sugar, and cow peculiar to their neighbors, but the point of the farm was not the house. The eternal exchange between meadow and barn pleased David, and lately his eyes filled with tears when he looked across the expanse to the patient and dignified cows. The woods where the meadow ended were filled with mist.

"Deer," David said softly.

"Do you see a deer?" Becky asked.

"Just talking to myself."

He wished another deer would appear for the little boy. It wasn't too much to ask. There would be a better chance of seeing deer six or eight weeks hence but by that time the boy and Becky would be in their Western home with its swift roads and empty vistas. Everything was different there, Becky had told them. There were no black and white Holsteins but herds of beef cattle, red Brangus and white Brahman, and the deer had ears like mules.

They reached the four corners in Lenox and were immediately in a traffic jam.

"Oh, no," Becky said. "Ryan, do you want Mom to refill your bottle? More juice-juice? Why is there so much traffic here?"

"Tourists. The Red Lion Inn. I don't know."

She inched along, too close to a van from Virginia, refilling the bottle and steering with her elbows.

"I don't like that," he said. "Not very safe."

"I know," she said, "but I've been doing it for thousands of miles."

Deftly, she passed the bottle back to the baby who tilted it up to his lips while Becky watched in the rearview mirror, her eyes everywhere but the road.

"Oh, hell," she said.

"What?"

"He took one sip and tossed it. He does that."

When the light turned green, the van from Virginia went into reverse, angling for a parking space. Becky inched back as far as she could, but the van driver stuck his head out the window, beeped his horn, and waved a hand at her.

"What an asshole," Becky said. "Where does he think I'm supposed to go?" and she leaned on her horn until the driver gave up, sped through the light, now yellow, and left them trapped.

"God," Becky said.

"Gosh," Ryan said, and touched his cheek in a gesture Magda found cunning and David thought was coy.

"If you're not careful that boy will be calling people all sorts of names," David said.

"Bottle. Bottle."

"Okay, honey. I heard you."

She put the car in Park abruptly, unclipped her shoulder belt, and turned around in her seat, her hands scuttling on the floor among the maps and soda cans for the juice bottle. She righted herself, wiped the bottle on her shirt, and handed it back to the baby.

"Do not throw the bottle again," she said, clipping her belt and putting the car in Drive in one gesture. "Don't throw bottle. Thank heavens."

They made the turn and were past the small row of shops.

"Some people drive just to get to Lenox. You're glad to leave."

"I mean, thank heavens Ryan didn't notice the s-w-i-n-g-s back there."

"Your sister took us out to the Red Lion Inn last time she was here. The food's very consistent year to year." Against his better judgment, he said, "She was very sorry not to see you this trip."

"She was hacked that we didn't come through New York. I can just see me in the city with Ryan."

"Lots of people in the city have kids Ryan's age. You were his age when we left. You could have taken the bus to see her one day."

"She didn't want to see us."

"She's busy. But she wanted to see you."

"She hates kids," Becky said.

"She's not used to them. They aggravate her."

"Everything aggravates her. If everyone in this family got as aggravated with her as she does with us—"

He held up a hand. "We are what we are. All of us. Too late in the day to do anything about it."

She looked as if she were about to retort but changed her mind, and he figured that they had come to the same conclusion: when he was dead, she and her sister could quarrel without impediment or make peace without giving him the satisfaction.

Arrowhead, Melville's house, was a handsome two-story affair, close to the road as houses of its era tended to be, for greater ease in and out in winter. Now proximity to constant traffic diminished the natural impression the house gave of solidity and permanence, though it was still a house a man might own who thought he had arrived.

The rain had stopped and they had a half-hour between the

guided tours given by volunteers from the Melville society, and had the choice of cooling their heels either in the barn where there was an exhibit of Melvilliana or outside on the damp lawn. The boy didn't last long in the barn where he pushed on the partitions on which the exhibits were pinned. Becky picked him up, whispering, "We'll be outside."

Melville's cigar case was pigskin, big enough to hold four twisters, sent to him by a secret male admirer after the publication of *Typee*. David remembered an account of Melville making Hawthorne sick with the smoke from his black cigars. Smoke from cigarettes and briar pipes, the fumes of Scotch whiskey and gin, those were the perfumes of David's youthful friendships but so long ago that time melted and it seemed that he and his friends might have shared the air with Hawthorne and Melville.

On to wire spectacles, small for that face with its bushy dark beard. If they actually were the great author's glasses, were they from the thirteen years he lived in this house, his era of stability and expectations? A man with a great pregnant secret, Melville wrote the book that he probably believed would encase him safe as one of his cigars in fame and fortune forever. All men wished for security, David thought, even brave men like Melville.

The exhibited detritus reminded David of clearing out Magda's father's apartment when the old man died. There had been no surprises beyond seven pill bottles filled with dimes from the years of the first world war and a dozen boxes of well-thumbed playing cards—When did he use so many? Magda wondered—though the amount of stuff the old and solitary man had lived with was astonishing. A cigar case, yes, and pairs of eyeglasses long disused, books, well, they expected books and records because he was a reader and loved music, but also newspapers, magazines, all folded back, some held with paper clips, awaiting filing with other crumbling bits of essential knowledge, and, of course, shirts, trousers, socks, and undergarments (these David had packed up, too personal for Magda, the old man's dignity), a top hat and tails, and his sticks of furniture too. Six months ago David had resolved to clean up his own mess, not to leave trouble for Magda and the girls and to preserve his privacy, but so far he'd done nothing.

David made his way over the uneven ground to the side porch, which Melville called his piazza, to the amusement of the locals. Even a hundred years ago, the major local sport was laughing at tourists, and everyone was a tourist who was not native. He and Magda had been there for thirty years, and they were still tourists.

"I guess Melville didn't have a driver's license," he remarked when he reached them, "what with no automobiles, otherwise that would be up in the barn too. Framed in gold."

"People want that," Becky said serenely. "It makes the man more real to see things he's touched and used."

She didn't sound like the same girl who'd called a visitor from out of state an asshole. The boy was intent on the grass and so was she.

"Toad," she said.

"Towad," said the boy. He held a stick as long as he. In the grass there was a profusion of black toads the size of fingernails, so that the lawn appeared to be moving. There was something sickening about so many toads. The boy waved his stick over them like a wand.

David wished there was a chair on the pleasant old piazza. The clapboards were yellow, which David never liked, the shutters shiny brown, courtesy of the historical society. The house lay about two miles off David's usual path through Pittsfield where he came every so often to the dentist or the specialty food store, but even if he'd passed, he couldn't have distinguished Melville's house from the other old houses around it. The Pittsfield Country Club right next door had also been in the Melville family, he'd learned in the barn, though the last Melville there had spelled his name in the old way, no "e." In his own family Rosenbergs became Rosses and there was Ryan, of course, where once there would have been Reuben.

"Look at the view," Becky said. "It's Mt. Greylock. It looks like a whale."

"Pretty far inland for a whale."

"Towad."

"Be gentle, honey. You can tell the house is really old," Becky said. "The clapboards are wide."

"They look average to me."

"Wider by three inches."

"It's aluminum siding," David said. "From the look of it."

"For God's sake, Daddy, why would there be aluminum siding on Melville's house?"

"I'm not suggesting he put it on himself."

"Gentle, baby. No hitting. Don't hit the toads."

David inched toward the house and laid his hand on the pale yellow siding. The color was more appealing with the sun full on it, bleaching it to wheat.

"No, no—oh, never mind. Yes. Touch with your eyes. Not the stick."

"You're right," he said more cheerfully. "It's wood. The real thing."

"Give the stick to Grandpa, baby. Grandpa needs the stick."

"Don't worry about the toad, Becky. There's more where that came from."

When Becky was young, she'd demanded a ceremony for every dead bird or chipmunk or toad, and David had been her willing sexton. She'd insisted on those animal funerals because she'd thought each death was something new. He took no comfort in prayer and burial, food and drink, cheek to withered cheek. He would attend no more funerals, he thought, but his own.

"It's time, Daddy," she said, and only then did David notice a snow-haired man gesturing to them at the corner of the house. They'd passed the time and the tour was beginning.

How did women cozy up so quickly? Perfect strangers a moment ago, Becky and the two old ladies chattered in the corner, examining the china display in the parlor as if they'd known one another for years.

David and the guide, who seemed to be deciding whether or not to clear his throat, stood before a fireplace decorated with Melville's words: *I AND MY CHIMNEY, WE SMOKE TOGETHER.*

Ryan, loosed from his mother, walked into the tiled precincts toward a cooking pot suspended by an iron arm. Ryan stooped and the pot swung, bumping his small and perfect head. He looked at David, surprised, then outsize tears sprang in his eyes and his mouth gave a perfect scream. David put his foot forward to grab the child but his body stayed where it was. Becky lifted the boy up, saying, "We'll go outside. Don't cry, little sweetie. We're going outside. Really," as if someone had protested, "it's better."

And it was. The guide cleared his throat: "The mantle of this fireplace. It is from a domestic piece...." His voice quavered like a bird riding the thermals. "Written after *Moby Dick* and before the great silence."

"Silence?" David asked. The larger of the women smiled at him, probably too timid to ask herself.

"I call it that," said the guide. "Until *Billy Budd*, the silence of the greatest prose voice. He wrote his poetry. And there was *Pierre. Confidence Man.* But what else would you call what might have been?" He closed his eyes and David was alarmed. The man looked as though he might cry like Ryan. "Nineteen years at four dollars a day, inspecting ships for contraband, the man who wrote *Moby Dick.*"

"Ships? From this house?"

"Oh, no, sir. Arrowhead was what you might call his dream house, and Arrowhead was sold when *Moby Dick* failed. Mr. Melville took his family to New York City. He's buried down there, you know. The Bronx."

David hadn't considered where Melville was buried. It was enough trouble to keep straight where all his friends were.

"This armchair," said the smaller lady, her ungloved hand hovering above a Windsor chair set at an angle to the fireplace, "is it original to Arrowhead?"

"Hard to say."

"Four dollars a day might have been a living wage back then," David said.

"And the paneling?" asked the larger lady. "Original?"

"Hard to say also. He became so discouraged after *Moby Dick,* you see, he invited dignitaries to visit Arrowhead to see if they would buy it for an insane asylum. Too small. Too close to the road, they said."

They moved in single file to the dining room which was papered in big red roses. The table was oval and shone with polish. Probably a reproduction, David thought, one of those places in North Carolina.

"Mr. Melville's household," said the guide, "consisted of his mother and his wife. His four children. The last of them born here at Arrowhead in 1855."

The house seemed small for all those people but families used to live closer together, unconcerned about physical privacy. He'd never slept in a room on his own until Magda decided she couldn't take the snoring.

"Daughters?" David asked.

"The first two children were sons, the next daughters."

"The sons weren't up to much," the smaller woman said, surprisingly. David thought she was interested only in furniture. "One killed himself," she told David. "The other wasted his life out West."

"To outlive a child," the other said.

"You know a lot about Mr. Melville," said the guide. He sounded annoyed. "Malcolm, the elder son, shot himself. Why did he do it? Why did no one hear the shot? The family was at home. Questions never answered."

David looked up at the staircase off the dining room as if Melville might come roaring his displeasure at this discussion of his dead.

"Things happen in families," David said. "Even in the Melville family."

The guide said, "Especially in the Melville family." He turned to the ladies and told them that the wallpaper was recent.

David thought, Not especially the Melville family. In his family there were the cousins who disappeared and an aunt who died suddenly and under circumstances that he didn't realize until years later meant suicide. He'd wanted to ask his mother about the aunt but hesitated to trouble her and now it was too late.

"Upstairs," said the guide, "two rooms are open to the public."

Above the dining room was Mrs. Melville's bedroom, pleasant and south-facing, catching the overpassing sun.

There was a brilliant shaft of light at the far corner of the room and David moved into it. He watched a white milk truck pass, the driver also in white, and heard the clink of glass bottles. How pleasant to hear the homely sound again. He had been told that the old and the dying have memories more vivid than their present, but no one had mentioned how sharp and sensate the memories were, or how satisfying. Even memories of pain had beauty at a distance.

"When they moved to New York," came the guide's voice, "Mrs. Elizabeth Melville decorated her room in white. Her husband's room was dark and the bed was covered with a black cloth. His room frightened the grandchildren."

"Grandchildren?" David asked. The life was moving along too quickly.

"Oh, yes. The youngest daughter had three daughters before her father died."

"More girls," David said.

One last glance out the window. Becky and Ryan were nowhere to be seen.

The ladies lingered to examine the appointments of Mrs. Melville's room. On the landing David stood with the guide, aware of how small the other man was and how frail. The blue veins on his forehead pulsed like waves, tide in, tide out.

"He was a disappointed man," the guide whispered.

David said, "I beg your pardon?"

The guide touched David's sleeve.

"Disappointed beyond anything you can imagine. He had pinned his whole existence on that book and no one understood it. He'd written the best book ever to be in American literature and no one liked it. They liked his seafaring adventure books! Hawthorne might have understood. He wrote a letter but Melville destroyed it. Well, it was a book that would frighten a man like Hawthorne. What did Melville expect? He knew so much but he didn't know enough to—" The guide's breathing became lower. "Crushing disappointment. Crushing rage. This house to support. The family." He moved toward a door half-opened to another room. "How happy he must have been in this room. Not knowing! Not knowing!"

The day before the news of his health or lack of it, David had ventured to a café that had just opened in town and tried a drink, sweet and full of chocolate and coffee, whipped cream bobbing on top, and he hadn't asked the price. Just like that, not knowing.

"And this room?" The lady's voice came shrill and David moved into the last room of the tour, while the guide's voice resumed its flutey tones, identifying for the ladies the type of pen Melville wrote with, and paper, all carefully laid out by the Melville Society.

The room was furnished simply: a table and chair, its back to the fireplace in the corner, one window giving a constant view of the little mountain that looked like a whale. On the walls, a yellowed canvas-backed map of Massachusetts in Melville's time, a few engravings. The floor was covered by a striped rag runner. Nothing was original but the room itself, David decided, and he wondered if the guide had really spoken to him outside the room—*Crushing rage!*—or if the words had returned to him from the college lectures so long ago. He understood the words *disappointment* and *rage,* as he hadn't ever before. It was too late for treatment, too late to try to save him, and he could do nothing but wait. The daughters whispered to Magda, *Better doctors, other hospitals,* and she repeated the argument and explicated it to the point of exasperation: he was too old and frail, the cancer too advanced to torture him with treatment or with hope.

The mechanism of the illness carried on oblivious to the words spoken about it. Nothing would be done for him and there was nothing he could do. The worst times, odd times, eleven in the morning, he would think: *They are letting me die.* Just like that, as clearly as if someone had spoken into his ear, and sometimes he half-rose from his bed or easy chair to cry alarm, but sense and the present overtook him.

Outside the window lay the whale Melville had never reached, farther away on rainy days and in the morning fog, closer in the clear sun. Melville's house was too far from the sea, no matter what the mountain looked like. His room was a shrine, a Lourdes of disappointment, so innocent, so hopeful, so serious. The furnishings never matter, he wanted to tell the ladies, it's the whale. You'd have thought they'd know that by now.

He heard voices, Becky's and the boy's, cooing to one another. David stirred, his neck stiff, his shoulder frozen. Becky was standing by the car door, the boy in her arms.

They were in the KMart parking lot, near the laundromat. The big store looked far away.

"I'll be with you in a minute," David said.

"Stay. Ryan's going to ride the horsie while the stuff dries."

So he'd slept through the journey and the unloading of the laundry.

"No," he said. "I have to get the numbers for your mother."

He watched Becky swoop the boy over the mechanical horse that stood guard at the laundromat door. She reached into her pocket, slid coins into the machine, and the boy began laughing as the horse tilted forward, backward, down and up.

After decades with only Rural Delivery to their name, they had a street address and Magda had been harping on the numbers, insistent that he put them on the mailbox though the deadline was weeks away. She had brought the subject up twice a day during Becky's visit as if to demonstrate his uselessness. It was his summer ritual to repaint their name on the box and he'd offered to do the same with the numbers, but Magda insisted on him buying numbers because, she said, she didn't want to be bothered repainting the mailbox herself.

When he'd first been diagnosed, still hale and hearty, Magda had made a long list of things to do to get the house shipshape, including his usual annual chores. Once he'd been diminished, so was she and requested nothing, letting many things go by that she wouldn't have before. The notion of the numbers she had clung to, insisting furiously that he buy them and stick them on the mailbox.

Assaulted by the fluorescent dimness and size of the store, he asked a cashier where the numbers might be and it took a while for her to understand what he meant. She looked at him as if she didn't expect such an old body to make sense anyway, then told him, "Aisle Thirteen."

Tube socks, though no human he'd ever seen had feet like tubes;

yellow buckets filled with pink curlers; and a table covered with seed packets, more than he'd ever seen, that bloomed as radiantly as flowers. He shook one packet after the other, listening to the seeds like delicate percussion instruments, and David saw sweet peas climbing the wire in his father's back yard in Brooklyn, sunflowers covering a field he'd seen once in France, brilliant marigolds whose sharp tragic odor he could catch through the paper. No other spring, not the lilacs blooming with Magda's red tulips nor the lilies of the valley along the stone wall, announcement that winter would be feared no more.

Becky turned the car toward home, and a northern breeze reached them from Canada. The boy gazed out the window, sucking meditatively on his bottle. Was he searching the fields for the deer or watching his own transparent reflection through which the landscape traveled? The reflection, David decided. Children had such an awful need to see themselves, to be sure they were really there.

"Let's stop at the farm stand for some corn?" Becky asked. "I'd hate to go home without eating some corn. The stuff from Florida's not the same."

"Our corn isn't the same either. I don't know if it's worth buying. Plus your mother's the one who buys the corn. She'll have the meal planned out."

"It's no big thing to boil corn," Becky said.

"Take that up with your mother. She opens every ear, gives it the once over. If the water's not boiling fast enough or she leaves it too long, you'd think she lost her best friend. Too emotional for me. Plus, I didn't buy the damn numbers," he announced. "It was a lot of trouble to put that mailbox up at the right height to please the mailman. Then the snowplow knocked it over and a tree limb fell on it during a hurricane.

"I disagree with your mother about these numbers. I told her I'd paint new ones on but she said she didn't want to have to repaint. She doesn't understand. I'll glue the numbers on and they'll fall off—they have to fall off a curved surface—and then your mother will be stuck with figuring it out for herself."

He looked at Becky's face and saw that she was appalled at what he'd said. David felt small for calling her bluff and thought of her friend who'd died. Had he felt the same, flaunting his imminent demise?

At the farm stand, instead of turning left for home, Becky parked in front of a display of Fall bedding plants.

"This isn't where your mother buys corn," he said. "We'll catch hell for this."

"It was my idea."

David saw the child she'd been, frowning, worried.

"Uppy," Ryan said, "uppy."

"Let's live dangerously," he said. "I'll pick it myself. It'll be on me."

David went alone into the produce shed, past the local honey and the jelly from last year, and approached the table of corn. He picked nine ears, pulling back the shucks to reveal even rows of yellow buds, all good. He considered trying also some white but Magda scorned it and he decided not to press his luck.

He felt good suddenly, like a man about to tie one on, and his mood lasted until they were nearly home. At the farm with the barn too close to the road, Becky asked, "Daddy, what will I—"

The boy began to fuss, and David wondered if she wanted to say, *Daddy, what will I do without you?* His jokiness left him. The last thing he wanted to hear was Becky saying forthright words. Her generation believed in saying everything. He and Magda did otherwise; they clung to their daily life, and maybe their charade had its own magic. The bag of corn at his feet shifted. He foresaw Magda's annoyance, Becky's defiance, and himself looking for shelter.

"Deer," the boy said.

David saw no deer out the window, then looked more carefully over the broad meadow filled with the slanting light of late afternoon. Near the trees at the edge of the grass stood a doe and a fawn as still as only deer could be. They might be mistaken for rocks or trees.

"Look," he said.

"Deer," said the boy.

The deer disappeared into the woods. Two fields more and the little car turned off the road for home.

In the morning, Becky hesitated, though the car was loaded up and the baby, kissed once and again, was in the car seat.

The air was so cold that mist rose from the lawn.

"I'd better get going," Becky said as if they were keeping her. "It's a long way home. Daddy." She hugged him too tightly for a second and then let him go.

David watched until the little car and its jaunty bumper sticker were out of sight. Magda had gone into the house as soon as Becky started the car. She had never been the one who stood waving long after the girls were out of sight, off to school, off to college, gone.

"What are you doing this morning?" Magda asked when he came into the suddenly quiet guest room. She was stripping Becky's bed and throwing the sheets and towels from the guest bathroom into a pile on the floor. She had flung the windows open as if to expel the odor of children.

"I plan to mooch around," he said. "Enjoy the peace and quiet."

"How about taking the laundry into town? And get those numbers! Honestly, David—"

"Fine," he said. "I'll get the damn numbers. I didn't have a chance, what with Melville."

"Becky said you were in KMart for a long time. I worry about you. Did you forget what you were looking for?"

"Is that a crime?"

"No."

Her shoulders slumped forward. She looked too tired to make it through the day. He was doing this to her, bending her shoulders with the burden of a sick man.

"Why don't you come with me?" he asked. "I'll treat you to lunch."

"No," she said. "Just drop the laundry off. I'll get it tomorrow when I go in to get my hair done. As you know perfectly well, today's the day I clean the house."

"Pack up the laundry," he said. "I wouldn't mind being alone either."

"Guests," she said.

"We're getting old," he said, as if that was what was wrong.

At the drugstore, David bought the *Times* and a fresh box of Kleenex even though it would be cheaper at KMart. The boy had gotten hold of the box David kept by his bedside and ripped out the tissues one by one. They'd fallen to the floor soft as snow. Becky had said she wished they'd come visit on Ryan's birthday in a few months but David had stopped wishing for things. Melville would have done better to write his best book when he was old and past his expectations.

In KMart, on Aisle Thirteen, he thought of telling Magda that all the numbers were gone but he collected the ones they needed—a grotesque five digits—and paid for them in cash at the Express checkout.

His parking space was far from the laundromat so he walked all the way to the car, left the numbers on the passenger seat, and lifted out the bag of dirty laundry. David concentrated hard on holding up the laundry bag so it wouldn't touch the ground. He did all right until the small step up to the sidewalk, where first the bag bumped and then he tripped. Something shifted then and he felt a quick vibration in his chest as he righted himself. He stood a moment on the sidewalk, dizzy, watching the parking lot, and it seemed that the cars were pulling away all at once. Then the moment passed and he hoisted the laundry higher and into the laundromat. Magda would pick it up tomorrow. It pleased David almost to tears that everything would be clean and folded for her; that at least would be easy.

He left the laundromat, forging across the sea of cars to his own.

It was a gloomy morning, and once past town he saw that the fog had not lifted. David drove with his parking lights on, hugging the edge of the road. Cars swerved around him, one flashing its lights indignantly at his slowness. David passed the new house that sat in a field of stubs, past the old schoolhouse, its flag wet at the top of a white pole. Near home, he reached the big barn with its doors open right onto the road. The meadow was filled with fog, a bowl, no, a sea of whipped cream with dark peaks that at first were scattered branches, then Canada geese, too many to count, part of a flock that was waiting out the fog.

Beyond the trees at the far edge of the whipped cream sea were the deer, a doe and a fawn, almost grown.

David relaxed his grip on the steering wheel and for the briefest time the car pulled to the right and sailed through the air before touching down, still in motion. He watched the car's flight through the barbed wire, which the car snapped like a hair, and he endured the jostling slalom across the rocky meadow. David closed his eyes, so close to home.

*The Natural Memory*

$\mathcal{L}$ooking up from the sodden path, Nicky saw the hump of the backpack beneath her husband's poncho. As he walked, the hump swayed from side to side as if he carried a creature on his back. In the pack were two Snickers bars, chicken sandwiches they'd bought at the lodge, and two cans of Diet Coke. His jeans were soaked to black after four hours in the rain forest.

All around her, above her and below her, was water and evidence of water. Even when it was not raining, the air was moist with droplets so small that Nicky couldn't feel them though they coated her glasses with a fine evenness. The rain forest was a lexicon of wetness. She thought of the Eskimos with their thousand words for snow.

Nicky followed because she was the faster walker and Paul had taught her the rule of the outdoors—the slowest walker leads. She'd had the same view of his back, sometimes covered by a poncho, for the three summers they'd been married, as they hiked into canyons along paths in the Rockies. Paul chose their turnaround point, invariably lunch at a water feature with a vista of uninhabited mountains.

Once, they'd come upon an abandoned silver mine, its entrance not much more than a hole covered by old boards. A sign from the Forest Service warned that the mine was dangerous and that it was illegal to enter it. Paul pulled away the boards and there arose the sharp smell of undisturbed dampness and darkness. Nicky didn't even want to lean over the entrance, but Paul stripped off his pack and climbed right in. She'd waited, wondering what to do if he didn't return. Anything might happen in the dark. She had the packs, a flashlight, her poncho, a soda, a chocolate bar, the map. When twenty minutes passed, Nicky peered into the mine, breathing in the cold, moist air. She heard nothing. She tried to imagine walking away from the mine, back to town for help. She'd paid no attention to the trail. What if Paul came up and she was gone? What would he think? She would stay until the sun set, calling his name until she ran out of voice.

Paul had emerged from the mine eventually, triumphant and more filled than ever, it seemed to Nicky, with the sense that he could have whatever he wanted in this world.

When Paul proposed that they hike in the rain forest on the Olympic Peninsula not far from Seattle, she had thought they'd be entering the precinct of death. Nicky had grown up in West Texas, in dry country where everything lasted, and so she conceived of the forest as a compost heap where everything ended in wetness. Instead she learned that nothing really died in the rain forest. The shallow-rooted cedars fell with regularity. The tallest cedar became a mother log, and on it rose not only ferns and moss and colorful mushrooms, but also a new cedar tree. The rain forest was growth upon growth and she saw this silent persistence in small scenes she hardly believed: a purple mushroom next to the greenest leaf; yellow, green, and silver fungi coating rocks and tree trunks. Fallen branches were covered by bright shaggy moss, stiff appendages frozen in animated postures as if, could she say the right word, they would come to life.

Paul stopped abruptly and turned to her, holding his fingers to his lips. His face was hidden beneath the peak of his baseball cap.

"What was that? Did you hear it?"

"I didn't hear a thing," she said.

For all its abundance, the forest was silent. There was no birdsong, no hum of insects, no sudden appearances by rabbits or marmosets. Here there was only the packed silence of growth.

"You didn't hear that crackle? From there?"

She looked where Paul pointed. Water rolled down her neck, a drop insinuating itself between her undershirt and her skin.

"No," she said. "I didn't hear a thing."

"I could have sworn I heard something."

Paul took off his cap, smoothed his hair back, and stared into the dense forest. He'd been sweating beneath the cap and with his hair dark and slicked back, he looked as he must have in his twenties, always the handsomest man in the room.

When they first became lovers he told her that he was beginning to be a ruin, a shade of his past glory. She had never had the least idea of herself as glorious. Her angular face, straight blonde hair, and long body made her a type in her family. She'd grown up hearing how much she resembled certain relatives, not how pretty she was.

Paul resumed his lead and they trudged on.

The ranger station at the head of the trail was closed and they hadn't bothered to sign in. There wasn't another car at the trail head, and they had the discussion they always did before a hike, if the car key was safer in Paul's pocket or on top of the left front tire. She hadn't slept well the night before, partly because she couldn't stop thinking and partly because of the sound of the rain thrown against their window like pebbles or a message, so the discussion went on longer than it should have. When she gave up, Paul pocketed the key to the rent car, and they started their walk.

Nicky had flown in two nights before, exchanging the brilliant heat of September in Austin for the grayness and chill of Seattle.

"Dark and cold is what you like if you live long enough in Texas," she said, but Paul said, "I'm a Texan born and bred and I feel like I'm growing things."

They'd stayed one night in an exquisite hotel up the hill from Pike's Market. Without Paul, even if she'd managed to get to Seattle, Nicky would be staying at a terrible hotel, always doing the wrong thing and being in the wrong place. She had come from the middle of nowhere, and four generations of his family had lived in Austin. There was a street named for his great-great-grandfather. Paul was almost forty when she met him and before she met his family she pictured him among others just like him; tall and solidly built, but in each of the others there was something amiss—a chin too small, a jowl too big, an eye wandering; only in Paul did all the features come together perfectly.

All of his friends, even the academics, had money or property or both. She flew with him to ranches for weekends, to beach houses and, once, to a private lighthouse, to chilly dinner parties in Dallas and barbecue eaten sitting on the fender of his truck.

That was after she left her husband for Paul. Before then the new planet was only Paul, his body, his energy, and finally his inexplicable wish for her.

When they were lovers, she became someone else. Before, she had always felt transparent. What you see is what you get, she would have said about herself. Once she had kissed Paul for the first unthinkable time, she found that she loved having the secret of being his lover and she savored the threat of the affair to her life which was the only one she'd ever wanted.

Paul was long adept at secrecy. An affair with his first wife's best friend had broken up that marriage, and after his divorce he had been with a series of women, some married, some not. What Nicky failed to notice in her excitement at the glamour of deception was that he was sick of it and longed for marriage once again. As their affair went from one afternoon to regular meetings, days to weeks to months, Paul came to see that he wanted nothing more than to transform himself into a husband.

One day the summer before, Paul asked Nicky if there weren't too many memories in Austin, if things wouldn't be easier if they lived somewhere else, and she'd agreed because she assumed that they would never leave. He had a chair in the history department. They were set for life.

Then he let it be known, as he said, that he might not mind leaving Austin and soon there were ripples: the chairmanship of the department in Massachusetts, a better chair in Illinois, and the deanship in Seattle. Their new location would be his choice because the decision to leave Austin had been hers.

He'd weighed the chance that Seattle might think him eager against his wish to have a weekend with her in the rain forest and decided that since he was paying for the airfare her presence the last day of the campus visit would only add to an impression of independence. He told her which dress to bring for the dinner in Seattle and arranged for her to join him and a few university vice-presidents and their wives, along with the outgoing dean and his wife. She wondered how Paul had known the restaurant would look so well with her dress.

When Paul had been her lover for only six months, he'd improved her wardrobe from time to time. With each outfit, scarf in a color unexpectedly flattering, earrings she would never have noticed without him, Paul transformed her into someone unrecognizable, a woman more glamorous and more sexual, mysterious to herself.

All through the affair she had waited for it to end. She had anticipated her sadness when he tired of her, her gradual return to the routine she thought of as her real life with her husband. She was convinced that she would keep her feeling for Paul always, somewhere inside her. She had felt like a present wound the pain and sweetness she would feel as she looked back on her time with him. Nicky had even thought that she would remember him by the beautiful clothes he'd given her.

Instead she had sat in a pale linen suit and waited for her first husband to stop her from leaving him. It wasn't that Chris didn't love her—she knew she was breaking his heart because hers was cracked wide open—but that he couldn't imagine trying to argue her out of something as serious as ruining their lives.

"We're going to the rain forest," she told the vice-president next to her at dinner.

"I grew up on the Olympic Peninsula," he said. He was a sociologist, a thin man with a pasty face who ate his food carefully.

Often people who grew up in vigorous places looked no healthier than basement dwellers. She looked frail but had a strong constitution. Paul was the only person she knew whose exterior self matched the interior.

She named the lodge where they would stay for the weekend and asked if it was a good place.

"It's about the only place besides a few fisherman's shanties. It's nice enough. Big stone fireplace in the lobby. Lots of easy chairs."

She would want to stay in the lobby by the fire but Paul wouldn't let her.

"Chintz?" Nicky asked. She was trying to make conversation but sounded like an idiot. The vice-president looked up from his plate and she wondered if he'd heard the talk about her and Paul, that she'd left her husband for him, Paul his wife for her, though when they met Paul had been divorced for years. She knew how they must look to him, a flashy couple from Texas, too well-dressed for academia, both of them too tall, her hair too blond. Only her glasses redeemed her. She still wore them because contacts never felt right. Nicky suspected that Paul tolerated the glasses because he hadn't wanted everything about her to change. In the end he'd wanted her not for passion or glamour but for marriage.

Across the table, Paul was charming everyone, exuding the warmth that was his family's manner. He gave a sudden hearty burst of laughter. She used to try for that laugh. Paul was simple, really, a man with a deep interest in his own pleasures that she had mistaken for imagination because she was poor at pleasure herself.

The man next to her was speaking and she turned to him, smiling automatically. She found that if she smiled, people paid less attention to her.

"—your husband. You know what they say about deans? They say a dean is a mouse who wants to be a rat."

"I never heard that," she said.

"Well, welcome to the academic world," her neighbor said, and as he turned away she realized that he disliked Paul already and didn't mind telling her.

They came to a bridge made from round logs, the bark still left on them. Like the colorful mushrooms and moss-covered branches, the bridge looked theatrical.

Paul set his backpack down in the middle of the bridge and rested his elbows on the railing. He hadn't shaved that morning and his dark beard showed gold and silver. He stared downstream. There were no insects on the water. Even in the deep pools there was no sign of life.

.

"Did you like the people at dinner?" she asked.

"They're all right."

"The man next to me said he was born here. He knew the inn."

"Lodge."

"This is like the place we found in Colorado, isn't it? The bridge by the post office on the Taylor. The fishing was so good there."

"It's just like it," Paul said, "except that there wasn't any bridge and the Taylor was too fast there for fishing. I lost my footing and nearly drowned."

She had remained on the bank, watching him, too cold to cast her line.

"I must be thinking of—"

"You have plenty of virtues, Nicky, but a natural memory's not one of them. You still can't tell a hawk from a vulture. You never remember one bird from the next no matter how many times I tell you the name."

Once Paul had told her he hated talking outdoors so she knew that this conversation wouldn't go on for long. She had learned to confine her outdoor talk to questions about birds and rocks, and she kept her drifting thoughts to herself.

"I remember a lot," she said.

"Of course you do. I'm just making an observation." He reached down and hoisted up his pack, adjusting his poncho in preparation for setting off again.

Paul was right. The lookalike bridge hadn't been in Colorado at all, it had been the day before when they stopped on the way to the lodge. She followed him once again deeper into the forest.

Back at the trail head, Nicky had glanced over the notices about lighting fires and camping out, and she read the warning about bears. She was about to point it out when Paul said he was ready to start walking. She'd never hiked in a place where there were bears though her friend Barbara had driven her kids all the way to Yellowstone and then discovered that she was too terrified of bears to get out of their van. She had forced herself to take a guided nature walk and had asked the ranger about the bears, hoping to be reassured. All along the nature trail were signs with a logo of a rampant bear. The ranger said that the previous year she'd been checking trails with her husband when they came upon a bear cub nearby and the mother appeared. The ranger had fallen to the ground and stayed there, flat on her stomach, motionless. The bear took the ranger for dead and left with the cub. The ranger, badly scratched, had lived to guide them along the nature trail.

It was true that Nicky didn't always remember what Paul told her but she knew more than he realized. Chris was a botanist and on field trips she'd been exposed to a litany of identification in English and Latin. If she had to, she could break down most of the flowers on Texas trails by parts and name their families, but she only liked to admire flowers and pass along, not worry about their names. She kept plenty of facts about airports, hotels, monuments, and restaurants stored in what Paul might call her unnatural memory. If he became a dean in Seattle, could she continue working as a travel agent or would it be more seemly for her to open a little shop and sell expensive soap?

Though Paul had picked out the pale linen suit, she had paid for it scrupulously with her own money. She had taken it out of the cleaners' plastic bag just before Chris came home and it smelled of chemicals. Sweat poured between her camisole and her skin, and she wondered if the linen would stain.

"I can't stop you," Chris said. "What could I do to stop you? I can't believe you're doing this. I don't understand what's come over you. What have I done to make you stop loving me?"

She hadn't even tried to explain it. For one thing it did seem ridiculous, not at all the way it felt when she was with Paul and he was helping her practice what she'd say. Now that she'd said she wanted a divorce she felt adrift. What came next?

After hours of Chris talking and her listening and then saying her words again, she'd driven across town to meet Barbara at a place near their office, up on a rise under an awning with shade trees and a breeze. They had their salads and iced tea, and Barbara was telling a long story about a customer who kept changing his mind when Nicky said, "I just left Chris. I'm in love with Paul." The secret which she'd kept in such complicated ways for a year was spread now before Barbara like the salt and pepper shakers, and Barbara didn't seem surprised at all, neither that Nicky had been unfaithful nor that it was Paul. Instead she asked, "But weren't you happy with Chris?"

Even now, in memory, Nicky was still struck by Barbara's instant use of the past tense for a marriage only over by hours.

"Well, that explains one thing," Barbara said. "Chris called one night months back and wanted to talk to you. I said you were in the bathroom and did he want you to call him back? No. He didn't."

"Was I there?" Nicky asked.

"Of course not. I never mentioned it to you because you never mentioned it to me."

"He didn't say anything."

"He didn't want to start anything. Up until then I thought you were happy."

Nicky's happiness had been like the silence of the rain forest before she noticed it. Her happiness had been an absence of trouble, and Nicky had discovered in herself a taste for trouble. Nicky hadn't said to Barbara, *I wanted some trouble, I made some, and now I'm stuck with it.* She didn't know enough to say it. It was too early then.

They were trudging uphill, Nicky's feet sinking into the deep soft soil. Usually even the most pristine trail yielded up a gum wrapper for Paul to scorn, but here there were few signs beyond the existence of the trail and the bridge that anyone had been there before them. Back at the trail head, Nicky had seen that the most recent signature in the sign-in book was two months before, and now it seemed that even the rangers hadn't been up recently because twice Nicky and Paul had come upon trees fallen across the trail that had become mother logs.

She was as wet as Paul. Water had wicked up her jeans, and her sweatshirt and t-shirt clung underneath her down vest. She was hot and cold at once as though she'd been struck by fever. Her feet were wet too, her hiking boots soaked despite the water-repellent Paul had rubbed on at home. She tried to wiggle her toes but her wet socks mashed them in place.

Paul waited for her at the top of the rise, folding the map into his pack.

"There it is, that's the water feature," he said.

The water cascaded furiously over a series of boulders, not staying long enough to form pools.

"Is it lunch now?" she asked.

"Across that bridge. We'll have lunch there and climb some more."

"It's after two," she said. "Shouldn't we be thinking of turning around?"

"Just a little bit more," he said. "Come on. I'll go first."

The bridge across the gorge looked sturdy, metal-framed with planks of lumber, but to get to it they had to walk through the waterfall.

"Why can't we stop here? Just eat lunch and turn around?"

"Stop whining, Nicky. This is easier walking than we've ever had before."

"Flatter," she conceded. "But wetter."

She followed him up to the waterfall then stood with him looking down at their path. First they would climb over a boulder that came to Paul's chin, then a quick step into the water, then a jump to the other side, then the bridge. The water fell with relentless force. If Paul slipped, how could she help him, here in the forest? And if she slipped? She wanted to refuse, to insist: Let's eat these sandwiches and go back to the lodge and sit by the fire, but she saw Paul's restless expression as he watched the water.

They'd met after a reception she and Chris gave for a candidate for a chair in botany, a college friend of Paul's. She'd told Paul about working at the travel agency and a few days later he turned up there, asking her to send him to Denver for a conference of Western historians. She knew the university had its own travel service but she made the reservation for him.

His marriage had failed, he told her at the Mexican restaurant where they went for lunch. She and Paul were the only ones eating there. She was trying to remember if the black bean soup was worth having when he said, "I wish I were married to someone like you. Life would be so much better."

"You don't know me," she said. "Why do you say that?"

"I want a companionable marriage like you've got—"

"Now you're being silly. You don't know a thing about my marriage."

"I can tell about you," he said. "I could tell when I first laid eyes on you. I saw your sweet house. I could tell that you're a companion to a man. You're smart and sexy—"

The waitress was approaching, a woman older than Nicky, pretty and tired.

"You can't know that either," she said.

"Oh, yes, I can. That's my specialty."

He ordered enchiladas and she had the soup. He drank a mug of dark beer and the bubbles clung to his upper lip as if they couldn't bear to leave him.

"We're always the same inside, cradle to grave, in our nature," he said, "so it's our obligation to live as many lives as possible to get some variety. My world is getting too small."

Nicky had seen such restlessness before from customers who looked for what they wanted in a new place when what they wanted a place couldn't provide. He was wrong about her house; it was sweet but Chris had done everything. Chris had painted the outside a soft apple green with cream trim and accents the color of red wine. He'd had the attic made into a bedroom, then painted the inside in creams and pinks that were almost the tint of face powder. Now she and Paul had their own domesticity in the hills across the river, their own house in pure whites and grays, their own velvet furniture and favorite TV shows.

When Paul was across the gorge, she struggled on top of and then over the boulder, which was poised over the small inevitable dip into the creek. She thought, If I do it fast enough, I won't know what I'm doing. The water—colder than any ice she'd ever known—filled her boot in one step. Paul caught her arm and pulled her over, and for a second she flew. Nicky laughed and looked back where they'd been. "That'll be fun to do on the way back," she said. "Are you soaked?"

"My legs are longer than yours," he said. "I stepped over."

What if she had sprained an ankle, slipped or fallen into the sickeningly swift and cold water, tumbled down to the rocks below? The bridge as they crossed made reassuring noises as the metal and wood answered their weight.

On the other side of the bridge, they ate, silently, packed up every scrap of trash, and walked on. Here the rain forest was filled with dog-hair growth, more like Colorado woods. Counting ten steps at a time, she almost believed that they were walking up a steep incline in a forest she knew. The only map they had with them wasn't exactly in scale but had been some use until the rain blurred the soy-ink line that was their trail. So long as they stuck to the trail, Paul said, they would be fine.

Near her boot she saw a tiny frog. Nicky stopped, letting Paul walk out of her sight. The frog was the first sign of animal life all day, and it rested as still as Nicky, as if it had nothing better to do.

They had gone too far. They had begun walking at nine and now it was three. Surely they had missed the division in the trail that the map showed as their turnaround point. Or maybe they were on the wrong trail. If there was one thing in the world Nicky could do, it was read a map but this map wasn't meant to be used for hiking into unknown territory, it was meant to lure travelers to the rain forest. That's why the chamber of commerce handed them out for free.

They should get out of the forest. It was hard to tell in the perpetual twilight if it was darker than it had been an hour before but she was sure they should turn back. They were moving deeper into the forest, their food and drink was gone, their time was running out. Even if she could persuade Paul to turn around she doubted they could walk the miles of forest and rain before dark.

The frog moved and she saw that it was a luminous green and perfectly made and that there were more frogs all around her, all small, exact, and beautiful. They lived here and would die here, naturally and without thought, as self-absorbed as Paul when he decided he wanted her, as heedless as herself when she first said yes to him.

Chris had moved to North Carolina, and their small cottage in Austin sold to people who repainted it khaki and white, unloving colors. She wouldn't leave Paul. Her new life had become through time and use her own, and there would be no other. She was stretched between poles of now and then and would remain that way, her self unchanging no matter how much change there seemed to be, as constant as the forest. She had made a mistake. No matter how long she waited for a summons from Chris, it would never come. No matter what she might see lacking, she was living the only life she ever would.

Paul stopped and turned back to wait for her, looking in his poncho like an old-fashioned figure of warning, Time or Death.

She should tell him that she was tired, that the map was wrong. Let's get out now, she should say. Let's leave the forest before dark.

*The Apprentice*

$\mathcal{D}$eborah set about making herself useful from the minute she woke up, and most mornings she was first in the household to rise. She pushed off the bedcovers, slipped into her robe, and washed in the bathroom, dressing cautiously and wincing if a zipper or button clanked against the closet door; her bed was in the attic, above where Quentin slept, and his wife and baby.

Deborah slipped down the back stairs to the kitchen. Her goal was to be like water, without stop or start, a useful presence that Quentin wouldn't notice except to be vaguely grateful and admiring. Certainly not to ask how long she had been there and how long she planned to remain.

In the morning before her first day off, she pressed the orange switch on the coffeemaker and kept vigil while it wheezed and crackled and steamed, and the coffee formed, drip by viscous drip, in the glass pot. The manufacturer, she learned when she replaced the broken one, called it a *carafe*. It was not her fault that the carafe had broken, only her bad luck. She'd noticed the crack but hadn't liked to call attention to it.

Once the machine was finished, she transferred the coffee into two thermoses, one a thin stainless-steel rocket with a black strap, the other a homely blue plastic with stripes. Most of the household's items fell into two categories: imported for him; domestic for everyone else. Coffee steam rose from the carafe as she poured and from the mouths of the thermoses as she rushed to screw on their lids, to capture the genii of the coffee before the morning air diluted it. Milk for her own coffee she heated in a heavy saucepan and into this she dumped the last of the coffee. She washed pot and carafe quickly—before the milk skin dried on the pot, before the coffee stained the glass—and the smell of detergent cut through the acrid meaty coffee odor. Then and only then did she settle at the table to drink her milky coffee, almost tasting in it the milk and honey solutions her mother insisted she drink on childhood nights when Deborah would not fall asleep.

It was the time she liked best in the Quentin household and it didn't last very long. Either her noises or the smell of coffee brought the rest of them to the kitchen.

Her mother had had an awful time of it, married young to a madman who lived now by the sea and was said not to recognize a soul from his past. This was Deborah's father and she had never met him.

The only father she'd ever had was Tony, her stepfather, who had the best manners of anyone she'd ever met. Even in situations that made her mother blow up, Tony never forgot to say *please* and *thank you.* He always thought of his guests' comfort. He remembered birthdays and even anniversaries. He was fond of Deborah, her mother had assured her, and now that she was adult, Deborah could judge that for herself. He had a special set of manners for Deborah that included warm smiles when she was all the way at the end of the dinner table and their house was crowded with guests.

Tony had gone to the same prep school and college as Deborah's father and claimed not to have known him sufficiently to answer questions. Her mother always answered the same: "It was a crazy time, Deborah. He just never came out of it." Her mother had come out of it and so had Tony, but even her father's name, Standish, spoke of being stuck in another time. Her mother had divorced Standish before his final madness and, in exchange for the house, her freedom, and custody of Deborah, had signed away all of Deborah's rights to his fortune, a decision she still debated, sometimes admiring herself, and at other times cursing her stupidity. Then she'd say, "Never look back! Pillars of salt!" She had whispered once to Deborah that she'd bargained with fate, that if Deborah never touched Standish's fortune, then his madness would not touch Deborah—she denied saying this when Deborah questioned her. Dreaming, she must have been dreaming, her mother said.

There were books in the library at home with Standish's name scrawled inside, a careless, skinny signature. Deborah imagined him walking along the sea wall in his town, followed by an attendant; his books, house, wife, and daughter forgotten in the dream where he now lived. Once in a beach house that Tony and Deborah's mother rented for August, Deborah had opened the door of an upstairs bedroom whose bright blue floor was covered with dead bees, the shells of bees really. They lay in groups, so many that at first she thought there was a yellow and black rug whose background matched the blue-painted floor. She'd had the sense to tell no one about it. Her father's mind was one of the bees, perfectly formed and hollow, supposed to be dead but perhaps only sleeping. They had tried everything: shock therapy, hydrotherapy, Lithium, anti-depressants, anti-psychotics, talking. A hot breath could blow him away.

———

121

That generation had all been divorced—even her stepfather twice—and at eighteen Deborah had given up on marriage for herself. Now that she was twenty-seven she had also given up the idea of becoming a great artist. She'd gone to art school and moved into a studio, but decided that though she liked to work with her hands and had thirsty eyes, she would never be any better than a good student.

She gave up the lease on her studio and moved back into her room at her mother's, for how long she couldn't say. Deborah needed something that would never leave her, she needed serious work, and for this she had come to the Quentin household, to be an apprentice to Quentin himself, whom everyone called by that name alone, even his young wife who was only six years older than Deborah. One afternoon when Deborah told her mother that she had discovered Quentin's latest work in a shop on Madison that was more like a gallery, her mother said that Deborah had been looking at his work all her life but hadn't noticed it. A screen in her mother's bedroom, always half-covered by clothing and robes, was an early example. Quentin was an old friend, her mother said, he'd even lived with them for a time when lots of people were in Standish's big house on the Cape that Deborah had never seen, all living together and, as her mother let her know now that Deborah was grown up, all together for a time and then parting. That's how it was then.

Her mother made the necessary call—Perhaps Quentin might be willing to take Deborah on?—then reported back to Deborah that she had come to an arrangement with him. The next week Deborah moved into the household and now had been serving as Quentin's apprentice for a month, entrusted only with a few simple tasks in the studio and learning new things all the time.

"Waffles! What a breakfast!" Ellen said. She sat in the chair Quentin usually took, the baby in her lap, so that Deborah had two pairs of wide eyes on her. It was the babysitter's day off, Ellen's weekly chance to concentrate her full attention on the baby, and she was glad for it, she told Deborah. The baby's eyes were wise and knowing, which meant good digestion, Ellen said. Ellen's eyes were wise and knowing but also satirical, as though Ellen knew a few things she wasn't saying. Every word she did say sounded chosen to Deborah, not rehearsed but pronounced with care and forethought. "You won't be here tomorrow, and I'll have to make the coffee and something for breakfast. Cheerios. Nothing special. We'll miss you."

"It's only a day trip. I'll make the coffee before I go."

"That would be so sweet of you."

Deborah had seen pictures of Quentin's farmhouse as it was before he married Ellen. He'd been five years or more between wives and the place was stark, its plaster walls and rough trim the same gray-white, the pine floors beat-up and dull. His furniture was simple wood, the one sagging couch the only piece of softness. Now the floors were waxed, the fieldstone fireplace sported a shining copper bucket for kindling, and tiger-striped curtains hung at the windows. The walls were stained a pale yellow and there was a fat couch with sausage arms dressed in a floral linen that looked as if it had faded over years of use. Black, yellow, copper: all variations and distortions of color blended perfectly.

Deborah had come upon a magazine story about Ellen's redecoration shortly after she'd discovered Quentin's work, and took the coincidence as a sign that Quentin would help her find her métier. The equation was completed when her mother arranged so easily for her visit. She had wondered, looking at the pictures, where Ellen had learned to decorate, and if she were born knowing which fabric houses to go to. If it had been up to her, Deborah would have left Quentin's house just as it was. Maybe she would have added an armchair. In her mother's living room there was an invariable group:

couch, two armchairs, and a big ottoman that doubled as a table; tweed in the winter, chintz in the summer.

"Will you be going far?" Ellen asked. "Where does this old school friend live exactly?"

"Near Gloucester." Too near the truth. She should have said Stockbridge at the opposite end of the state. She might have gone to Gloucester anytime in the years since art school, or even when she was at boarding school. But she'd felt timid with the past and had been waiting for her father to call for her at school, the way other parents did sometimes, surprising their boarded children. Her mother's visits were planned long in advance and Deborah's schedule cleared so that not a moment of her mother's time would be wasted waiting for Deborah to finish class or change from her gym clothes. In her last year of art school she'd studied a map of Massachusetts and located Gloucester, which became her true north, the place she would go when she was ready.

"I've never gone to Gloucester. Have I, sweet little baby?" Ellen's little lips cupped like a rock singer's when she addressed her child.

"I probably won't go there, to Gloucester itself," Deborah said. "She's out in the country, near Gloucester." She'd never been good at lying but was doing all right so far.

"Roommates! It's wonderful you've kept up. I haven't had the time."

Deborah had known girls like Ellen at school, pretty and accomplished, girls for whom things went smoothly. Except Ellen had married a man old enough to be her father and had a baby who looked like the man's grandchild, so that strangers looked around for the missing young husband. Just what Ellen would do in time, predicted Deborah's mother. She said that Quentin never kept his wives for long. Ellen looked as though she'd stay until it was her choice to leave, unlike the wives and women Quentin had rejected. Certainly

Deborah was no threat to her, unpresentable in baggy work clothes and her new hairdo. Deborah had always been her mother's creature, dressed in her mother's severe, expensive style, her hair shaped by her mother's reliable man who knew how to soften Deborah's features and make her look more feminine, more like her mother. On the way up to Quentin's, Deborah stopped at a mall and had her hair cut as a sign of her new life, a different look to go with the work clothes she'd bought used downtown. She was on her way to an apprenticeship, she told the girl at the salon, and didn't want her hair to get in the way. A month later it was barely an inch long all over her head, making her look less like a gamine than a newly released convict.

"Is your roommate an apprentice too? What does she do?"

Deborah glanced at the clock. She was usually in the studio by now, safe from Ellen's questions. Ellen liked to chat while Deborah made the studio lunch or breakfast, planting herself where she and the baby could watch Deborah's every move. Deborah liked Ellen more than she had expected to when they first met. Ellen knew how to make herself cozy with Deborah, and Deborah found that throughout the day she tried to remember interesting thoughts or observations to share with her.

"She's a broker for Merrill Lynch," Deborah said firmly.

"Out in the country near Gloucester?"

"Computers," Deborah said. "There's lots of widows who only trust a woman with their money."

"Funny. As a rule, women like to trust men with their money, not younger women. Of course, she's not so young. Your age."

"Younger than you," Deborah said.

"Not by much. The years mean something when you're a child, most when you're an adolescent. Then it fades. Or it all rolls together."

"Maybe that's why she's so successful at what she does," Deborah said. "The old ladies don't mind."

"Interesting," Ellen said. "When I'm a widow, I might have a younger woman take care of my money. Something I never considered before. If there is any money."

"Of course there'll be money. Why shouldn't there be?"

Ellen laughed. "The golden goose will be dead. Gander."

Deborah widened her eyes in imitation of the baby. "He's not all that old. My mother's age. Younger than my stepfather. He doesn't seem at all old to me."

Ellen loved to speculate about her widowhood and did so often with Deborah as an audience. Deborah would take part only by wondering about Ellen's emotional future, how she would cope without Quentin, and what the baby would do without him. When Quentin held the baby, as he did each night religiously, he turned the child toward him and gave the baby his most serious concentration. Would the baby remember?

Probably not. Ellen liked to calculate how young she might be at the break of widowhood, if she'd be young enough to marry again or if she'd even want to (exhausted by Quentin). She knew a great deal about Quentin's ex-wives. Like everyone else from the crazy time, Quentin had married a lot, and some wives did better than others, depending on the market value of his work at the time of the divorce. In gloomy moods, Ellen feared the return of the ex-wives to make *ex post facto* claims, however outlandish, on Quentin's estate.

One thing Ellen didn't have to fear was her status as the mother of Quentin's only heir. Though he'd married carelessly, she said, he must have been cautious about something because until her baby there had been no offspring, "legal or otherwise," she always said. They lived as high on the hog as they did because Quentin believed that living in the moment was the only practical thing to do, but Ellen had ticked off several times for Deborah the annuities and mutual funds she had set up in the baby's name whenever Quentin let loose some cash.

Deborah watched him from the foyer outside the studio door, through what he called the observation glass. She thought it odd that a man who prized his privacy would keep unveiled the clear glass panel in the studio door, and she'd offered to cover it with tracing paper. Of course, there weren't very many people on the place to peep through the glass.

Quentin was not very tall, taller than Picasso, and dressed like a super in khaki pants and a matching shirt, or blue pants and a blue shirt, his work uniform. Deborah never saw him in anything else. He usually came directly from the studio to the dinner table and disappeared after the meal with Ellen and the baby into their end of the house. So what he wore for relaxing Deborah didn't know.

Quentin was famous for his lacquer work, and he had a niche creating furniture, objects, and screens. He was so famous that he had become invisible, and when Deborah had discovered his work she was surprised not so much that he was still alive as that he existed; his name was synonymous with his work which had taken his name away from him, as the Eames chair had from its creator. Quentin's latest pieces went beyond his old, beyond the decorative, and they were garnering him new attention as a master, a national treasure. He was applying brilliant technique to pure art with freedom and magisterial imagination. Some said it was a mistake, but Quentin said that it was so hard to know about your own mistakes, how could those fools be sure of his?

At first he did not allow Deborah to spend many hours in the studio with him. She worked in the foyer, a kind of anteroom, preparing his materials in small quantities. Because of the glass door into the studio, she called her foyer the glass booth, as if she were Eichmann on trial. While she waited for Quentin to call her, she read Trollope, her stepfather's favorite novelist.

Quentin's studio had been a surprise to Deborah. It was more like a storeroom than a workspace, big enough to accommodate the mess and the work, the file storage boxes piled on one another (each box stuffed and labeled *materials, clippings, old photographs, bills;* the platform on which a model might once have stood, was also piled with boxes. Quentin's studio was the densest place she'd ever been. Her mother's rooms were paper-thin, decorated and orderly.

Deborah had offered to go through Quentin's archive and to file everything. Perhaps among the old photos were some of her mother and father, when they and Quentin had been on the Cape.

He'd laughed at her idea. *They're for the funeral pyre,* he'd said. *Who the hell would care to go through that junk? I never look at it, why should anyone else?*

Why did he keep the boxes then? Deborah wondered. His biographer would care, of course, as Quentin must realize. He was at an age when biographies of his contemporaries, dead and alive, were emerging. He was not so careless of posterity's opinion as he claimed, because, after a week, he let Deborah alphabetize and file business letters and reviews from the last five years. He gave her a corner of the studio for her own, clearing away a stack of art magazines.

She valued the hours when they worked in silence and listened to the classical radio station Quentin liked. His work was, of course, beautiful, but so was his concentration, and she found herself imitating his slight hunch as he stood before a piece. He watched her too. Sometimes Deborah looked up and found him staring at her.

Her mother had asked her if Quentin was still attractive and she had answered yes without hesitation. Ellen joked about the flesh on his chin and neck that was ceding to gravity; about his farts one terrible Sunday when he stayed in bed with a cold and took Vitamin C in quantity. Deborah's mother told her that Ellen was probably threatened and playing down his magnetism. "You're younger than she," her mother said. "Quentin's wives are always jealous, usually with cause."

At night and sometimes in the early morning, Deborah heard Ellen moaning for a long time and then one gasp from Quentin. She heard the baby cry and laugh, and Quentin and Ellen talking in low tones and sometimes arguing. She couldn't make out the words. She wished she had a room far away from theirs, but the babysitter was established in the guest cottage. She couldn't help hearing the sounds and listened for them.

When she reached Gloucester she would walk along the seawall and meet her father.

The story she'd once overheard her mother telling was that their old friend Grace had gone to Gloucester to visit a cousin, and there, walking by the sea, she'd come upon Standish and his attendant. At one time Grace and Standish were an item. When Deborah's mother and Standish fell madly in love and were married, Grace became their dear friend, she and her husband, now dead in a single-car accident that Deborah's mother referred to, though not in front of Grace, as a suicide.

By the sea, Grace had approached Standish. She said that he was wooden-faced, erect as ever, with his head held at an odd, fixed angle, a difference only someone who knew him well would notice. He and the attendant were walking very slowly and they did not stop at Grace's approach. Grace finally put herself in their path. (Later, a shopkeeper told Grace they walked that same way every day.) *Standish,* Grace said, *it's me, darling. How are you?* He didn't recognize her. He looked at her through eyes she did not recognize. A stranger lived within, Deborah's mother said Grace had said. Grace had retreated. Deborah imagined Grace stepping backward like a Graham dancer, in flowing black dress, the lift of her leg creating a pie slice of fabric. Standish and the attendant moved on as if there had been no interruption to their routine. *He's mad*, Deborah's mother sighed, to change the topic.

When Deborah got to Gloucester she would find the shopkeeper and the road by the sea where her father walked daily with his attendant. To ground herself in reality she recited: *He is old and has been ill and he has not seen me since I was an infant.* Nevertheless: They walked in their usual direction, eastward perhaps, the sun to their backs, and moved slowly, in a stately fashion or perhaps a shuffle. She, waiting, saw them coming, and moved onto the road, deliberately, carefully, not stirring the air to alarm them. They paused, or rather her father did, and the attendant, surprised, stumbled. Her father, stony-faced and stony-eyed, recognized Deborah, through all the years and the long absence of physical image, and he said: *Deborah?* Or, *Daughter?* Or, *It's you. I've waited so long.* He saw her and was surprised back into the world. And then? To his house for hot chocolate? She could not imagine any further and would rather have died than have anyone know what she imagined, which contradicted everything she had heard of him in particular and fathers in general except in fairy tales. Still, she believed or wanted to believe enough so that she always came to the same place after wrangling with herself to be sensible: *What do you have to lose, you who have nothing? And everything to gain. Your father.*

*How do you do this? How do you do that?* She asked Quentin endless technical questions. "Didn't they teach you anything in your fancy art school?" He was bald on top of his head and kept his white hair cut short and neat, accentuating the strong bones of his skull and his black eyes. He looked like the china bust her mother kept in the library, a man perfectly formed. Now, as he bent over his drawing table, Deborah could almost see the dotted lines and small print labeling the regions of his brain. At first he explained his process patiently, but he must have caught on that she couldn't listen. She could understand but not listen. Her eyes overpowered her ears and her unlabeled brain, and she let them roam over his broad muscled shoulders and his workman's fingers. In early photographs of him—her mother had one tucked in a volume of Pound's poems that she had never read—he had a mustache that concealed the thin meanness of his lips. Deborah's questions stopped him from working, and he commanded her to be there and not to be there. Her apprenticeship would be silent, or at least non-verbal. He kept music on all the time in the studio and unlike her stepfather didn't care what it was: Berlioz or Bach or "Carnival of the Animals." But she needed talk. Quentin had a secret that Deborah needed, knowledge of her mother and father when they were young and in love. He didn't answer direct questions. He gave her unhappy looks and shrugs and turned away when she compromised her dignity and asked what her father was like.

Quentin looked up and addressed her for the first time that morning. "I have a job of work for you, if you're willing to work."

"I always am." If he needed her, she would stay tomorrow too, go to Gloucester another day or week.

He said, "I'm tired of this mess. Sweep the floor, if you can find it."

"Is there anything you want to save that's on the floor?"

"Of course not," he roared. "Are you deaf? I just asked you to sweep it."

She was trying to be thorough. She was trying to let him know that whatever he wanted from her, she was willing to do it. She saw herself with his sparkling black eyes, a lumpy, overgrown girl with very little hair, good only for sweeping. She turned and got the broom. When she had finished an hour later, having swept slowly and carefully, he glanced up from his drawing table and looked at her over his bifocals. "Good work," he said. "I won't need you anymore. Maybe Ellen needs a hand. That girl's off today, isn't she?"

"Yes. I'll be off tomorrow."

"Will you?"

She thought he looked relieved. Two months, he'd promised her mother, a two-month apprenticeship.

When there was company Ellen cooked French food—a piece of meat or poultry with sauce (wine or cream), rice or noodles, a vegetable. Quentin loved sweetbreads, brains, and liver, and the local butcher saved them for Ellen, along with what he called veal, grass-eating calf. "It will do in the country," Quentin said.

He'd lived in the country for twenty years and his trips to the city were few and far between. Ellen complained that she never got to wear her city clothes. One afternoon while Deborah was supposed to be looking after the baby, Ellen showed her all the jackets and trousers, skirts and silk blouses, creamy cashmere sweaters she'd bought in the last year, covering the bed with them. In the clothes, Ellen looked like another person, oddly like Deborah's mother in her daytime outfits.

Tonight for the second time in a month there was fried chicken for dinner. Deborah had walked the baby in the stroller up and down the long winding driveway while Ellen dipped, dredged, and fried. Deborah would feel greedy for the chicken the next day at lunch, not now, for she disliked chicken when it was disagreeably warm.

Conversation was sparse when they ate together like this, more so without the babysitter who kept up a running inquisition of the baby—was he hot or cold, did the food disagree with him, was he a sweet baby?

"I heard," Deborah said, "I was told once that Standish was genuinely talented. As an artist. And that's what made his madness an even greater shame. The loss—"

132

Quentin laughed. "Who in the world told you that? Your mother? I thought even she knew better than that. Standish was no genius. Nothing of the sort. First he was a dabbler and then he was a promoter."

"Quentin," Ellen said.

"A collector but not in any big way. Not enough to really help anyone. He was a succubus. He had just enough of an eye to pick out your best work and then snatch it for pennies when a fellow was down and out."

Deborah stopped chewing the drumstick and stared. No one had ever talked about her father that way, using any but the one note of pity. She had been right to come here. If she learned nothing else, she learned that when her father, her own father, was young and not mad, he had the capacity to annoy someone like Quentin. A vein stood out on Quentin's forehead.

"Your work?" Deborah asked. "Your wonderful early work?"

"Hah! You look just like your wicked mother when you say that."

"For God's sake, Quentin, what is the point of telling Deborah any of this? And keep your voice down." Ellen looked at the baby who was sculpting mashed potatoes. "Baby doesn't like cross noises."

"Honesty. That's the point."

Ellen rolled her eyes and said, "Someone always gets hurt when you start talking about honesty. It's an overrated quality."

There was a thin layer of grease around Quentin's thin lips, like a clown's painted mouth.

"Didn't they teach you anything in your fancy art school?" His schedule was like her mother's—drinks starting at six and on through the night—so Deborah was used to emotion at meals. "There have always been people like Standish. Auxiliaries, handmaidens of the arts, patrons, agents, people who oil the market machinery. But are not artists themselves. You've heard of Vasari?"

"I know who Vasari is," Deborah said.

"Your mother. Another handmaiden. Another apprentice! She and Standish fed the artists, let them have a room, a room and a studio. And food and drink. They were generous with food and drink, all right. All for their good hearts. Not so generous. Not so selfless. No one is selfless except the boring dead. All the art! We used to joke about the second-rate drawings we gave to Standish and your mother to pay for room and board. All gifts! Never asked for. Of course not. All gratitude. Some of it first rate, inevitably. I've wondered over the years. What happened to the art?"

"Some of it's there," Deborah said. "She has a lot of art. Some she sold before she married Tony, but I have no way of knowing what. I mean, there are drawings and paintings in the house, and those are all I've ever known. One of everyone who matters, my mother says."

"My screen."

"It's been there all this time. In her bedroom. The first time I knew it was your work was—"

"When she called, called about you, she said it was in perfect shape. That's how we made the arrangement, of course. Room and board for the screen. Very fitting, I thought." He wiped his mouth. "She never cared about anything but herself. Stupid of me to be surprised she never told you. I wanted to meet you, of course."

"Quentin," Ellen said.

"When did you actually know them?" Deborah asked, to move the conversation along. "What years?" She didn't want to witness a fight between Ellen and Quentin and then hear about it all the next week.

"You must know," he said. "Didn't your mother tell you anything?"

"If Deborah knew she wouldn't ask," Ellen said. "Would you like some fried chicken for the road, Deborah? Unless you're worried about making the steering wheel greasy. I'll pack a napkin. Deborah's going to Gloucester tomorrow, Quentin. To see an old friend."

"Near Gloucester. Outside Gloucester."

"Will you go to see Standish?" Quentin asked.

"Oh, no," she said. "I've never met him. And he doesn't recognize anyone anymore."

Ellen stood and began clearing the dishes, and Deborah helped her. When she reached for Quentin's plate, he clamped her arm and she was surprised by the strength and warmth of his grip.

"Deborah," he said in the voice he got at the third drink.

"Why did you say that my mother was wicked?" she asked. *Playful,* Tony said, *your mother is being playful.*

"You don't look much like her. A beautiful woman. Is she still beautiful?"

"Yes. Do I look like my father?"

He was stroking the inside of her arm.

"The eyes," he said. "The mouth. The shape of your head. Your hands."

"But—"

"Dessert?" Ellen asked.

Deborah broke away from Quentin and took the plate into the kitchen.

She leaned toward the dappled mirror that hung crooked over the attic sink. Her dark ovals and the pale rounds in the blurry photo that she liked best of Standish were nothing alike, her straight line of a mouth, his cupid pout. Maybe her masculine hands were like his. Maybe the photograph lied. She undressed in a hurry, and put on her old flannel gown that Ellen laughed at, calling Deborah a marvel for keeping a nightgown so long.

Quentin and Ellen quarreled that night, and Deborah did her best not to hear. The attic had two dormer windows and she couldn't stand in most of the room. The baby's room was just below the attic door; Quentin's bed below Deborah's. She pushed aside the worn rug that Ellen said fit nowhere else in the house so perfectly as the attic, and she took to the floor with a glass, which worked only medium well on the bumpy floor. "Original," Ellen had said, unsanded and rough. *Baby's* something. Baby's nights? Baby's right? *Baby, baby, baby,* the only word Deborah could make out in a blur of words. She might have been dreaming one of her annoying dreams with lots of talking, Tony kind of talking, background noise, when she couldn't make out the words in the dream or when she woke, yet she heard it throughout the day, a buzz in her ear.

The music of their quarrel came to an end. Deborah waited until it was as quiet as the morning, then searched in the dark for her socks and robe, and descended the bare wooden stairs, her hand on the wall for support. In the darkened living room, the tiger curtains—the perfect balance of yellow and black—buzzed like bees on a summer afternoon, and she glided past the sound without making a sound herself. The baby's room was on the other side of the door and she paused at the crib. Baby had a nightlight shaped like a fat bumblebee, its black stripes shadows, its yellow hills glowing. Baby slept on his stomach, his mouth a little open, his wide eyes closed. She ran her palm over his little vertebrae, no bigger than peanuts. In and out, and Deborah counted his little warm breaths until he stirred and moved from her hand.

The door to Quentin's bedroom was open. She navigated carefully the smooth polished floor and fat rugs until she stood at the bottom of their bed. Their feet were intertwined like a vine and a tree, and at first she could not tell whose leg was where. Ellen's foot was smaller and at the very bottom of the bed, caught in the fold of the sheets and the blankets, her toes discernible, tangible, the arch swelling the blanket. Bending, Deborah felt the outline of her toenails, like seashells in sand.

Ellen's eyes were on her. "Deborah. What's wrong?" No answer possible, and then, "You're frightening me," and movement in the covers, legs scrambling up beneath them.

Deborah withdrew her hand. Quentin rolled on to his back and put his hands behind his neck, raising his head the better to see her.

Deborah sat on the bed in the bumblebee's light, where their feet had parted. "Did you love her at all?" Deborah asked.

In the dark it seemed that there was only Deborah and Quentin.

*That Boy*


e'd been trying to buy hay, my husband and I. When Bob drove into the city to work, he noticed signs along the road, "Hogs & Pigs For Sale Soon"; "Hay"; "Coastal Hay, Bales and Rounds," but he never stopped. He didn't mind the ride into the city but he didn't like to stop. In the morning when I watched our old dog do her business out on the front lawn, checking her to be sure she didn't wander off the way she did sometimes, I'd pick up the giveaway newspaper from the sidewalk and look in the classified ads. I guess if one of the ads had said, "I'll bring the hay to your garden, clip the wire, and spread your mulch for you," I might have called. As it was, I strolled to the trash can at the curb and dropped in the paper. My husband called it as close to nothing as you'd want to read.

We lived in Garland for five years, and each year it was like we were starting the garden all over again. One year it was tomato blight, another the drought stunted everything. One year I went up to Colorado to visit my sister, and it was a storm of tomatoes; my husband's busy time, and he'd come home to an evening of picking tomatoes and making sauce. When I got back the garden was full of weeds, purple native morning glories twining tight around each tomato cage, Johnson grass into everything I'd worked so hard to clear in the spring. But the tomatoes were there if you looked, starting to be too much for the two of us, even with sauce.

I made a practice of not saying things like that—just the two of us, the two of us in that big house. There were kids all over town from morning to night, walking or riding their bikes to the school a few blocks from where we lived on Guadalupe Street, dragging their jackets behind them in the winter, running past in their little shorts on the hot days toward summer. After school there were more of them—two boys on a bike, one riding the handlebars—and when I went to the high school track to jog my two miles there were the cheerleaders, and every time I went to the Wal-Mart there were babies grabbing for candy at the checkout. At night, driving through town, I'd turn a corner and my lights would catch a child on a bicycle riding silent through the dark streets. There were kids and mothers everywhere, and at first when we moved to the town it was a continual reminder of what I didn't have in a way that it wasn't in the city where there's plenty of kids but more grown-ups, it seemed to me.

I didn't plan to be childless. I didn't think of myself that way. I tried, and I let the doctors have their day, but there it was. We didn't plan to live in a small town either, but most of the time it was fine. Sometimes in the evenings when I had supper cooking and I was cleaned up from the day in the garden or working on the house, I'd go back out to see how the garden was doing after it had time alone to settle down, and I stood looking at Marie Pavie, my favorite little rose, or the Louisiana hibiscus, tropical and almost gaudy. I heard the Mr. Softee ice-cream truck on the next street, playing an old tune to gather in the children.

Bob and I were doing square-foot gardening, and that meant laying out pieces of wood and measuring where to plant. It was a fussy way to garden but it looked like it would work. It gave order, though I liked the twenty-foot rows we used to have. This way it was like little rooms in a house, and I was moving furniture around inside each room.

We were pretty desperate for hay when my friend Johanna, who was more industrious than I, called to say she'd found us three bales each.

"Is two dollars too much?" she asked. "I don't know from shinola about hay, so when my neighbor said two dollars, I said fine."

"It's fine," I said. "I've seen it for one-fifty, but it doesn't matter."

"Oh, hell," she said. "I knew I should have asked you. I just figured it would be okay and it didn't seem like—"

"It isn't much, Johanna. For pity's sake, it's only fifty cents."

"I just figured—oh, well, I'll bring it by this morning, after the kids wake up from their nap."

Johanna had two girls, terrors both of them, though the younger, Tracy, was worse. Sugar had some manners. When she went to school the next year she got even better.

"What time's their nap?" I asked. I never remembered and felt like I should.

"I usually get them down by ten."

"I'll be by at ten-thirty," I said.

"It's no trouble for me to do it."

"Johanna," I said. "You're the one who went to the trouble of getting the hay. There's no call for you to haul it, and anyway it'll take two of us to get it in the car."

"I hope it's all right," she said. "He's my neighbor, you know, and he was mowing his yard and I asked him to dump his grass into my compost heap. So when he did that we got to talking, and I asked if he knew where I could get some hay. Turned out he has a farm out somewhere and he said he'd bring some by, and he had no idea when, but then he showed up Saturday when we were having supper. I did-n't have a penny to pay him but he said that was fine."

"I can pay him," I said.

"Oh, Teddy paid."

"Well, I'll give you my money and you can do what you like with it."

"I'll give it to Teddy," she said. "There's no need to piss him off."

I was gardening pretty hard because there were two guys working on the upstairs bathroom, a two-day job (they said) in its second week. It wasn't really their fault. This old pipe or that would come out or break or give them some kind of time-eating trouble. Twenty dollars an hour for Donnie and his helper, a sweet flat-faced Mexican kid named Ricky. I liked them fine but I was used to being in the house all day by myself. It improved the garden no end, though there was always more to do than I ended up doing.

I pulled into Johanna's driveway and she was standing there with the two little girls. I wouldn't stay for coffee, I decided.

"Hi, girls," I said. "I thought you were napping."

"No way," Tracy said. "No way, José."

"Some days you win, some days you lose," Johanna said.

She was a large, skinny woman, full of energy for everyone in the world but herself. Johanna was voted Volunteer of the Year at her church and delivered Meals on Wheels and did a lot of things I did-n't know about, though I'd admire her for them if I did.

"That hay looks good," I said. It looked a little fresh for my pur-poses. It was better to mulch with spoiled hay, but this was a gift horse if ever there was one. I opened the back of the station wagon and was fooling around, trying to fold down the back seat.

"The boy across the street hung himself this morning," Johanna said. "There was an ambulance there real early, and I wondered what it was."

I turned and climbed out of the station wagon. "Which boy?"

"The Harvey boy," she said. "There were police cars too." Sugar was pulling on Johanna's baggy jeans, and Tracy was getting ready to stop being shy.

"Which house is it?" I'd never noticed that side of the street much before. The houses were alike, bungalows, not the grand kind but the humble variety. One was a kind of medium green, a color of paint that might have been bought on sale, and the other was peeling and gray, like Johanna's house. The green house had a bunch of cars in the driveway and, in front, an old pickup. Johanna and Teddy didn't lift a finger on their house because it was a rent house. She would have, but he wouldn't let her.

"I called my other neighbor," she said, pointing to the new brick fourplex next to her house. "He works on the paper so he knew."

"Which house is it?"

I looked at Sugar, who'd heard the story before and was starting to look antsy, tugging more at her mother and sticking her thumb in her mouth.

"Is it the green house?" I asked.

"That's it. The Harvey house," Johanna said, gesturing. The green looked sad to me now, and I could imagine what was going on inside: the phone ringing, the calls to relatives, people arriving, hesitating at the door, looking scared to enter, then the bursts of sobbing and embraces.

"I saw him in the driveway the other day," Johanna said, "with his girlfriend. He had his arm over her shoulder and was kind of leaning on her. I thought, What a cutie. My God, I was in love from the time I was ten years old and every time I got my heart broken, but I never ever thought of killing myself."

I looked down quickly at Sugar, who was frowning and starting to droop, and I wondered what she was making of all this. Tracy was hunkered down on the driveway, gathering stones, looking up at my hubcaps, as if to measure the distance. I'd never known Johanna to lower her voice, and I hoped the people in the green house couldn't hear her.

"It's different now," I said, just to have something to say. "There are lots of kids doing it."

Sugar broke away and headed into the backyard, which was fenced in, and when Tracy saw her sister moving along, she got up and toddled after her, leaving her stones behind.

"All I can think," Johanna said, looking after the little girls, "all I've thought about all morning is that our kids are growing up in this mess."

I watched the girls too, until they'd disappeared around the corner of the house. It's always amazed me first of all that mothers let their children out of their sight and second of all that they can stand watching them so long.

"Let's load this hay," I said, "and I'll give you your money. I have it in quarters so you can wash your car."

Johanna said, "I'll buy us some ice cream. Or dinner."

I got home and drove the car out to the back. Donnie and Ricky followed me and unloaded the bales, putting one by the garden, the others in the shed. Ricky went back to the house to finish touching up a wall where he'd left a big handprint the day before.

"So you spread the stuff around," Donnie said. "Now why would you do that?"

"To keep the weeds down," I said. "And it breaks down and lightens up this clay soil."

"I just went to the lumberyard," Donnie said.

He went to the lumberyard three and four times a day, to pick some little notion, and always came back with news that he and Ricky mulled over together.

"They're taking up a collection for that boy who hung himself."

"Word gets around fast," I said.

"His father's a roofing contractor," Donnie said, "so the father knew everyone at the lumberyard."

"How come there's a collection?"

"They don't have the money to bury that boy," Donnie said. "Don't ask me why, they just don't."

"That's terrible," I said. I looked around at the scrawny little tomatoes in their big cages. The week before we'd had a hard freeze and I'd lost half of them, and the other half still looked pretty shook up.

"Ricky knew the boy. It was drugs. He was in trouble with the cops for drugs and he told on his friends. They don't like him so much anymore."

So it wasn't love.

"He was a friend of Ricky's? How old is Ricky?" I had never thought about Ricky's age, or whether he lived on his own or with his family.

"I don't know. Eighteen or nineteen. Same as that boy. Maybe he's younger."

Donnie wandered back to the house as soon as I started to work, and it was an hour before I got hungry.4 I was in the kitchen, making myself an apple stuffed with peanut butter for lunch, when Ricky knocked at the kitchen door and came in, holding a dry brush.

"You got a bigger brush?" he asked. "I'm starting on the floor."

"Somewhere," I said, and we went into the tool room. "Did you know that boy?" I asked. "The one who hung himself."

"I knew him," Ricky said.

"What was going on?"

"He was in trouble," Ricky said. "He got picked up for drugs and told on some friends. The other kids wouldn't talk to him."

"What kind of drugs?" I asked. I handed the brush to Ricky and saw his face close over.

"Just some kind," he said, and I knew he wouldn't say anything more about it. "This won't work. It's too messed up."

"Did he graduate?" I asked. "That boy?"

"Yeah," Ricky said. "I think he did. Last year maybe."

After lunch, I stayed in the kitchen. I thought I might go out to the garden once more, to see if the mulch was shading the tomatoes excessively, but I didn't have the heart to do it. With Donnie and Ricky upstairs working, I didn't feel right taking a nap, which I liked to do sometimes after lunch. I thought of going over to the lumberyard to make my contribution, but instead I took out a bunch of cookbooks and when I settled on my old favorite, I began to make the cake that I made for all occasions. It was a six-egg cake and called for real butter, which I had to thaw, and I had to add some heavy cream to the skim milk and hope that it would do. When the batter was done and the layers in the oven, I started grinding up pecans for the sugar icing. It had been a good fall for pecans and I had a gallon shelled and frozen in the freezer. I'd made the same cake for our anniversary the month before, and it stayed in the refrigerator on the good cake stand for a week while we nibbled away at it, telling ourselves not to.

Donnie and Ricky came downstairs a few times, saying how good the cake smelled, but I didn't offer them any, nor did I say what the cake was for. I just smiled and looked mysterious in the way my own mother did when we kids were begging for something from her.

They left as I was icing the cake. At first the silence when they were gone was heavenly; then the house felt too big and empty without them. I finished the cake and carried it into the dining room, the only room in the house not suffering from the work going on upstairs. It was the way it always was, summer and winter—dark and clean and cool, waiting for people to fill it up, our family room. I set the cake in the center of the round oak table beneath the big ceiling fan. The stained-glass window was full of the evening light. Just after the icing, before the cutting, was the time I let a cake settle, let it become itself before it was given away, sliced up, and gone forever. I took a seat at the table to admire the cake. I almost put out a finger to touch it. It would be a wonderful cake, I could tell, light and sweet to taste, but not too sweet.

I thought of carrying the cake over to people I'd never laid eyes on, especially at such a time. I would appear at their door, the cake on a plastic plate that I wouldn't expect them to return. Why burden them with returning a plate at that moment? I knew I could get Johanna to give it to them for me, but that was the coward's way out, and still they'd know it was from me and they'd be obliged to find out who I was and to thank me, a stranger—and why add to all they needed to do?

I would bring the cake myself. I would knock at their door as if they expected me, as if they knew me now, and knew that we were all alike.

I would stand at their door, a nice woman holding a better-looking cake, someone who looked like nothing bad had ever happened to her, and I'd be the sign that trouble was in their home for good.

*Hagalund*

That winter in Stockholm we ate brown rice from the People's Republic of China. The embassy where we bought it was a bus and a train ride away from Hagalund, the outlying district where we lived. I made such a trip daily to attend Swedish language classes, the free course for immigrants, leaving in the morning gloom, returning mid-afternoon when the mercury-vapor streetlights spilled pink pools in the darkness. Bill and Barbara went to the embassy for the rice, and I was in the kitchen when they returned. Bill set the ten-pound sack on the table, and told me that they'd asked a young Chinese man up on a ladder, washing the windows, if the embassy was open. They assumed that he was the janitor, but he was first secretary of the embassy. He sold them the rice, and Bill invited him to dinner. He came about a month later, and Judy and Eric from upstairs came also. Mr. Win didn't speak much English and, except for Judy who studied hard and Eric who was gifted, our Swedish didn't extend beyond simple present-tense declarations. We smiled and he smiled also. That was the last we saw of him.

By the time Mr. Win came to dinner, I'd learned to pick over the rice. It was awfully good rice, fat grains that kept their crunchiness, but it was the dirtiest rice I'd ever seen. When I told Bill and Barbara how long it took to sort through it and cook it, they said that because it was real rice, it was more demanding, naturally. There were rocks in the Chinese rice and hard clumps that looked like rocks but burst when I squeezed them into a fine sand that I had to rinse again and again. I was home anyway, so I didn't mind. I wasn't complaining, only telling.

Our first morning in this Colorado resort I sprained my ankle, trying to skate. Now I sleep a lot, night and day, my only obligation limping to dinner between my husband and my son. They spend the day skiing, and there is a smell that comes from them of cold health and sunburned skin. When the wine appears at the table for my husband and me, they start yawning, and I skip dessert because they can't stay awake. We walk back to our rooms, and I kiss my boy good night. My husband and I talk until his eyes close. I don't have much to say about my day which I've spent on the balcony of our room, hurt ankle raised and pillowed, looking out on the snow and the mountains, hot and cold at the same time.

There must have been a lot of snow in Stockholm twenty years ago just because it was Stockholm in the winter. I remember a walk that might have been many walks that I took in the cemetery nearby, in the late morning before dark, while the pleasant dry snow covered the gravestones. Lawyer, Worker, Mother: the occupations of the dead were carved on the stones. Another short walk I took in the snow or rain was to the shop down the hill. It was in a two-story yellow building; on the south wall was painted a window with a shade half-closed, lace curtains in the background, a red geranium blooming in a terra-cotta pot on the sill, and next to the plant, asleep, a black and white cat. *Trompe l'oeil*, but I took comfort that the open window, the sleeping cat, the blooming geranium were always there. The shop offered only a few things—bread, eggs, milk—and displayed unidentifiable cuts of meat and parts of chicken in its dimly lit case. I was too shy to use the little Swedish I knew. Good day, I'd say. Good day, the grave grocery lady would reply. I was relieved when we needed milk because I knew the word for it.

I own a Volvo now, a 240, the square design that was uninvented then. At the bus stop in Hagalund I studied the Volvos parked along the curb, all with blankets over their engines, the blankets plugged into the parking meters, all cozy and careful like the geranium and the cat, and I hated the Volvos as an orphan might loathe a much-loved only child. I was in Sweden the way and for the reason a Frenchman might have joined the Foreign Legion. I had a broken heart and I was hoping something better would follow. I was waiting it out in Hagalund.

To get to our apartment from the bus stop, I walked past open fields of rubble, keeping in sight on either side the new white high-rise apartment buildings. Each apartment had a balcony but since it was winter there wasn't a soul up there. I walked until I saw the stone carver's hut and outside in the little yard between his shop and the sidewalk, stones, blank and carved, some unclaimed the whole time I lived in Hagalund. Beyond the hut was the cemetery that was a garden compared to the fields. Between the rubble and the cemetery was our block—the stone gray apartment building we lived in, one private residence (yellow wood), and down the street the grocery with the cat and the geranium. This incomplete set was a part of what Hagalund had been when it was filled with wood-fili-greed cottages. In the city museum that winter, we went to *Hagalund på hjärten*, "Hagalund in Our Hearts," a photo exhibit of the pretty cottages with gardens and cats, the residents of the old Hagalund in charming dresses. Each afternoon I heard the blasting and knew more cottages were lost. The yellow one next to us was left because the owner and occupant, a well-known painter of village scenes who'd been born in the cottage, announced to the papers that if his home were demolished he'd commit suicide. The government decided that his cottage, our building, the grocery, the hut, the cemetery might stay. Everything else would make way for more white high-rises.

We kept the tile stoves burning that winter with scraps of wood from the cottages, trim from the porches, weathered shutters and railings we broke with our hands and feet. When the workers left for home we set out, stepping over places where the fires were still burning, to find our fuel for the night. I didn't save one curlicue. We were cold and money was thin. Besides, I didn't believe that I'd ever have a house to decorate with scraps from Hagalund.

To get to the apartment, I crossed the courtyard, a square expanse with a wooden door to the apartments and an iron door to garbage and storage. Some of the apartments had narrow balconies with iron railings. Ours didn't and neither did Judy and Eric's upstairs, but Mrs. Lindblom's did and she watched as I brought down the garbage. Her daughter's two-wheeler sat next to the cans. On Saturdays Mrs. Lindblom beat her sisal carpets and her daughter helped her drag them to the balcony and back inside. One Sunday the little girl was playing in the courtyard and I saw cuts on her palms.

⌒

It suits me to have a sprained ankle. I wish I'd had one the whole time I was in Sweden. This way I have an excuse not to ski, not to put myself into the Colorado view, and I may watch as I watched my son in the bath when he was two and wanted to hold water in his hand. He wanted also to hold the full moon. It was stupid of me to go skating.

The reason I was in Hagalund, along with my broken heart, was more or less the same reason I visited Judy nearly every afternoon of her high-school bout with hepatitis: I was lonely and bored, and Judy was stationary.

I met Judy at summer camp when we were sixteen, and though we went to different schools, we lived near each other on the Upper West Side, so that our friendship continued after camp.

Both of Judy's parents worked, so when I visited we had the run of the apartment. The most daring thing we did was paw through her mother's vanity to inspect her cosmetics and her nest of hairnets. We never tried any. We never ate more than the three cookies left for each of us on a plate in the refrigerator beside two glasses of milk. I assumed Mrs. Silver poured milk and allotted cookies so that we shouldn't eat or drink too much. Now I see that it was her way of being home with Judy.

I too had working parents. My mother was a social worker who helped the helpless through the city bureaucracy, her profession the remnant of her socialist youth. My father was a tax lawyer who worked downtown. He made partner when I was in ninth grade, but it didn't seem to make our family richer or any more free. Only when my father retired did I see how unhappy he'd been at his job for years.

Mr. and Mrs. Silver had a shop on Broadway where they sold medical equipment, prosthetic devices, wheelchairs, canes, and crutches. Mr. Silver had been studying medicine in Vienna when Hitler invaded Austria, and Mr. Silver fled. No place for a Jew, he said. When I left Judy at dinnertime, I passed the shop and waved to Mrs. Silver who sat behind a desk, her hairdo perfectly in place, her lipstick bright. Mr. Silver was often out on a call. Only rarely was there a customer. I wondered even then that Mr. Silver didn't seem mad at anyone, not even Hitler, that he was selling bedpans rather than being a doctor.

Lying on her sickbed, surrounded by a cloud of crumpled white Kleenex, Judy was the embodiment of resignation. She had blond hair that was almost red, and pale green eyes. Her illness made her skin yellow, and she looked like a doll. I fixed weak tea for her and threw away her used Kleenex. I made her brush her thin hair and change her sweaty pajamas. When she was settled again, we ate our cookies. One time Judy told me that she used to talk to Kleenex in the hours before I arrived. The few times I skipped visiting Judy I couldn't enjoy myself, thinking of her alone with her Kleenex, and I accepted Judy's illness as mine, though she didn't come to the same conclusion. When I rang the apartment bell, she'd greet me by name, "Miriam!" as if she were surprised to see me.

⌒

Barbara and Bill shared a large bedroom on one side of the living room and I slept on the opposite side in what had been the dining room. In my room there was a stove, a *kakelugn*—white tile, brass doors—which I never used, identical to the one in the living room, where we burned the scraps of wood. Three windows overlooked the street, each split vertically and intended to open like the doors of a cuckoo clock. I would have opened them but there was a set of storm windows between me and them.

Bill and Barbara also had three windows and storm windows. We had heavy shades though I rarely pulled mine down unless the streetlight seemed too bright. Their bedroom was a lair—shades down, the bed a rumpled mess of comforters and pillows. They thought they had the best room; they got there first and chose it. Their room was nearer the bathroom, further from the kitchen, but it had a small room next to it so their privacy was curtailed.

I don't flatter myself that Bill offered me the dining room to rent because he liked me or even because they needed the money, though I've wondered since if Judy hadn't asked him to take me in, to get me off their kitchen floor. I remain convinced that I owed my square room with its big bed and three windows and the view across the rubble to my ex-boyfriend Terry. Bill had met Terry at a pow-wow for movement leaders in New Hampshire. I don't know if Bill was a movement leader (I'd heard of him vaguely, I thought), but Terry was included in a chart of the antiwar movement in *Esquire,* and the *Voice* ran an interview with him when he was in the Tombs. He'd been in jail in New York, Chicago, Washington, California, and Mississippi. I don't know if Terry was involved in the bombings he was wanted for; they happened after my time. He redefined everything between us, asking, "Why should it drive you crazy that I make love with other people? Why should it bother you any more than if I told you I went to a meeting with them?" Terry was monitored by the FBI as were his blameless parents in Far Rockaway, and, for all I knew, I was too. Terry wasn't underground when I was with him; he was halfway between this world and another.

In Bill's eyes, Terry's virtue attached to me. I was treated as the widows of great men are, and I lived in my comfortable room on false credentials. I lacked Terry's ruthlessness and courage, his ability to transform himself into a person who lived out of a suitcase, slept wherever with whomever, traveled constantly. Terry was a person who was the same inside and out; in other words, a person with no personal life. I could no sooner follow him than burst spontaneously into flames. It was a lack in me, my need for a private self, and if I'd been so wrong, thinking he was mine, what could I ever be sure of? Even Judy, who disliked him, couldn't see why I'd left Terry. She thought all through college that we were the perfect match.

But now that was over, and I was waiting for the next thing to happen though it was happening already. I was stuck being myself, as Terry was also, wriggle as he might. Terry's time was not his own, and neither was Bill's. Both were dedicated to something they thought was larger than themselves while I was dedicated neither to myself nor to something larger.

During college I didn't see Judy often, though we went to movies together on vacations if we were free. I was disappointed when I first met Eric. Like Judy, he was small but he had a more elfin quality, with round pink shell ears resting in the field of his red curls. His father was a plumber in the Midwest, his brothers journeymen electricians. Eric was the family's first college graduate, majoring in Chemistry at the state university where he met Judy. He decided against graduate school to get married, and he hoped changing draft boards would slow things down. He found a job as a lab chemist, and Judy acted as though a one-bedroom apartment in Queens was her life's dream. Eric slapped people on the back and squeezed you right above the elbow to emphasize a point. Two weeks before their wedding I left Terry, and I was sure that couples were smug cowards, like the animals sauntering up the ramp to Noah's Ark. A week before the wedding I asked Judy why she was marrying Eric. I thought I was being honest. It astounds me that I would do such a thing. In the next year I saw Judy once when I went to dinner in Queens and ate off their wedding china; then Judy and I went to a demonstration on Wall Street where she would have been trampled by a police horse if I hadn't pulled her out of its path. I mentioned it later, thinking she'd be grateful, but she hadn't seen the horse. A few blocks away, the air was clear of tear gas. It was spring in New York and full of promise.

Eric was drafted and I think he might have gone into the army but Judy objected so strongly that they bought one-way tickets to Sweden. I told her I admired her conviction and courage, and she said, "I don't have any big ideas, Miriam. Eric could be killed, you know."

Mr. Win from the People's Republic was not our only guest. Deserters and resisters, their wives and girls, came to meetings and stayed long into the night. An American boy lived for a while in the room next to Bill's. He'd been arrested in Israel as a Palestinian spy and imprisoned for three years. He glanced cautiously at the knives we used in the kitchen and for the table. He sat with his hands folded on top of the table until Bill gave him a signal to start, and then he wolfed down his food. He didn't trust me because I was Jewish, but he ate the food I cooked. He glanced at Barbara as he did at the knives and tagged along after Bill who liked being admired usually, but something about the spy got to him.

Bill spent his days reading Lenin on the window seat in the living room. He got one paperback after another at the Red Star bookstore in the center of the city. He must have imagined that he and Lenin were alike, exiled in gray cities. Once or twice I'd disturbed Bill going through his box of clippings: Bill occupying his local draft board for a week; the wide support his act rallied; and finally Bill, bleeding and barefoot, being hauled off by the FBI. He was snickering as he was arrested but after his conviction he looked dazed, as if he'd missed a crucial piece of information. Between conviction and appeal, he jumped bail. He and Barbara went to Canada and then Sweden. Barbara talked about its going to Bill's head to read Lenin, as if he were eating too much fudge. I meant to find Bill a biography of Lenin so that he could study a long exile, but I always forgot when I was at the library. I imagined that Lenin and Bill had similar afternoons, occasionally looking at the sky over Stockholm or Geneva, the exile's sky.

In Hagalund we had plenty of food, not only for the three or four of us and Judy and Eric a few times a week, but also for the deserters and resisters who dropped by and stayed a few days. It was a long way to Hagalund from the districts where most of them had managed to find housing they could afford. It was better than Malmö where deserters were kept in a hotel and never had much in the way of jobs or a home, though in Stockholm few managed to find work. There wasn't money from home. They'd lost their families when they left the army or refused to join; one a bank president's son from Kansas, a farmer's boy from East Texas, a plumber's son from Minnesota. It's been twenty years and the rules have changed, but at one point if they wanted to come home and do some jail time, they could resume their lives. Aging parents, time advancing without them, Sweden—they must be home by now, though the ones that married Swedes would be there still, indistinguishable. They hated it when I first got there that I used current slang when they were three years behind. During meetings, the women, except for Barbara and Judy, drank coffee in the kitchen. They weren't sure what I was doing there, but no one asked.

Barbara knew her way around the kitchen, though she scorned it. Before she discovered boys and drugs, she and her mother watched Saturday afternoon cooking shows and planned menus. Nothing came out the same as on TV because they couldn't find exact ingredients in their little factory town. Barbara and Bill looked made for each other, tall and broad. He was blond and might have been Swedish. She was dark with flat features, one-eighth Iroquois, she said. We had one cookbook, *Easy Meals,* which I've never seen since. I should have been stirring up heartening meals from nothing in Hagalund, Nail Soup, but I was inadequate. It might have given meaning and shape to my days to cross Stockholm to buy Minute Rice and Cream of Mushroom Soup, the basis for so much in *Easy Meals* and available at the Food Halle, but the imported convenience foods were too expensive and the Swedish ones too odd. I made Strawberry Soup. Barbara set it aside for dessert. Bill and the spy ate it up. It's a very particular use of language, label language, and the Strawberry Soup made me see that an imitation is only as valid as your knowledge of the real thing. Maybe to Swedes the pink liquid was summer and everlasting light, but all it brought to me was a pudding my mother made from a mix, a rare concession. To my mother, anything easy was probably unethical. One night I made Sardine Soup. Only the spy ate it.

Not long before the spy moved out, Judy invited me upstairs for lunch. I let myself in with the key she'd insisted that I keep when I moved down to Bill and Barbara's. I hadn't been back often and it was much the same as it had been when I walked in, suitcase in hand, from the airport. The apartment was tiny; a short dark hallway leading to one room that contained a bed high with pillows, a student's desk, a blue tile stove with brass doors, Eric's easy chair. The kitchen was narrow and spotless, the deep sink dull from scrubbing. Some of the decorations were from the Upper West Side: the worn rug that had been by Judy's bed at home placed by her bed here; a china ballerina on the window sill; a flowered teapot with matching cups and saucers. On the desk, an old-fashioned black telephone that looked like an instrument of murder, and Judy's family photos in silver and wooden frames. Their wedding gifts had covered tables but they'd brought only a few souvenirs of the old country. Judy provided me with a cup, chipped and no saucer, to be used during my stay.

I hadn't intended to stay in Sweden and certainly not to sleep on Eric and Judy's kitchen floor for a month. Each night as I dragged my mattress from the hall closet and made up my bed, I hated myself for being there, but I couldn't figure out how to leave. Then Bill told me about their spare room and I was gone the same day. The things in Judy's apartment, though the same, were no longer the familiar and only boundaries to my Swedish landscape.

"I'm in here," Judy called. "Soup for lunch. Carrot and potato. Bring in the desk chair."

Within minutes of my arrival it was as if I'd never left, and I was reminded that Judy was my friend first.

"How did you make the soup?" I asked.

"I just used some of the bouillon cubes."

Judy and Barbara's food always looked normal and tasted better than mine. Both of them began their cooking explanations with, "I just—," Barbara to demonstrate that she had more important things to do, and Judy that she practiced the domestic arts so well.

"Some meeting, wasn't it?" she asked.

"I was in the kitchen. You tell me." I refused to go to the meetings.

"There's a basic disagreement, Miriam. It's a turning point. It isn't just talk anymore. Sam saw to that."

Sam had shot rat poison into his arm because he heard it made you high. The newspapers were full of it, fanning isolationist flames by blaming the Americans for Swedish drug use.

"If the community's trying to be respectable, he's set them back," I said. "The Swedes are so freaked about drugs."

"It isn't just embarrassing," Judy said. "Get two bowls, would you?"

At the meeting, Barbara had reported, there had been a split between the social workers and the politicos. The social workers argued that if there had been an organization for Sam, he might have had something better to do than shoot rat poison. The point, said the politicos, was not the problems of individuals, the point was to end the Vietnam War and get amnesty so that all deserters and resisters could get home. The secret politico thinking was: And continue to fight the revolution once home. I suppose there was a secret social worker thought that most of the boys were less like heroes than travelers who'd missed the last train out. The social workers thought that the deserters should adjust to life in Sweden. The politicos thought that life in Sweden should be ignored. Had Lenin joined the Kiwanis Club? Barbara told me about the meeting before she left for the day—she had a job then, typing—and before Bill took to the living room and his reading, the spy near him on the floor like a nervous, faithful dog.

"What are you going to do?" I asked. I didn't feel neutral. I wasn't comfortable with the politicos, but I wanted to be more like them than like Judy and Eric, who went to graduate school in Chemistry while Judy stayed home and studied Swedish. Actually she did more than anyone in the group, even Henry, the mainstay, a thin guy from Nebraska whose wife confided to Barbara that he beat her.

Judy had been on the phone every day, collecting addresses of resisters and deserters in Stockholm, even some in the hotel in Malmö. She spent hours at their desk, the heavy black telephone receiver propped between her shoulder and neck. She copied the addresses onto unlined white paper, writing in her clear hand. Eric and Judy were social workers, Bill and Barbara politicos. No one would get far without Judy's list.

Though I didn't live as the deserters and resisters did, like Lost Boys, taking drugs and not learning enough Swedish to do anything but buy more drugs and sweep floors—and for that Swedes preferred to hire Finns—I felt like them. Most of the deserters had joined the army because it looked like a good opportunity, and then—on impulse—they'd blown it. I couldn't predict anything about my future. Though I was free to go, I stayed.

"Well, if you want to know—" Judy balked, then dove in. "We're going to split off and form another group. Our goals are too different. We're going to get in touch with everyone and start to organize. Get them started."

"Who's we?"

"Well, we hope you and Bill and Barbara."

"I don't know," I said, though I did.

I had heard from my mother that Judy's father had been in the hospital, so I asked her about him. Bill and Barbara wouldn't be content caring for the less fortunate. I'd once asked Terry if he thought a bomb in a bank would really help anyone, and he said, "We're not in the helping business. We're trying to stop a war," in the same way he called terrorism low-budget war.

The soup was thin and tasteless except for saltiness. Still, it was homemade. Judy had laid out two crackers apiece. After we did the dishes, we walked in the mid-afternoon twilight to the cemetery.

"Don't tell them," she said. "Don't tell Bill and Barbara yet. Eric will want to do it when the time's right. It's fairer that way."

I understood two things at once: Eric and Judy were capable of wanting victory, and I was incapable of not telling. Childlike, dog-like, I would be faithful to whatever kitchen fed me.

The spy was alone in the living room. His name was Paul and he came from Pennsylvania, not the Philadelphia of Bill's Quaker people nor the factory town bordering New Jersey of Barbara's family. The spy's people worked in the coal mines of Western Pennsylvania, so far west that it might as well have been Ohio. They'd lived and died for the mines, I'd heard him tell Bill. He was holding the book high to catch the light from the street; Lenin, I assumed, but when I got closer I saw that it was an English mystery, one of an armful I got from the Stockholm library each week.

"Are you enjoying it?" I asked, and I pointed to the book when he didn't answer. "It's okay that you borrowed it. I have lots else to read. Do you want me to turn on the light?"

We were always telling him not to be afraid, that it was all right to eat and sleep and use the bathroom, but he hadn't grown more comfortable nor did he seem able to break his habit of waiting for permission—except for taking the book from my room. "It's dark," I said. "Would you like me to turn on the light?" I was about to start cutting up a skinny chicken according to *Easy Meals*.

"Why are you here?" he asked. "What are you doing here?"

I didn't pretend to misunderstand his question. "I came to visit Judy. We're friends from camp."

"Judy." The way he said it—Jew-dy.

"Yes. Why do you ask?" I felt brave, returning question for question.

"You're here for me, aren't you?"

"For you?"

"I wondered why they released me."

"You said you'd served your term."

He looked at me contemptuously.

"So they expected me to come here. I never told them."

"Here to Hagalund?" Our lives in Hagalund, Hagalund itself, seemed so accidental that even if I'd been able to believe that the Israelis cared enough about the spy to follow him, I couldn't believe that Hagalund was part of anyone's plans.

"To Stockholm." He waved his hand to indicate the larger area, the only spontaneous gesture I ever saw him make.

"But it was pure chance that you came to Bill and Barbara's. And no one put me here. Bill invited me. I needed a place. Just like you."

"Not just like me. Not just like me."

I turned on the light, and Paul said, "It hurts my eyes! Why do you do that? They kept the light on my eyes for hours."

"It's too dark in here," I said, but I switched off the light. "I have to start supper."

"I won't let you report me to them."

"Report what? That you're a picky eater?"

He relaxed, his fear and hatred confirmed. I stopped feeling sorry for him and began to feel afraid.

"I have to joint the chicken," I said.

Bill volunteered to dry the dishes and he stood close to me, taking up too much space in the little square kitchen. He kept the pantry door open for the convenience of putting things away, but there was a hole cut through the thick stone exterior wall so that the pantry could be a cold closet, almost a refrigerator, and the added cold made me more tired and sad. When Barbara dried, she laid out the dishes on the table and put them all away at once.

"You sure told him," Bill said.

"What are you talking about?"

"'Report what? You're a picky eater?'"

During dinner the spy had been expansive, reaching for the salt without asking permission.

"He's a worm," I said. "An anti-Semitic worm."

"Not all Semites. Just Jews."

"I don't see too many Arabs around here."

Bill closed the pantry door and the sudden warmth was suffocating.

"Him or me," I said. "And where were you, anyway?"

"In my bedroom. Eavesdropping," Bill said. "I'll get rid of him for you."

"Not just for me," I said. "I have other places to go, and he—"

"He's getting on my nerves," Bill said, shrugging like a movie gangster.

I let the water drain from the sink. I meant to say that I should be the one to go but when I turned around Bill was admiring me, noticing me, and I said, "Good," as I said when Bill invited me to live with him and Barbara, forgetting to think, forgetting to go home. "Judy and Eric—" I said. "They're going to start another group."

"It's the next logical thing for them to do," Bill said.


The only deserter I really liked was a tall, honey-skinned boy from Georgia, and after we made love and we lay in the dark of the night that was lit by the streetlight that had been the only light for twelve hours, he said, "I sure like you. I never thought I'd be here with you like this."

"Why not?" I asked.

"You'd never look twice at me at home," he said, pulling me closer to him. "You're too smart for me."

"You're wrong," I said, though it was true that he bored me. It didn't occur to me until years later that he was smarter than I, smart enough to tell the truth.


Early on, Barbara and I went to the Aunts, a giant brick establishment two trains away, all thrift shop. There were tables of hand-embroidered linen and an expanse of ancient, neatly folded union suits. One corner of the top floor had rack after hanging rack of the sheepskin coats used in the Swedish Army. I tried one on and my knees buckled beneath its weight. We bought napkins and heavy institutional forks, knives, and spoons, and thick white plates, some with glaze crackled by time, others with the crest of a ship or a hotel.

"It'll be like living in a diner," I said, eyeing thinner, only slightly crackled green-flowered plates.

"These are serviceable," Barbara said serenely, sure that the choice was hers. "They'll last."

She found drapes for their bedroom that she made long enough by sewing on a blue border.

On our way home, Barbara told me that she'd divorced her husband when she met Bill. She'd gone along, living the same life as her mother, waiting for her first pregnancy to surprise her, and working in a canned-soup factory. One evening when she left work, a girl—black leather jacket, jeans torn at the knees—handed Barbara a movement paper, antiwar, antiracist, a few years early for the women's movement. I'd produced one for Terry's group before the bombing. Maybe it was ours that Barbara read. I'd always hated it and done it as a duty, the one thing I felt capable of contributing. Those movement papers were an illegible mess of jargon and blurry photos of atrocities in Vietnam and demonstrations at home, but here was Barbara, living proof that such a thing could change a life. She was ripe—against the war though she'd never said it aloud, bored. The scruffy girl looked wild and free to Barbara, and Barbara probably looked to her like a working-class victim. Barbara joined a local protest group and met Bill before his trial when he was travelling around and speaking at rallies, raising money for his defense fund. "I left with Bill when he left town," she said.

"Ran away with the circus."

"That's what my mom said. My brother owned the only headshop in town, and Mom sank to begging me to stay and sell roach clips."

Barbara's mother sent her packages every month containing tollhouse cookies, a long letter filled with family news, and Tampax. Barbara thought the Tampax meant that her mother thought she couldn't buy it in Sweden, but I thought that the Tampax was her mother's wish for Barbara not to get pregnant and trapped with Bill for good.

The thick white plates outlasted me in Sweden and traveled with Bill and Barbara back to the States when he returned to serve his prison term for jumping bail. The government dropped the draft-dodging and destruction of government property charges. So Barbara was right to buy the heavy plates which had their own aesthetic anyway. Like so much else, the choice of plates was none of my business, though I felt as if I were conceding to Barbara. I did it often, conceding, deferring, and imagining that she liked having me around.

"I envy you," Barbara said. "You're free to go."

"You have a passport," I said, ignoring her other difficulties.

"I can't leave yet," she said, "but I will if I have to carry him on my back."

"He wants to go," I said.

"He's safe here," she said. "I'm glad you're here. I hate being alone."

"You have Bill."

"Yes," Barbara said, "but I'll always have him and who knows how long I'll have you."

That afternoon on the train back to Hagalund, we held our packages in our laps like refugees, and I drifted toward infantile sleep as I do when I travel. I was imagining Barbara behind the counter of a powdery-dark, sweet-smelling shop. I was imagining that if I met her years later in a street of stone buildings—something like West

End Avenue, something like Stockholm—that I might call her name, might think, Here is my friend, and that Barbara might look at me as if she'd never seen me before, not out of unfriendliness but because she'd left so far behind the life in which she knew me. And I imagined, incorrectly, that I wouldn't mind.

⌒

Nothing reminds me of Sweden, not the snow from my balcony, not the Rockies as twilight gives way to the night sky. I have more sensational memories of Venice where I once spent three days. I know I was in Sweden but I cannot call up an internal witness to verify it.

At home in a red wooden box are three marbles made of stone, not glass, one violet, one dull jade, the third a pitted, dusty ivory. Bill found a whole jar of them one day in the attic in Hagalund, and he offered me some. I stopped at three. I don't recall if Bill urged me to have more. I used to wonder—How do lives take shape so that you move from one stage to the next? How does a person make the first decision that in turn determines all the other decisions? If I found the marbles in a fairy tale, I would roll them between my fingers, and they would open in my hand like flowers and explain what I don't understand about the past.

⌒

One day I got home mid-afternoon from language school and the spy was gone. His room was empty, the bed stripped, the thin mattress naked to the world, and the window was open though the room still smelled like him.

"The lawyer's got him," Bill said. He stood behind me in the doorway.

"Is he in trouble?"

"No. The lawyer who gave him to us. I called and told him Paul had stayed long enough."

We sat in the kitchen, Bill pulling the cheese cutter slowly and carefully across the yellow slab and laying the paper-thin slices on a plate for me. I buttered Wasabrod and ate the cheese and the tough cracker greedily. Until Barbara came home and told us that there would be a special meeting the next week, I did not wonder why I was there.

The day before I decided to leave, Central Stockholm was filled with Christmas decorations whose lights broke the gloom. I started across the square called Hötorget where I'd been the week before on a march celebrating the tenth anniversary of the Democratic Republic of Vietnam. We took shelter from the snow in the lobby of a theatre where photos of Vietnam hung on red-brocade walls; streets exploding and the flayed bodies of children on country roads replaced stills of actors in Strindberg dramas. Oddest of all, for we knew the other images, was a map of the United States with its military bases marked with blue paper dots. The city where I live now with my husband and son was obliterated by blue dots; at the time it had marine, air force, and army bases. I was alarmed: were these secrets betrayed? were the dots targets for attack? Then I realized that the dots were supposed to demonstrate American invincibility.

We walked through Hötorget to the American Embassy. Stockholm police and American soldiers guarded it side by side. When we reached the embassy, it began to snow harder and we sang the "Internationale." There were speeches in Swedish. A passerby said, "If they hate Americans so, why do they all wear dungarees?" Or so Eric translated for me. When the march broke up, the corner hot dog stand was swamped. When I think now of the march it is my hunger that is most vivid and the sharp nasty taste of the hot dog—more than the words and the war, the people I lived with and the flat blue-dotted map of my country. It feels histrionic to say *my country*.

⌒

I was sure I saw Judy last September. I was waiting for a green light in the turn lane when a yellow Mercedes swerved toward me. The woman driving was small and shaped like Judy, but she wore mirrored sunglasses which Judy never would, and Judy wouldn't own a German car. Wherever Judy is living now, it isn't anywhere near me.

I say this with assurance—she wouldn't drive a Mercedes or live in the city I plan to inhabit for the foreseeable future—though I haven't seen Judy for twenty years. If I had about myself only the information I had about Judy twenty years ago I wouldn't have predicted the life I now live. It would have looked like a jail cell to me, a life sentence. When I saw women doing what I do now—clean the house, keep a job, pick up my boy and take him to soccer, Little League, cook the meals, look forward to the summer drive to fishing in Colorado and, now that we've done it once, a week in the winter to ski—I pitied the women. My life is similar to the lives I imagined for the Swedish women with gleaming hair who paid outrageous prices in the Food Halle for Kellogg's Corn Flakes. But I like my life and what more can I ask? I fear that it will end too soon and I keep my head down.

It was just after Rosh Hashanah that I thought I saw Judy barreling at me in her yellow Mercedes. For three hours in temple I'd thought about the New Year—who will live and who will die, who will prosper and who will lose, who'll have health and who the misery of a failing body, whose children and husband and old parents and sisters and brothers will be snatched from them, and to whom will be given the blessing of sameness, of a year in which no one will be lost? The rabbi said that only God knows but if we pray and study and are righteous, we can bear whatever is written. It is no wonder that I should have seen Judy coming at me full speed in a vehicle heavier than mine, her eyes become mirrors, her life a stranger's.

⌒

With the spy gone, we had an extra room, and immediately Bill invited another American boy to live with us. The boy was tall and dark, with an odd mechanical way of moving, as if every gesture were rehearsed, a little like Richard Nixon. His name was Gordon Macintosh, and he said he was from Ohio though his family had lived all over. At the time Gordon came, I was getting low on money, and Bill and Barbara always were. Eric and Judy were prudent as ants, and they were successes in Sweden. They were advancing in the language and could curse, "Twenty-seven," in Stockholm dialect. Eric was on a student stipend; as we thought of it, he was paid for taking graduate courses.

Though I suppose in Stockholm in those years, as in America, there were plenty of people who went for days without thinking of the war in Vietnam, it was on our minds all the time. Bill and Judy and Eric were stuck in Sweden indefinitely. And I was waiting. The week I arrived in Stockholm, Terry's group blew up the house they were staying in over in Jersey. I thought I'd met the boy who died, and I said his name over and over for weeks afterward to try to remember. The picture in the *Herald Tribune* was from his high-school yearbook and he'd changed in five years. After the bombing Terry vanished and was wanted. Terry was always wanted.

I'd come to Stockholm with all my money in one wad of traveler's checks which I kept in the top drawer of my dresser. The list of check numbers and my record of cashing I kept with me. Sometimes at night I compared one to the other and took comfort in the symmetry.

One night a week or so after Gordon moved in, the four of us were in the kitchen after dinner. Gordon and Bill had been inseparable—both fans of Crosby, Stills and Nash, both with a fondness for the hashish Gordon had plenty of, both inclined to confide their adventures and theories and to shut up when I or even Barbara passed through the living room.

"I saw a red sweater today in a store window on Sveavägen. Little gold buttons. Cashmere," I said.

"My mom has an old cashmere sweater of my grandfather's," Barbara said. "She mends it every fall."

"They make cashmere," Gordon said, "from the underbellies of special Mongolian goats. The peasants track the goats and gather the wool from the thorns and thickets the goats get snagged on."

"So does the cashmere oppress the peasants or the goats?" I asked. Gordon laughed his percussive *hahaha*. "It doesn't matter. I can't buy it anyway. Anyone for dessert?"

"Wait." Gordon signaled with a chop of his hand that I should sit down again. "I know a way to get more money."

"Rob a bank," Bill said.

Bill had broken several laws but not to gain money. The blending of criminal and political activities that was taking place at home bothered him when he read about it—partly because it repelled him morally and partly because he felt left out.

"Nothing violent," Gordon said as if he'd considered violence and rejected it. "A tiny swindle. Miriam, you have your traveler's checks, right?"

I knew then that he'd searched my every thing and I was too cowardly to call him on it.

"It's all the money I've got."

"You won't lose a penny. We'll double your money. It's a terrible company, you know. Who cashes checks in Saigon?"

"If we're taking an action, Pan Am's my choice," Bill said. "Soldiers in, body bags out."

"What about it?" Gordon addressed me as if Bill hadn't spoken.

I wanted to refuse, not so much from scruples as from my fear that I'd lose my money and not be able to go home. I wanted to turn from Gordon's rigid face to Bill and Barbara, and to ask them what I should do, or to Judy and Eric who suddenly seemed at a terrible remove.

"How does it work?" By asking, I was committed and I knew it.

He had a friend and the two of them would take my checks to Malmö for the weekend and cash them all, buying small expensive trinkets worth ten or twenty dollars and paying for them with fifty and one hundred dollar checks. I'd get the cash, they'd keep the trinkets; this was implicit, not stated. On Monday when they returned, I'd report the checks missing and get the refund the same day, probably on the spot. That was what the company advertised, Gordon argued. I'd seen a wool shirt the color of Bill's eyes in the shop window where the red sweater lay. Christmas was coming. My language class, which would end before the holiday, was learning all about Saint Lucia, who is celebrated with candles. It was the turning point of the year when it grew so dark that the change to light was inevitable.

What did we know about Gordon? He'd caught Bill's attention at a meeting when he'd proposed an assault on the U. S. Embassy which wasn't always so heavily guarded that a few people couldn't cause some trouble, a kind of kamikaze mission because there would be arrests and deportations, if not first a term in a Swedish jail and then deportation. Maybe his name wasn't Gordon Macintosh, which sounded too Scottish. I looked at Bill and Barbara who looked away, leaving it to me.

The weekend Gordon went to Malmö, the emergency meeting of the deserter's committee was held in our living room. Judy and Eric urged me to attend.

"But I never do," I said.

"You should," Eric said, squeezing me above the elbow. "You're in this too."

When Judy and Eric arrived in Stockholm the committee had its office in Central Stockholm in a room donated by an international relief organization. Surrounded by posters of bone-thin children, the committee discussed the latest war news, sent representatives to the annual Stockholm conference, and issued statements of support and solidarity that were published only rarely in Swedish and American newspapers. Henry the wife beater kept careful files as though he expected a postwar audit. During the breaks in the meetings, Bill told me, they usually went for coffee at a *konditori* nearby, ate pastry and drank coffee, and gossiped about jobs and apartments. When the relief organization needed the room back, the meetings shifted to Hagalund, and I'd buy cookies and make coffee. Henry carried his files with him to every meeting. Now, at what promised to be the last meeting of the group, Judy sat primly, hands folded over the list of names and addresses she held in her lap.

I didn't like the political people but I didn't like the implication of Judy and Eric's plan—that all that could be done was to try to live as best one could, given present conditions; no grand actions to be taken, only quotidian difficulties to solve. I carried a tray of steaming coffee cups and left it on the carpet in the middle of the room, glancing as I left at Judy's list and Henry's box of files. Judy's list was a road map. His files were dead letters.

In the kitchen with the straggly girlfriends and wives I watched the steam cover the window and listened to the seesaw Swedish murmur of which I caught isolated prepositions, nouns, and adjectives. Bill and Eric were shouting in the living room, a percussive background to the kitchen melody. Then the front door opened and the extra storm door to the stairs, and both slammed shut in sequence. Silence from the living room followed by laughter and a cheer. Judy and Eric and two deserters were gone. The inevitable split had occurred and by a fact of geography (my location in the kitchen) I was with neither one nor the other nor both.

⌒

One of the things I left behind in Hagalund was the winter coat my mother mailed to me when it became clear that I wasn't coming home right away. Bill had no winter coat and made do with a sweater

I'd bought at the Aunts and his leather jacket from high school. When he came in once from a walk, hands and face red and painful, I asked him why he didn't ask his mother to send him his coat. He said, "I've asked my mother for as much as I can," and I smiled as if I understood what he meant but it's hardly clear even now if he meant that jumping bail (which cost his parents their summer cottage in the Poconos) and leaving America had been all he could ask his mother to endure, or if he'd used her up long before the war came along. We liked making fun of our parents when we talked about them at all. Bill's parents were antiwar and hoist on their own convictions, angry at him and at themselves. His father, a lawyer, wrote letters proposing deals, but all the deals would result in Bill going to jail. *Not perfect,* his father wrote, *but acceptable.* At his age, Bill preferred to wait for the perfect deal. Bill and Barbara didn't worry about spending their old age in Sweden. He rejected personal speculation. She was sure she'd get him out of there. Probably it was my uselessness and my reluctance to return to New York that made me think that I would stay in Sweden forever, always single, never quite speaking the language, status uncertain. I couldn't imagine a happy life.

Neither did I imagine that two decades later I wouldn't know where Bill and Barbara, Judy and Eric were.

I do know where Terry is. I couldn't have imagined his parents' old age and I can't say how they spend their time between visits to him in one federal prison or another. He's moved around from prison to prison, and kept in isolation much of the time. I wonder if they blame themselves or if they blame Terry, whose brightness never respected moderation or craved safety. Probably his parents have been taken down to a simple state in which they are grateful to be able to see Terry and to talk to him.

⌢

When we took an acid trip we prepared as though we were going on a voyage, cleaning the apartment and ourselves, laying in supplies of fruit juice and bubbly water, and scented candles. Mostly we tripped at night, though after one p.m. it was as dark as night anyway. Maybe it was to avoid the blasting. We had no television or radio, our news came from our halting reading of the Stockholm dailies and the thin *Herald Tribune*. Still the noise of the war was with us. We listened for it.

Clean and in clean clothes, the kitchen counters and table cleared, the beds neatly made, the deep rough bathtub scrubbed and the cement floor and drain beneath the wooden platform sluiced clean—we three went to the living room, lit candles that we'd place on the tile stove, and put tiny transparent squares in our mouths. Bill liked music and talk. I liked talk because the absence of it frightened me. I suspected that Barbara would have liked music and sex and candle gazing. Bill wanted us three to make love and I was silent. Barbara refused with a slow shake of her head, perhaps because she didn't want me or because she didn't want to share Bill. Most of the time she seemed happy to sit in her corner and listen to us talk about the war, Terry, demonstrations, and the Mafia which Bill began to believe was behind everything, making even the government work for its profit. Then Bill decided that there wasn't much difference between the Mafia and the companies that ran America, then we saw very clearly that all power was one. Or, in silence and candlelight, I closed my eyes and saw a river, was rushed along the cold water not in a boat but above the water. I was invisible, the world no longer framed by my eyes.

When the talk and the rush was over, we'd get restless and walk, most often Bill and I. I was glad when Barbara stayed home and too acutely aware of my happiness.

We walked out of the apartment, down the hill toward the little store with the cat and the geranium, and up a steep hill to a tower that I never saw unless I was on acid. The ground was hard and dry, the snow cracking beneath our weight. The tower might have held electrical equipment or plumbing for the cemetery. The tower was Europe to me, back where my people came from. We tried to open the door to the tower and couldn't. Then we realized that we were cold, awfully cold, and half-ran, half-skidded home, not slacking the pace until we were through the courtyard and up three flights of stairs to our front doors, open shut open shut, and there would be Barbara and the apartment still lit with candles. She was now in the kitchen, waiting for us with hot cocoa and bread and cheese, as if we were children home from ice skating.

⌒

Tomorrow is our last day in Colorado. At dinner I pointed out that we needn't leave for Denver until after lunch, so why not ski again in the morning? They'd thought their last run today was the end of it, so they discussed it. Did they want the extra hours? They're worried that I've been bored.

When my father was ill a few years ago, I flew to New York to see him. I remembered him when he was a young man, younger than I am now, and he skated on weekend ponds, his hands crossed behind his back, serene. The illness made him an old man suddenly, the ice skating inconceivable even in memory, something another body did. But it was my father who'd skated. I told him that I was beginning to think a lot about the past, without fondness or judgment, just rolling things over. After a point, it's all a constant stream of reminiscence, he said, and he asked, How old are you?

I might be reading the books I brought to Colorado and haven't touched. I might hobble downstairs to share the couch before the midnight fire with other travelers. I prefer to stay beside my sleeping husband. I prefer my silence and the words I speak to myself.

⌒

Judy was sick with a cold the day Gordon left for Malmö with my traveler's checks, and naturally I visited her bedside, letting myself into her apartment when I knew that Eric would be at the university. Judy lay against the bed pillows, Kleenex crumpled on the quilt and spilling over into the floor. As always when Judy was sick in bed, time had come to a stop, as in the minutes before morning light and evening darkness. She gave her illness—hepatitis or a head cold—her entire self and willed the world to stop.

"What else can I do for you?" I asked. I'd made chamomile tea. Two cups steamed on the desk by her bed. At Judy's request I'd emptied the wastebasket of soiled tissues. Her nose was red and she'd pulled her curls away from her face with a pink ribbon that had seen better days.

"Nothing else," she said. "Sit down and drink your tea. Any reaction from downstairs?"

"Talk, talk, talk," I said. "What a relief. No more squabbling." The split made Bill as happy as I'd ever seen him.

"The squabbling's just started," she said.

"But why? It's not as if they're rival teams."

"They? What about you?"

"I'm not taking sides," I said. Judy blew her nose and tossed the used tissue toward the wastebasket, where it draped over the edge. "But if you want an opinion from me—Share the list, Judy. It's not going to hurt you, and if you're right about the deserters needing to be taken care of, well, you'll have your hands full. You won't have time to worry about politics, Bill's or anyone else's."

Bill had instructed me to tell Judy whatever would work and to promise anything, however unrealistic or false. He needed the list to make his case before the deserter community that his was the right way to go, politics and not charity, to make a devastating argument against what Judy and Eric would offer, so that the deserters and resisters wouldn't see themselves as boys who had screwed up and who needed help, but as heroes.

"You're wasting your time, Miriam. You'll never get what you want from him. He'll never leave Barbara." She shifted in bed to get more comfortable, as if we were telling each other the dreams we'd had the night before.

"What are you talking about? Of course Bill won't leave Barbara. Why should he?"

"Exactly," she said. She sipped her tea tentatively, then nodded, as if in confirmation. It had cooled enough to drink. I picked up my cup and put it down again. "There's no reason for him to leave her," she said. "He's scared and she protects him."

"Has your cold made you the Delphic oracle or something?" But I thought, She's right. Bill will never leave Barbara. Barbara will leave him and by then it will be too late. "Judy," I said, all business, "if you don't share the list, it doesn't mean they won't start a group. It'll just take them longer."

"But what will they use my list for?"

"To send out a notice or something that the group is split. You know, notice of the next meeting or something. Without an office and no notice—it'll all fall apart, it'll be just one more thing falling apart for those guys."

Judy frowned at me and sneezed. She reached for more Kleenex and tended herself. "Are you going to say anything bad about us? I mean, I worked hard on the list. It's practically all I've done for months and I don't want to be denounced by Bill—"

"That's another thing. You were working on the list when the group was together. Doesn't that make it communal property or something?"

"Oh, Miriam," she said. "Next thing you'll be demanding alimony."

"It's neutral information. Most of those addresses will be obsolete if you carry on like this much longer."

She reached for another Kleenex, setting the used one carefully beside her. A cloudy nest was forming, shaped like a sleeping kitten.

"Eric says I shouldn't do it."

We'd always made fun of women who hid behind their men that way; her own mother saying, "This is your father's final decision," but I would have given anything at that moment to have someone to hide behind, not Terry or Bill, but someone who cared about me.

"Oh, well," I said, "if Eric says no."

Judy finished her tea and sank back on the pillows, and she let her puffy eyelids flutter shut as if sleep were overcoming her.

"Oh, for God's sake," I said. "I can take a hint."

"He's using you," she said, eyes still closed. "Don't say I didn't warn you."

When I had my hand on the doorknob Judy called me back to her bedside. She pulled herself up and said, "Look on the desk, Miriam."

"Where?" But I saw what she meant, a green and white marbleized cardboard folder with black strings to keep the sides together.

"Open it," she said.

I untied the strings and flipped it open. There in Judy's neat writing was the list of more than 100 names of deserters, resisters, Swedish politicos, lawyers, religious people—what Bill called the deserter community, of whom six or eight came to meetings. She had recently stopped using circles over i's but it was otherwise the same hand I knew.

"There's two," she said. This was in the days when it was hard to make a copy, and I imagined Judy in the bowels of a yellow Swedish building, waiting patiently for the duplicate list. "You can have it on two conditions," she said. "You have to give me your solemn promise that this list isn't going to be used against Eric and me. Our group. I'm serious, Miriam."

"I can tell."

"The second condition is harder. If you take the list, you have to leave."

"You're kidding."

"I told you I was serious."

"Why should I leave?"

"Because you've stayed long enough." Now I thought of earlier times when I hurried up Broadway at dusk, relieved to be out of Judy's stuffy sick room, which I'd been wanting to leave for an hour but didn't know how. "It's because I love you," Judy said.

"Oh, come on." I replaced both lists in the folder, closed the cover, and tied the strings.

When I got downstairs the apartment was deserted. Gordon hadn't returned from Malmö, Barbara and Bill were out. I was sorry I'd skipped Swedish class, my next to last before the Christmas holiday. I went into Gordon's room, which he hadn't decorated except by nailing a much-folded Jimi Hendrix poster to the plaster wall. I went through the heaps of t-shirts and sweaters, jeans and boots, and I found a blue tie with a red stripe but no papers, no identification, no letters from home, no diary, no books with his name written in the flyleaf. The clothes looked like they came from the Aunts with no American labels. Not even his sleeping bag had initials written in it, nothing except cleaning directions in French and English. He claimed he'd refused induction and fled to Sweden, but it looked as if he had no life at all previous to Sweden. If Gordon never returned, it would be impossible to trace him. Bill and Barbara's room next door was dark, their bed at the center of the room, enthroned. The drapes from the Aunts made the room even darker than the dark of a Swedish day, for Barbara was planning ahead for the light of summer I'd never see.

It didn't take me long to decide to return upstairs. I never really decided. I moved with all my attention on doing it quickly and not using any more words. If Judy had said anything when I got upstairs, it might have gone differently but Judy was sleeping when I let myself in. She slept like an angel and the silence of the apartment was complete. I glanced at the pictures of her wedding, her parents, his parents. I took the copy of the list from the folder and I laid my key to their apartment where the list had been, then I let down the stiff cardboard top. I did this soundlessly and then I found the door.

In the afternoon I went to Sveavägen to report the lost checks. Going to Central Stockholm at an unaccustomed hour, I felt like an escaped prisoner, and I wanted to be back safe in Hagalund. I would get my money the next day, the bland-faced clerk told me in uninflected English. I said, "I thought it would be today."

He looked at a clock on the wall, one of many. It was much later in New York. "Too late for today. Tomorrow first thing. Bring along your passport," and he slid it back to me.

So when it was over, so quickly and unfruitfully, I was unwilling to turn around and go right back to Hagalund. I walked along Sveavägen, visiting the shirt the color of Bill's eyes and the red cashmere sweater. I stopped at a *konditori* and settled into a soft gray armchair. The waitress came, and I ordered coffee and a *franska*, my favorite pastry, two thin waffles with cream in between. There were people who would enjoy my life more than I, appreciate being free in the afternoon to eat pastries and look in shop windows. I knew this even then, but I felt rushed and pursued. The other customers in their gray armchairs looked ordinary and peaceful, as if there weren't a war on, as if the most urgent thing in the world were the packages beside them or their silent contemplation of their coffee cups and plates of pastries. They'd already made it from youth, where I was trapped, to where I wished to be but couldn't hope for, middle age. I was landed temporarily in a comfortable chair, made nervous by the small ease it represented.

That night Gordon returned with a hand-knit sweater for himself and a bottle of wine, much better than the usual Algerian red. He gave me the cash, counting it carefully note by note, and then he regaled Barbara and Bill with a story about a deserter he met in Malmö who warned him that Bill was a CIA plant. As Gordon counted the money into my hand like a careful clerk in an expensive store, I felt for the first time a little hope. It wasn't just money, anymore than the list underneath my pillow was ink on paper. When I got back to New York I went to the bank on Ninety-sixth and Amsterdam where I'd deposited my weekly dimes as a child, and there I deposited the roll of bills Gordon had given me in Hagalund, losing a little in the conversion. The money stayed for a long time in the bank, sometimes tempting me, but I left it until my life began to turn on its own, and then a long time later when the money bore no mark, I used it. It is a drop in the river of money that flows through my hands and might be paying for the rented car, my son's skis, for room-service coffee.

About a year after I left Hagalund I got a letter from Barbara that has survived the years along with a few love letters. She wrote that she was in a women's group and they were getting close and letting down barriers—Bodil, Sandy, Barbara—and attacking their sexism. Also that after I left, Gordon and Bill became very close, though there were rumors of a guy of Gordon's description who had hung around cafes near the American bases in West Germany, insinuating himself among the soldiers who were doing drugs. The guy always had drugs, enough money, and no source of income. Barbara was writing to movement friends to see if anyone had heard of the exploits that Gordon entertained Bill with night after night. Maybe Gordon was a spy. His reports may still be in a file somewhere along with other facts that no one can use. I see him in Stockholm, waiting. I see me in Stockholm, waiting also.

I'd come to visit and didn't intend to stay. Still, my second week in Stockholm, I had signed up for the free government course in Swedish for immigrants. Judy was in the Advanced class and told me that a

Beginning session started the next week. "Why not?" she'd suggested. "You could always drop out." Going to language class gave me the skeleton of a life, for my class took place at a different time from Judy's, and I went to school and returned home alone. Most days I went straight home as if the path to Hagalund would disappear unless I used it immediately. Other days I forced myself to dawdle for the pleasure of letting myself into the apartment and hearing Judy call out, "Miriam? Is that you? Where have you been?" When I lived with Bill and Barbara I went straight home and I waited for them shamelessly.

The school was in Central Stockholm, two buses from Hagalund. Dagny, our teacher, was clean-featured with yellow hair and blue eyes, and it seemed as if she were really interested in our hours of repetition. It was a class in sound, designed for herding immigrants into a quiet room and giving us the chance to make Swedish noises. There was a Polish couple, middle-aged and stolid, he in an eternal gray leather jacket, she bundled in sweaters. They sat like adults waiting at child-size desks for a parent-teacher conference. I never learned the names of the Greeks and Turks who'd come to Sweden for the work. They had a harder time than the rest of us because they knew only the Cyrillic alphabet. Our well-designed Swedish text with amusing line drawings was almost useless to them, and they kept their books closed, hands folded on top. Antonio was from Portugal and he'd refused to fight in Angola. Antonio was at odds with Sweden. When Dagny told us that there were many words for darkness in Swedish, Antonio asked, "Why learn more than one word when it is one thing, only one?" I accepted his desertion casually, incapable of believing in more than one war at a time. He might still be there, have married to someone like Dagny, who was full of the plans one may have in one's own country—the apartment that she and her fiancé would buy when they'd saved enough money, the cottage on an island in the archipelago that they hoped someday to be able to afford, holiday visits to her family in the north, and Sunday dinner with his family in Gamla Stan.

At our very last class, Dagny gave us a taste of the future tense, letting us know this was way out of turn but she was trying to entice us to sign up for the next level. I dreaded the next level. Having punctured the ice on top of the language, I sensed how deep and cold the water was.

"Yes," said Dagny, "for example. It will soon be Christmas. At Christmas my fiancé and I will travel north on the train. At Christmas, Miriam, what will you do? What will you do at Christmas, Miriam?"

I turned red as I always did when I had to speak Swedish. "I will cook," I said. "I will—" She waited. I would like to have said more to the patient audience of teacher and students, she looking forward with trust in her future, they swaying in the wind, but I didn't have the vocabulary.

"Antonio?" she asked, and he answered, "I will turn on the light."

After class, a group gathered to go out for coffee. They beckoned but I shook my head, hesitated, and left the building.

The checks were ready but in the place of the sallow clerk, against the same background of posters of sunny Spain and foggy San Francisco, was the first fat man I'd seen in Stockholm. He was light-haired and ruddy, with the blue eyes of the nation. When he'd counted out the checks and watched me sign my name to each one, he said, "Good to have that settled. So now you may go home for Christmas."

"I don't know. I don't know if that's possible."

He put his finger to the side of his nose and smiled.

"New York?"

"That would be all right."

"Just this moment a young man canceled. A flight on Christmas Eve."

"But that's tomorrow."

"Too soon?" He seemed disappointed that the coincidence might not play out neatly.

"I have some library books," I said.

"It's an evening flight," he said. "You will be there by the break of day."

"Daybreak," I said. What I did next was a tremendous relief, like putting down a sleeping child too heavy to be carried for another minute: I slid my passport to him and let him make the reservation for me, my second signature on the checks looking much like the first though everything had changed.

I shopped in the biggest department store to avoid speaking Swedish in the elegant shops along Sveavägen. I found a notebook for Bill to use as an exile's journal, and for Barbara a pair of Norwegian mittens. For my parents and for Judy and Eric, I bought lap blankets. Nothing for Gordon. Nothing for another soul in Sweden. At the time I felt smug that I bought nothing for myself, certainly not a red cashmere sweater, but I wish that I had bought something. I didn't know whether or not to mail the blankets to New York, and the saleslady explained that it was so late they might not arrive until February. There was a line of shoppers in back of me, impatient to be finished, but I took the time to say, using the future tense, "I will carry them with me," and she handed me two shopping bags and wished me good day and a happy holiday.

The bus wasn't crowded, and I got a window seat on the side I preferred. The shops of Stockholm passed and the yellow stone buildings that reminded me of West End Avenue because both kinds of buildings spoke with confidence that nothing would ever change. Then came the plain white buildings that looked the way Hagalund would in a year, then the cemetery, and it was time for me to get off the bus.

I felt burdened by my shopping bags and the schoolbooks I clutched to my side. I wished Bill would appear to help me carry them. The cemetery was peaceful and well cared for, the trees with their amputated stumps, the wetness blackening the stone monuments. The way up the street was long and I took it slowly. From a distance I saw our windows, lit up and swagged across with gold tinsel. Barbara and Bill had decorated the apartment and bought a tree for their first Christmas in Sweden. The boarders, Gordon and I, hadn't been let in on the preparations. Across the courtyard, past the closet that held the dustbins and rug beaters, up the cold stone stairs and through the doors to the apartment, Bill and Barbara would be arranging gifts for each other beneath the tree, kneeling like the Magi. I stopped and studied the garlands on the windows. I had been waiting for him all this time, waiting patiently for Bill to give me a reason to be in Sweden. Perhaps I'd thought Barbara would melt or go up in a puff of smoke, but it was I who would disappear.

Bill came to the window. For a moment I hoped all over again. He looked over the ruined blocks of Hagalund as he sometimes did all night. He might start to pace, trying to guess what he should do next, playing out scenes that would never happen. At dawn he might decide he'd had enough, and he'd walk through the cemetery, breathing the dark air, imagining jail.

When I was a child, I read fairy tales over and over. In them, one episode was part of the next and all were part of the moral. Rarely has my life matched the fairy tales, but I've examined each episode for the shadow it might cast on the next. In Hagalund there were no shadows cast, no touchstones to reassure me, only one foreign day after another. I left my winter coat in Hagalund, as if New York would be sunny and warm, not the March it turned out to be. I took the money and the address list, and the list I left on the airplane, stuck in between an airline magazine and the chart of the plane's emergency exits.

*Sympathy*

The occasion was so miserable and had weighed on her so heavily for the days since the death, that the rain didn't surprise her. It was a cold rain with an extra wind that teased the hem of her long skirt. She should have worn boots. She should have worn a heavy petticoat. The church was across town, and she went to the curb, sticking her reluctant arm into the wind and wet to signal a cab, if one existed.

But one did. An old, fat Checker cab, the kind she loved from childhood, waddled into the puddle in front of her and stopped carefully, it seemed, so that it shouldn't splash her. She opened the door and let herself fall into the cab, onto the cracked leatherette seat that had been repaired neatly with tape in a similar shade of brown. She laid her umbrella by the base of the jump seat, her bag beside her, closed the door behind her, and said, "Our Saviour. Park Avenue around—in the Thirties. Or lower Forties. That's all I know."

"Don't worry, lady. I know the one you want."

Through the clouded plastic boundary, she could see his license, but only that it was there, and the back of his head. He wasn't very tall. His name had a lot of letters in it.

From the window of the cab, deep against the back of the seat, the rain didn't look so bad. She had thought in the last week that if the weather would only hurry up and be spring, that her friend might rally again. He would be able to eat and could put a gentle layer of fat between his thin skin and his hard bones, he would be able to hold his own spoon to his mouth to sip first soups and then mushy solid foods, and then the day would come when he would leave the hospital, leaning forward to get out of the requisite wheelchair, and at the door he would stand on his own two feet and lift his head and smell the air like his dog whom he loved, and he'd say—something funny and gallant. He hadn't been gallant before his illness, or if he had she hadn't noticed. It had occurred to her also in the last week that it had been so long an illness, punctuated by rallies and retreats so often that maybe he should die since die was what he must do sooner or later, and being dead might be better than this. She had confided her thought in no one and when he did die one morning between friends at eleven a.m., she had tried to forgive herself and to say that she was just so tired.

"Mass?"

"I beg your pardon?" She hadn't been called *Miss* in years.

"There's a good quick Mass at Our Saviour this time of day. My dad used to drive us across Brooklyn to find the quickest Mass. Force of habit, finding the quick ones."

"It's a memorial service of some kind. I don't know. I'm not Catholic. I didn't have anything to do with this."

Churches made her nervous. It wasn't that her friend had been so religious, but he was a person of curiosity and when he admitted his illness was fatal he started to bone up on it, buying books that ranged from *Why Bad Things Happen to Good People* to pamphlets he found God knows where with important sections in bold; and, of course, bi-

ographies of stars who'd had various diseases. Along with research-
ing the afterlife, he tried to read his way back to health with books
that encouraged him to decide that he just wouldn't have any of that
death stuff the doctors were shoving down his throat. When his eyes
faltered, he went back to his childhood religion which it seemed had
been waiting for him all the time. Out of nowhere popped numbers
of friends who'd been Catholic all along or who had just returned to
the Church. It was they who were organizing the service.

"Won't be quick," the driver said. "These days there's a lot of extra
talking. The way we used to after Mass, now they do it in church."

"Great," she said. She did not look forward to hearing people talk
about her friend, reciting lovingly composed summings-up of his life
and his presence that would, by their inadequacy, prove to her that
he was dead. She wouldn't know when to stand, sit, or kneel. They
were passing the hospital now, where she hoped she would never be
again. She would never forget it. Was it right to grieve so? He hadn't
been her flesh and blood, not even a lover, just a friend.

"My girl died four years ago last week," the driver said.

"Girl?" He didn't hear her. "Your daughter?" It was unthinkable.

"It was an accident," he said. "Sudden. She was..."

She felt the withdrawal of her sympathy, swift as an accident.
Maybe the girl didn't suffer because it was sudden. In the church everyone else would be crying and she would comfort them. This was
her only chance and now it was ruined. Why hadn't she gotten a
driver who would go on about the mayor or the weather? They were
only blocks from the church and if she were willing to be a little
brave she could walk the rest of the way and keep the time for herself. She leaned forward and made out his name through the holes in
the plastic barrier.

"Was she very young?" she asked, and she said his name.

*Sunny*

$\mathcal{S}$unny turned from where she stood at the living-room door and walked down the long hallway. She was leaving them all behind: her parents' best friends, her aunt and uncle, her older sister—who was now like one of the adults—even her father, who sat in his usual armchair, more distracted than ever.

"Nothing dies easy," Sunny heard her aunt say in her matter-of-fact way. Her aunt lived across the river in New Jersey, and had grown up in Alabama with Sunny's mother, her baby sister. When Sunny was a little girl—now she was twelve—she thought people from New Jersey talked like her aunt and her mother. "You know," her father would say on family occasions, "if only New Jersey had won the Civil War—no income tax." Or, "Grits—you know, like they eat in Jersey."

"Raising rabbits is nothing," her aunt was saying. "Any fool can do that. But the harvesting was beyond me."

Sunny had entertained the company earlier, when they'd just gotten in from the cemetery and everybody was shivering, their eyes

191

and noses red from the November cold or from weeping. She told them about her summer work camp, run by German refugees, where the kids sang folk songs and the Mozart Requiem, wove belts, threw pots, and where the sporty kids, the tennis players, were the odd-balls. She looked up during the laughter and saw her father staring out the window, the other adults beaming at her.

On her way down the hallway, Sunny passed the kitchen and bathroom, her parents' room and the mound of coats lying damp on the bed, and, at the end, the room she shared with her little sister, who had been sent to the upstairs neighbors for the day. A few feet beyond was the apartment door. Sunny hesitated and then she lunged, opening and closing the door behind her with a slinky, practiced motion, breathing in the air of the outer hall with relief.

Sunny rushed down three flights of dimly lighted marble stairs, her feet passing over grooves made from years of tenants' walking up and down. She slid along the mosaic-tiled hallway mopped by Luis, the super, twice a week, and arrived at Betty and Russell's door, on the side of the building that faced the street and got all the noise.

Betty and Russell had moved into the building after Sunny's family, and their daughter, Bebe, who was six, was born around the same time as Sunny's little sister. Sunny could remember when she was the baby of her family. Bebe looked like Betty, and they both wore their straight blond hair in bangs like Mrs. Eisenhower's, across broad foreheads. Sunny and her sisters looked like their mother—dark hair, thick eyebrows, lips that were shapely and full, as though they might burst at any time.

Sunny pressed her forehead to the door of Russell and Betty's apartment. She knew the bumps and lumps of the shiny brown paint job better than she knew her own face. She leaned against the door for coolness, and listened for sounds from inside, trying to hear if

Betty had the radio on, if Russell and Betty were talking, or if Bebe was playing in her room.

She rang the doorbell, heard its echo: they weren't home. She'd been good all day. She hadn't cried or laughed, hadn't complained, but now she might cry. Then she heard the swing of the peephole above her and Betty's voice: "Sunny? Is that you?"

Betty'd had polio when she was a child, and from it had a little crackle in her voice, so that Sunny loved hearing Betty say the most inconsequential things. Russell wasn't around as much as Betty. In the years Sunny's family had known him, he'd been a medical student, then an intern and a resident, and now was a pathologist at a hospital downtown. He had chosen his specialty for the regular hours, for which Sunny's mother, who usually didn't comment on people one way or another, praised him at the dinner table to Sunny's father. Later, recalling her mother's remark, Sunny wondered if her father had criticized Russell. He'd once told her never to trust a pretty man.

When Betty met Russell, she was engaged to another boy, a basketball player, and she'd broken off her engagement twenty-four hours later, she told Sunny, not because Russell proposed right away—he'd never do such an impulsive thing—but because, seeing him once, Betty understood what real love could be. Russell's voice was as smooth as Betty's was crackly, sweet as butter toffee.

"It's me," Sunny said, just above a whisper. "Can I come in?"

"Sure," Betty said, in two syllables, like Sunny's father. She opened the door and put a finger to her lips, saying, "Bebe's just started her nap. I didn't expect to see you today."

"They're all up there," Sunny said. "We just got back from the cemetery."

"Maybe I should go," Betty said, looking at her jeans and sweat-shirt, a hand up to her hair.

"Daddy would probably like it," Sunny said, "but that's not why I came. I don't want you to think—"

"Don't worry, chickie. Russell's got to go to the hospital soon. I'll change into a skirt and go back with you for a minute."

Russell and Betty's apartment was like Sunny's, a series of rooms off a long hallway. At the end was the kitchen, and off that the maid's room, where Russell and Betty slept. They'd given the big bedroom at the beginning of the hall to Bebe, and had to leave their dresser in the hallway. To get to the kitchen, you had to turn sideways and squeeze.

Russell stood at the kitchen counter, the evening paper spread before him, spooning Cheerios and milk into his small mouth. "Hello, Sunny," he said gravely. Russell was in his whites, pens sticking up from the pocket of his baggy jacket. When he looked at her, Sunny didn't know what to do. She wished she were in the bedroom with Betty, who was looking in the crammed closet for proper clothes. Her mother had been in a hospital uptown, not the one where Russell worked.

Sunny watched as he finished his cereal, slowly and deliberately, washed the bowl and spoon, and laid them on the drainboard, where they dripped. He wiped the counter, then tossed the sponge into the sink.

"We were awfully sorry about your mom," he said. Russell looked straight at Sunny, not avoiding her eyes, as some did. Others stared too long, and Sunny didn't know what to do. Russell had probably seen lots of dead people, Sunny thought. It was his job to look at dead people.

"I know you were," she said. She examined a headline in his paper. There had been a plane crash out West, caused by the first blizzard of winter. Sunny had never been West, nor had she been South. Her mother and aunt had talked about jumping into the Studebaker and taking Sunny to Alabama. They'd shown her their favorite photograph of themselves as girls—in braids and middy blouses on the porch steps of their childhood home. The whole idea of travelling South, of leaving New York and going past New Jersey, had always frightened Sunny, for where was the guarantee that they would be able to return? She had once believed that if they went to Alabama her mother would change back into the girl in the middy blouse.

"Now I'm ready," Betty said. She wore a dark pleated skirt and a white top that made her look like an auditorium monitor. She lacked only a red band across her chest.

"Russ," she said, "stay a minute. I don't want to leave Bebe alone."

"Don't stay too long," Russell said.

Betty kissed him, and Sunny looked away and started down the hall.

"Bye, Russell," she called out when she heard Betty's footsteps behind her.

"Bye, Sunny," she heard him reply faintly.

They stopped at Bebe's door and watched her sleep.

"She just falls off like it was a cliff," Betty said.

When Betty closed the door to the apartment and turned to double-lock it, Sunny wanted to push her aside and open the door, to rush down the hall to see if Russell was still there and Bebe was really sleeping in her room.

Since her mother had grown ill, and even more since she died, Sunny had heard people take deep breaths coming into the apartment, as if they were coming into a place with a bad smell. But the apartment was the same. There was still a faint odor of mothballs in the living room and of wax on the hall floor. Today there were also good food smells from the kitchen, where casseroles, roast chickens, cakes, and cookies had been set on the counters and table, helter-skelter, some not even unwrapped. Sunny wanted to be hungry, but she wasn't.

Sunny's father was still in his armchair. Her older sister looked prim in stockings and her best dress, squeezed onto the couch with their aunt and uncle.

Sunny's father half rose before Betty reached his chair, saying, "Don't get up, please." He introduced Betty as their neighbor, then Betty brought a chair from the kitchen and joined the circle. They'd run out of stories, Sunny thought—something that had never happened before.

"Betty's getting her Ph.D.," Sunny's father said, naming the university where Betty was studying. "She's so smart she's going to straighten us all out. Once she gets her Fud."

Betty looked embarrassed, but she smiled and asked Sunny's aunt how her daughter in Mexico was doing. The conversation picked up. Like a kite, Sunny thought. Just when it looked as if it was coming down, a puff of air came by to save it.

Sunny's cousin in Mexico had left New Jersey when Sunny was three, and married a man from Oaxaca. Every year she promised to visit, but there was never enough money or one of her children got sick at the last minute. Once Sunny's aunt had gone down there and returned with a stomach bug, and now she was telling Betty that her grandchildren spoke English like foreigners. They shouldn't have been talking about her cousin, Sunny thought.

Her father stood abruptly, and everyone looked up at him. His voice sounded the way it did when he had hay fever. "I thank you for coming, folks," he said. "But I'm afraid I've had it. It's been a long day."

Sunny looked out the window, to the right, to the west, where she could see the Hudson if she craned her neck or leaned out as she'd been told not to over the nine floors of apartment building below. She was afraid that her father would go to his bedroom and close the door, and the company would stay. She had been taught always to knock before she opened her parents' door. Her mother had been behind the door, ill, for months, and yesterday Sunny had opened the door to find her father sunk in a frightening, deep sleep.

Everybody rose as Sunny's father reached the living room door, and they crowded together, shuffling down the hallway, gathering from his room their coats, pocketbooks, umbrellas, saying that they, too, must leave and they hoped they hadn't stayed too long and how sorry they were. They didn't say if they were sorry, too, that they let the conversation drift to rabbits and Sunny's cousin, to summer camp, sorry that they might have, even for a second, forgotten why they were there and whom they had just buried, seen for the last time.

When Sunny was a child her little sister's age and younger, she woke sometimes in the night and stood at the door of her room and cried into the hallway for her mother, calling softly and repeatedly. Her mother came—pulling her robe around her, hurrying to Sunny—saying that Sunny sounded like a baby bird chirping for its mama. She accompanied Sunny down the passage to the bathroom and guided her back into bed, tucked her in, smoothed her way to sleep past her dreams.

Now Sunny stood, her sleeping sister behind her, peering into the hallway. It seemed to her the same as it ever had, dark and endless, too frightening to enter.

Tonight Betty was meeting Russell at their favorite restaurant in Chinatown, and Sunny sat on the bed in the little room, helping Betty dress. When Betty dressed to go out, not to a seminar or to study in the library, she tried on different outfits in front of the closet mirror, buttoning blouses and dresses wrong, pulling up zippers halfway, and then she stripped them off and started again. The year before, Sunny had come after school to baby-sit while Betty attended her seminars two afternoons a week, but now, Betty said,

Sunny was old enough to stay with Bebe at night. Betty seemed to be settling on a yellow angora sweater set and a straight wool skirt that matched it perfectly.

"You look nice," Sunny said. Betty looked grownup and comfortable for once, just like Sunny's mother when she was dressed up to go out.

Betty smoothed the skirt over her belly, stroking the soft fabric. "It's not too tight?" she asked.

"I don't think so."

Most of the time now Sunny wore the same clothes—a wraparound hopsacking skirt and an army shirt, sometimes with a bandanna—and tried not to think about it. She had gone to Broadway the week before to buy underwear for her little sister, but she dreaded the time when her own clothes would wear out and she'd have to ask her father for money for new clothes, then go and buy them by herself.

Betty turned, keeping an eye on her reflection in the mirror, patting her stomach, then said, "Oh, well. I'd better get going."

When Betty left, Sunny played a few rounds of Chinese checkers with Bebe, until the little girl grew bored and began rolling the marbles all over the metal board. Sunny tucked her in, though Bebe said she wasn't ready for bed yet, and turned off the light and sat on the edge of Bebe's bed, telling her the story of Hansel and Gretel until Bebe fell into her usual heavy sleep.

Then the apartment was too quiet. The clock on the hall dresser ticked. Sunny looked in the refrigerator and didn't find anything. She checked the cabinets and extracted a soup cracker from its box.

In the living room, she looked through Betty and Russell's records. First she played a Weavers album, letting her tears well up at "Greenland," a dreadful place where the land was never green; next she put on an old Woody Guthrie album. On most songs he sang too fast and the sound was uneven, as if the recording had been made in the back of a pickup out on the road somewhere.

Sunny stared at the picture of Woody Guthrie on the front of the album. He was looking down at the guitar he held in his arms. A deep shadow cut into the hollow of his cheek. Sunny sucked in her cheeks and wished they had less flesh to them. She stared at the picture, straining to hear everything in the music. She wondered what the Weavers and Woody Guthrie said to one another—if they talked like Betty and Russell and her father, or if they had a special way of talking that sounded like the words to their songs.

While Betty dressed, Sunny had talked. Now she couldn't recall a thing she'd said, only the sound of her voice rattling on, talking and talking. She wished she could talk about her mother in an ordinary way, but she couldn't talk about her at all without crying. Lately, her mother seemed farther away than dead, down a passage too dark to see into, too thick to call out in. Sunny only talked fast to Betty. At home she felt so silent that sometimes she thought she would never speak again as long as she lived.

When the record ended, Sunny went down the hall to Bebe's room. The floor was covered with linoleum, and Sunny slid along the slick surface, feeling the bumps in the floor through her socks. She stopped herself by grabbing onto the molding on Bebe's door, and she pushed open the door quietly.

Bebe always slept the same, curled on her right side, her bangs shoved off her forehead. A jigsaw puzzle of the United States covered the floor, complete but for Florida, which lay scattered in pieces across the room. Sunny's mother had given Bebe a poster of the Cheshire Cat, which hung over the bed, pinned to the wall with thumbtacks Betty had brought from school. Nothing was ever taken from Bebe's room; more toys, dolls, and books were added. Sunny decided not to listen to another record that night, because she might not be able to hear Bebe if she woke and called out. They trusted

Sunny to baby-sit at night now because her mother had died and that made her older. Sunny walked back down the hall, touching both walls as if she could not move without their support.

After Christmas, Sunny's father hired a housekeeper—Desi, a gigantic black woman with a scar from ear to ear across her throat. Sunny's older sister said it was from a knife fight. Their father said it was probably from a thyroid operation, but no one asked Desi, who was silent and methodical in her work. She overcooked the green beans and used canned fruit, which Sunny's mother would never do.

Sunny's older sister was applying for college, and she and Sunny's father talked each night at the dinner table about her prospects. Her little sister had started to take violin lessons, and she walked all by herself twice a week to her teacher's house on Central Park West. Often when Sunny went to their room after school, she found her standing in the middle of the room, violin clamped between her chin and shoulder, frowning until her two eyebrows were one. When Sunny saw her with her friends in front of the building, she seemed older than Bebe, yet Sunny had to swallow hard and stop herself from ordering her upstairs at once, where she'd be safe.

During dinner, while Desi waited in the kitchen for them to finish and her sisters talked, Sunny kept her eyes on her plate. If her father asked her a question, she ducked her head and mumbled. If he asked her to say it again, she looked up and spat out what she'd already said.

"Big news from downstairs," her father said one night. "I bumped into Russell in the lobby. They're expecting another child. Isn't that marvelous? She gets her Fud at the end of the school year, a new baby in the summer, and they're looking very seriously for a house to buy in the sticks."

"What do you mean?" Sunny asked, looking up from her plate.

She'd been cutting her liver and bacon into smaller and smaller pieces, hoping it would go away.

"Just what he said, dummy," her older sister said. "Betty's having a baby and they're moving away. Don't you talk to them? You practically live there."

Sunny couldn't imagine why Russell and Betty wanted a baby. Nor could she imagine their becoming people like her parents' friends in Larchmont and New Rochelle, people with plenty of room. Betty and Russell, Bebe too, would forget her, and everything else about their city life. Once they left the street, that would be the last Sunny saw of them. When she thought this, she felt as if they were already gone and she was only a memory.

Sunny met Betty by accident in the elevator the next day, and Betty told her what she already knew. Betty stood, holding the elevator door open with her foot, her arms full of books and a grocery bag.

"I started to tell you a few times," Betty said. "I'm sorry."

"It's O.K.," Sunny said. She kept her eyes fixed on the panel above the door where the numbers of the floors were illuminated. She could hear thumping from below. Someone wanted the elevator.

"Russell's at the hospital late tonight," Betty said in her crackly voice. "Come down and keep us company?"

"I don't know."

"Come down for noodle casserole?"

"O.K.," Sunny said quickly. Another time—when her mother was sick, before Sunny knew Betty and Russell were moving—she would have been happy for the invitation. She grasped the wooden railing at the back of the elevator and said, "You'd better let go. Someone wants the elevator."

After that, when Sunny went to dinner at Betty and Russell's or came to babysit for Bebe, she didn't talk in her old way. Now it was Betty who talked—about the baby kicking, or finishing her dissertation, or houses they'd seen on weekends. Sunny listened as Betty once had, and she wondered what she could say or do to make things the way they had been.

One night when winter was over, Betty told Sunny that they'd finally found a house. She had made Sunny's favorite meal of lamb chops and frozen green beans with almonds, and when she told Sunny the news Sunny felt tricked into feeling good. She put down her fork and asked, "Where is it?"

Betty said, "It's on the other side of the river, Sunny. But it isn't the Confederacy, it's still New York State. You'll love it. I want you to come out a lot."

"Sure," Sunny said.

Her father had been talking about sending her to camp again, trying to get rid of her for the summer, but she wanted to see the city in the hot months. When her mother was alive, the whole family went for the summer to New Jersey. They rented a house down the street from Sunny's aunt, from people who went home to Canada to visit their relatives. Sunny wished everyone would stay in one place. She never wanted to leave Manhattan Island. Now her father would tell her to visit Russell and Betty, as if a trip across the river would serve some medicinal purpose.

Betty said, "It isn't for two months. We still have lots of time."

"Sure," Sunny said.

"The house has a white porch," Betty said.

Sunny thought of the house in Alabama, the little girls in braids on the porch steps.

"That's just peachy," she said, and then was ashamed of herself. To make things better, she said, sounding a little like her mother, "I can't wait to see it."

School was finally over, and Sunny helped Betty pack, and she baby-sat for the last time for Bebe while Russell and Betty went out for Chinese food.

All through the week of packing, Betty wore the same blue-and-white checked maternity dress. She washed it at night, and the smell of ironing greeted Sunny each morning. Sunny's mother had taught Betty to iron the right way, the small parts first, but Betty still rushed and left deep, neat creases in the fabric.

Sunny made trips each day to the liquor and grocery stores for empty cartons. The pile of packed boxes at the centers of all the rooms grew, until on the last night nothing was left in the apartment but one dish for each of them.

The morning they were leaving, Sunny woke feeling that she'd missed something important or had forgotten to do something she'd promised. She put on her clothes from the day before and started downstairs. She was out in the elevator before she remembered that nothing had really happened yet. She decided that after they left she'd go back into Betty and Russell's apartment and stay for a while. She wanted to know what it would feel like to be there without people or furniture, or the poster of the Cheshire Cat. She wondered if she might be able to see what was no longer there. No one would know where she was. Even she wouldn't be quite sure.

All morning she helped Russell and Betty by playing with Bebe until the moving men showed up. Then the apartment was emptied faster than anyone could have guessed. Two small suitcases—one for Russell and Betty, one for Bebe—were loaded into the old brown station wagon in which Betty, Russell, and Bebe would drive across the river.

When they were in the car and she was still on the sidewalk, Sunny was startled when Betty said what she herself was thinking. "You should be coming with us."

For a second, Sunny thought she would do it, cram into the

backseat with Bebe and her dolls, not say a word to her father or sisters.

"Oh, there isn't room in the car," Sunny said. "I'll come soon."

She waved goodbye and watched as the car disappeared around the corner. Then she turned away and went back into the apartment house. She rang for the elevator and thought of the heavy, solid door of Betty's apartment.

In the elevator she pushed the button for Betty's floor. She leaned her head against the elevator wall, her spine pressed against the wooden railing. She could remember when she was so small that she could reach up to the railing and hang on like a monkey. Her mother told her not to do that, that someday the railing would come off in her hands. So when Sunny was alone in the elevator she usually grabbed the railing, stretching her arms and bending back, walking herself up the wall. She liked to imagine that if the railing did pull free she would fall backward very slowly, through the floor, straight down the dark elevator shaft. But now Sunny knew that if she did pull until the railing came off in her hands and she did fall, that even the darkness would have an end.

*Buddy*

here were footsteps on the stairs, flights below, and I tried to guess if it was a man or a woman, young or old. It might have been my sister's landlady, Madame Lansky, a spinster who lived in the ground-floor apartment. Years before, the brownstone had been divided into apartments; closets were made into kitchens, hallways into closets, the curving wooden staircase covered by a patchwork of dark carpeting. Skinny and full of wrath, Madame Lansky spied on everyone who came and went, and though she didn't mind my brother-in-law's admirers or the people my sister helped with problems, she dreaded family. She'd stopped me once on my way upstairs, accusing me of trying to move in with Marilyn and Alan, saying, "You, you," as if I'd committed a crime against her in the past. Now, I thought, she'll see my suitcase and make a fuss. I looked around the landing for a place to hide the suitcase, but before I could drag it to the corner Marilyn came up the last half-flight of stairs.

She was beautiful, my sister. I'd spent years of my childhood staring at her, waiting for her beauty to disappear. She was carrying two bags of groceries, and her head was lowered in an unaccustomed, tired way. Her expression, when she reached the landing and looked up, was abstracted and uncertain, like a dreaming child's.

"Louise," she said. "How did you get into the building? I hurried as fast as I could and then you weren't downstairs, so I thought you'd come and left."

"Let me take those bags," I said, trying to be another person, one who wasn't angry with Marilyn and never would be.

My sister had a different sense of time than I—for her, days passed as hours, minutes as seconds. I'd waited on the street until another tenant let me in; then I'd climbed four flights of stairs and assumed my place on the dusty landing. Once or twice, I'd kicked my suitcase, moving it an inch at a time.

"There's more downstairs, Weasel," she said. "If you wouldn't mind."

I was imposing on Marilyn and Alan, which put me in a weak position for indignation. The night before, I'd telephoned from Boston after midnight. My brother-in-law answered out of a deep sleep.

"I'm sorry I woke you," I said, but he insisted that he was glad to hear my voice.

"I guess I'm at the end of my rope," I said. I didn't tell him I'd been crying as I sat there, and trying not to telephone. I asked if I could speak to Marilyn, though I knew that Alan would have listened patiently and would have found a word to say to help me past a trouble he would regard—as he did all trouble and all happiness—as a momentary transition.

"Of course," Alan said, and I thought I could hear the rustle of bed linen, the groan of the bed, the fissure my call created in the solid wall of flesh that was Marilyn and Alan. At times, talking to them, I felt that they loved me as much as they loved anyone, yet my presence or absence was the same to them, and that they might be wishing I'd leave, so they could be alone again.

When Marilyn came on the phone, sleepy and thick-tongued, I asked if I could visit for a few days. "Come tomorrow," Marilyn said, and then she promised to be in the apartment waiting for me.

Once I'd called, I felt a little foolish for begging to be let inside their warm circle. As I settled down for sleep, I waited for this blow to my pride to jolt me awake or to start up the tears that had plagued me for weeks. But I slept deeply through the night.

When Marilyn and I were growing up, it was unthinkable that we'd live far apart, unimaginable that we'd go through a day without talking several times. We were close when I'd lived in New York, but I'd been in Boston for three years. I wondered what we'd find to talk about this visit, now that we had nothing in common day to day. Traditionally, when we ran out of things to say we'd turn to the topic of my boyfriend, Josh. But in the month since Josh and I had parted company, I'd decided not to talk about him any more—not one memory of him in happier times, not a mention of his status, his opinions, his good or bad qualities—no small reference to the fact that I still loved him. I would try to act as if I were all right, even content. If I couldn't stop thinking about Josh until my heart was sore, I could keep it to myself and hope that my silence would help me through this time which I saw as a chasm too wide to jump, too deep to walk.

In the fourteen years I'd been with Josh, I'd grown used to everyone I knew treating me as though I had a slight but crippling infirmity. If there was a general discussion of love and I spoke, my friends and family listened, paused, and resumed the conversation as if there had been no interruption. I knew I loved Josh more than he loved me, but this was only another form of love. What other people thought, or where the balance of affection was achieved, didn't matter so long as he and I were together. Josh was a folksinger, with a small following in places like Saratoga Springs and Burlington. He was on the road a lot, and even when he was home, in Boston, we didn't see each other every day, sometimes not every week, but it didn't matter. He was in my life, if he was there or not, and when he did come around or we traveled together I was happier than my friends, happier even than my sister. Because I was so empty when he wasn't there, pitched so far forward toward the reunion, when the moment came for us to be together I was sometimes sick with excitement.

"Are you all right?" he'd ask. "I'm great," I'd answer, and then Josh would tell me about a new song he was writing or a performance he'd given. "Never argue when you're on the road," he liked to say, finishing up a story of bad food or a car accident he'd witnessed, any of the obstructions a traveler faces. I took this to mean that I should never argue, or attempt to quarrel with my fate.

I'd met Josh when I was sixteen and he was twenty, and since then my time had been divided into good time when he was there and disposable time when he was gone. For years, I lived in New York, taking classes, working at one thing after another: typing for a temporary agency, waiting on tables in restaurants, or selling in department stores at Christmas. I thought I was living like this until I discovered what I really wanted to do. When I moved to Boston, I saw that I was doing what I wanted already.

Much of the time, I waited: for Josh's set to be over, for the tour to end, for him to wake from travel-weary sleep. Forever, it now seemed, he was up on stage, a small, red-haired man with a light tenor and an adequate ability to play guitar. I would sit at a table a little too close to the stage, a little too tall for Josh, plain-looking, grateful when someone recognized me as his girl. Josh sang old Carter Family songs like "Will the Circle Be Unbroken," and sometimes he dedicated "I'll Fly Away" to me, and I'd feel as though he were touching me as he sang. It made my skin crawl now to think of myself that way. My time was good only for marking off the calendar, and I lived for his return, which might come days or even a week past the promised hour because, as it turned out, Josh wasn't counting.

Women are fools, to judge from my experience. Josh was married now to a pretty little girl from Maine whom he'd got pregnant on one of his short hops around New England. The girl's parents owned a club he sang in. One Thanksgiving, years ago, Josh had taken me to see them. I'd been one of twenty or more people at tables they'd set up all over the big hay barn they'd made into a house. The ceiling extended without a break to the peak of the roof. The men and women at the tables were a few years older than I, and they looked hearty in their country clothes. I could disappear and no one would notice, I thought. There was a diamond ring on the hand of our hostess, a former debutante, now a housewife in the woods. Her husband, like most of the other men, was going to fat a little from all the home-grown, home-cooked food, his plaid wool shirt straining at the buttons. The men wore long graying beards and braids, as if nothing would ever change. Across the table from where Josh and I sat, my hand on his knee for comfort, was a girl of eleven or twelve, with almost coffee-colored skin and almost blond hair, staring at us. I smiled, but it wasn't me she was looking at.

When he came home a month ago, Josh told me she was pregnant. I asked him if she was out of high school yet, and he straightened his shoulders and said she was going to get an equivalency certificate. "I feel like I'm getting old," he said, "and it's time to start a family." He would live with the girl and her parents in the barn until spring, when the child was born. And then? He shrugged. We'd always been so careful. He'd worried that I would get pregnant, and then what would we do? I would have had his baby, gladly, had I only known what he wanted. And I would have laughed at the idea that he was going for good had I not felt a rush of blood to my head that I thought would blind me. I didn't know what to say, so I followed him speech-less around the apartment as he packed up his third-best guitar and made a pile by the door of his books and shirts, the laundry he'd left behind. He called that night, from a phone booth on the road, to see if I was all right. He was sad, too, he said, but I'd get along without him. I'd find someone better. "Don't worry about it," I said. "I'm not your business anymore."

By the time I got back upstairs with the shopping bags, Marilyn was in the kitchen, unpacking groceries. She'd left the apartment un-locked, and when I opened the door I saw that she'd put my suitcase in the guest room, a nook of the living room that Alan had framed in. Its one window saved it from being a closet with a bed. I stood for a moment, recovering from the stairs. "Close the door! Quick!" Mari-lyn called from the kitchen.

"What's wrong?" I asked.

"Close the door," Marilyn said. "It's Buddy. Madame doesn't know we have him."

I looked down, and there was a white cat, half grown, looking up at me with eyes like cracked green stones. He turned from me to the door, but I brought it shut just in time. Buddy sank to his back legs and licked a front paw energetically, as if that was what he'd meant to do all along and he hadn't been thwarted.

Marilyn came and took the bags from me. "Alan went to Savannah to visit his folks," she said, "and he found Buddy wandering around the streets, just a little kitten then, wearing a red collar with bells. He must have belonged to someone. He would have been run over for sure."

"So Alan stole him," I said.

"He saved him."

"Who named him Buddy?" I asked.

"Alan's dad. They had a dog named Buddy when Alan was growing up."

"Cute," I said. I reached down to pet him, and Buddy stiffened, waiting politely for me to stop. When I did, he hid beneath the round oak table.

"We're eating a little meat now and then," Marilyn said. "I bought a chicken for later in the week. Don't worry—I'm going to freeze it."

Marilyn worked in a luncheonette on Broadway, not far from the apartment. Passing it, you'd think it was a regular place: frozen orange juice, American cheese, thin hamburgers with grease popping from every pit. But the luncheonette served only fresh vegetables, virtuous steroid-free meats, juices thick with authentic pulp. Marilyn cooked lunch there weekdays; for holidays she baked pies with whole-wheat crusts and fructose-sweetened fruit.

I watched as Marilyn unpacked food in the cramped galley kitchen and put it away. She was shorter than I, more like our mother, Sadie. Marilyn had bright-blue eyes that made Buddy's look like counterfeit gems, the curly locks of someone pure and modest, and dark, smooth skin. I had my father's lean frame and fast metabolism. Like Sadie, Marilyn was a food lover, always looking for ways to deprive herself of what she wanted to eat. I never gained weight, no matter what I ate, but then I didn't care much for food.

"You have to wash a chicken, Louise," Marilyn said, turning on the faucet. Her square hands opened and then closed the chicken's wings and legs, raised the flap of skin over its empty neck, and forced water in and out of the plucked carcass, gently, as if the bird might feel it. "And before you freeze the chicken," she said, "dry it well, then wrap it in freezer paper. You wouldn't believe some of the chickens we see at work." When she was finished and the chicken was swaddled in white paper, taped up neatly, Marilyn said, "O.K., we're taken care of for the next few days, except for lunches, until Alan gets back."

"We can always send a scout out for supplies," I said. "Where's Alan gone?"

"Oh, Alan's very busy these days," Marilyn said. "He's in Philadelphia—he teaches there once a week. Then he flies straight up to Boston. There's a conference in Concord of transcendentalist scholars and writers. Alan's giving the keynote address."

A philosopher by training, a naturalist by inclination, Alan had written a book of meditations on a year he'd spent alone in Vermont, just before he married Marilyn. The book, brought out by a small press, did surprisingly well, and every week some backpacker appeared in search of Alan.

"I wonder if Henry David Thoreau would have made a good keynote speaker," I said. "Probably too shy."

"For Christ's sake, Louise. He has to pay the rent," Marilyn said.

"Of course he does," I said. "So do I. So does everyone. Should I help with dinner?"

Marilyn's expression softened. "Let's have tea. Then I'll cook. I'm sorry, I just hate being late."

After we'd had a cup of tea, it was more like old times. Marilyn lounged on the chintz couch and I took the armchair that used to be in the library at home, where we'd sat and talked before dinner every night. Buddy sat on Marilyn's lap. She had changed into a dark chenille robe, and when the cat purred, stretched, an ambled to the end of the couch he left behind ghostly white hairs.

"How did you smuggle Buddy?" I asked.

"Their vet in Savannah gave him a knockout dose, and he traveled in a box. Then it was late when Alan got in from the airport, so Madame was asleep."

"And she still hasn't caught on?"

"Buddy hasn't gone anywhere." Marilyn pulled on a lock of hair, an old signal that she was about to say something disagreeable. "I worry if it's good for him, being in the apartment."

"What do you mean? He has you and Alan. It's better than being road pizza."

"That's disgusting," she said, laughing.

"Or being put to sleep at the humane society, or whatever they do to strays."

"Buddy's a cat," she said. "He needs room to roam around, things to climb besides furniture. I wonder sometimes if I shouldn't just hand him over to Sadie, so he can be outdoors." She lifted Buddy to her face, giving him a squeeze. He let out a small squeal and rearranged himself on her lap.

"If you love him," I said, "why not keep him?"

"It seems wrong," she said. "I don't know why."

I reached for my cup, and Marilyn stretched to touch my hand. "It's good to see you," she said.

I pulled my hand away before she got to me, pretending I was fixing my hair. While her mind was on wrongs, I was tempted to tell Marilyn about Josh and his bride; all she knew was that it was over with us.

"Is he deaf?" I asked.

"What?"

"Is he deaf? White cats are frequently deaf," I said.

"Blue-eyed white cats," Marilyn said. She brought the cat to her face again, kissing him on his long white whiskers. I smiled at the two of them despite myself, then felt foolish for regretting the smile.

For dinner, Marilyn said that she'd cook peas in a cream sauce over buckwheat noodles, and I could sense the start of the home feeling that overcomes me when I'm with my mother or sister: the feeling that everything else in the world is inauthentic compared with home, making home no less irritating a place to be.

I sat on the kitchen stool and watched Marilyn chop and mince proficiently. From the refrigerator she took a package wrapped in newspaper and opened it, spreading the paper over the counter. She began shelling the mound of peas, placing the pods in a pile, the peas in a glass bowl.

"Here," I said. "Let me do that. Only you could find fresh peas in October."

"I just bought them," she said, "I didn't grow them. Sadie always said she'd settle for peas out of all that stuff she planted."

Sadie planned her garden over every winter, drawing a new scheme, sending away for seed. In the spring, she planted in the same plot, and every time deer would come down from the woods behind the house and little by little eat everything in the garden. Sadie tried a higher fence each year and invented more elaborate cages for the rows of tender vegetables. She spread blood meal. She buried pop bottles in the ground, their necks sticking up, to make an eerie music when the wind blew. The summer before I moved into the city to go to college, I used to wake early to watch a doe and her fawn come to feed in the garden, the doe alert, the fawn so small that I wanted to cry at the sight of such a baby. With no trouble, they were able to leap the fence, and they left as easily as they entered.

"I don't know why she persists," I said. "I think she does it to have the same stories to tell every summer."

"She always believes that the garden will work if she just manages to think up the right fence."

"Maybe," I said, because Marilyn wouldn't abide anything that sounded like criticism of our mother.

There was something melancholy about shelling peas, though it reminded me of the joy of a similar task. "Do you remember all the corn we shucked?" I asked. At sunset on summer evenings, Sadie would give me the newspaper from the day before and ears of corn from the farm stand down on Route 17. 1 used to sit on the kitchen steps, listening to the crickets and the birds, watching the lawn grow deeper and the light recede as I stripped the shucks and golden silk from pale kernels.

"I remember eating corn," Marilyn said, "but not shucking it."

"Never mind," I said, and I shelled more peas. "What's so terrible if Madame Lansky finds out about Buddy?"

"She could claim we broke the lease and kick us out—but she likes us. She might try to raise the rent. Meantime she'd scream, for certain. She must never find out. I carry Buddy's used kitty litter out every morning and throw it away at the corner." Marilyn made a face in imitation of crabby Madame Lansky as she searched her tenants' garbage and listened at their doors. "She trapped me on the stairs this week and demanded that I let her in the apartment. She hasn't been inside since we first moved in."

"You said she liked you," I said.

"She does," Marilyn said. "She likes me fine. She can't help it. She's just a mean person."

I cleared a spot on the newspaper and came upon a four-day-old horoscope. For me, there was love trouble, which I knew all about, and vehicular trouble as well. Marilyn was a Taurus, same as Josh.

"For you," I read aloud, "it says, 'Avoid arguments.'"

"Those things in the newspaper are fraudulent," Marilyn said.

"I know," I said, "but reading it here like this with peas all over it, isn't it fate?"

"Everything's fate," my sister said briskly. "If you want your chart read, I know a terrific woman here."

"That's O.K.," I said. "I had my chart read in Boston." I'd had it done when Josh left—his and mine—but nothing changed.

"Speaking of fate," Marilyn said, "I wanted to tell you—I don't know what you're going to do now, but in case you'd even consider moving back here, there's an apartment right in this building. In a month or so. The cellist who lives in the front apartment one floor down is moving to Milwaukee."

I looked at Marilyn and she looked down at the shallots she was chopping. I saw circles beneath Marilyn's eyes that hadn't been there the last time I'd visited, the beginning of lines on her brow. We would both grow old, I thought, believing it for the first time.

"I don't know," I said. "All my friends are in Boston, except you and Alan. I don't know if I can keep moving back and forth this way. Not back and forth—just back. Let me know, O.K.? If she really is moving to Milwaukee, I'd like to know."

"There's something else I have to tell you," Marilyn said. "I should have told you as soon as you got here."

"Is it Alan?" I asked. "Is everything all right?"

"Alan?" she asked, looking puzzled. "It's me. I'm going to have a baby, Weasel. What do you think?"

I thought it couldn't be true, she couldn't be pregnant without my knowing, but I felt very calm, as if the worst had happened and, having happened, was over at last.

"When did it happen?" I asked. "How far along are you?"

"Only nine weeks," she said. "The baby's not even due until spring. When I found out for sure, I cried. I've always wanted babies, but this seemed so final, as if I'd never have another thing to say about anything ever again. Then I told Alan and it was all right. You think it'll be all right, don't you?"

"Of course, everything will be all right. It always is," I said. "You're just the right age to have a baby. And you're strong."

After dinner, I volunteered to take down the garbage while Marilyn had a bath. I could hear the water running as I tied up the two garbage bags. I opened the apartment door and turned to tell Marilyn I was leaving. She stood at the bathroom door, her robe untied, holding the cat to her. When he saw the door, he moved in her arms and she held him more tightly to her. His white fur made her skin look dull.

"Buddy likes to sit on the sink while I'm in the tub," Marilyn said.

"Cozy," I said.

I met no one on the stairs or in the lobby. Outside, I put the garbage into the already full cans, and set the tops at rakish angles. I shook my arms to get the blood moving, and looked down the street to the park below the sparsely leafed trees, to the lights lining the paths. Would my life be any better if I lived there? I went back to the building, ready for the day to end.

In the middle of the night, the phone rang. Marilyn answered it in one ring, but it woke me. I got out of bed and listened at the door, wanting to hear Marilyn say that the call was for me. I guessed that it was Alan, that Marilyn was telling him I'd arrived. But I couldn't hear what she was saying. I went back to bed, rubbing my cold feet one against the other, to warm them. As I waited for sleep, I remembered how one winter, when Marilyn was a toddler, a neighbor gave us some chops from a deer he'd got on a hunting trip. Sadie fried the venison and served it to us, cutting Marilyn's chop into small pieces for her. Marilyn screamed and wouldn't eat hers, finally scattering the pieces on the floor. I tried to swallow mine. It was like fudge gone wrong, too rich and dense, but I remembered that I chewed it, that I chewed it very well.

In the morning Marilyn left for work, and I enjoyed the silence. Buddy slept on the table, looking up once in a while to see what I was doing. I made coffee from a small package of beans Marilyn kept in the freezer for guests—she didn't take in caffeine, she said—and I looked over the Sunday *Times* from the previous week.

"I love having you here," Marilyn had told me before she left, when I was waiting for her to go so that I could be alone. She surprised me by saying, "I miss you, you know."

I pushed my chair back from the table, stood up and stretched, hearing my bones crack in the effort. In the kitchen, I fixed a cheese sandwich. Buddy came and sat at my feet, gazing at me steadily. I ate standing up at the counter and I smacked my lips to show the cat how good it all was—Marilyn's homemade bread, pure butter, non-chemical cheese. I cut a sliver of cheddar and held it down to Buddy. He sniffed it, batted it with his paw, and walked away. "No dairy products?" I asked.

Marilyn and Alan's apartment looked as though it had been the same for thirty years, partly because they had so much old, mismatched furniture (gifts from Sadie) and partly because they never changed anything in it. Above crowded bookcases, family photographs and old engravings from home covered every inch of the apartment walls. It was as if not only Marilyn and Alan but their families had been linked together always. I found myself at Marilyn and Alan's wedding, on the lawn at home, wearing a long skirt that I remembered catching my heel on with each step I took.

Late in the afternoon, I left the apartment and walked over to Broadway. There was a two-story wooden building on a corner a few blocks away that I liked, and when I visited Marilyn and Alan I made a point of checking the picture windows on the second floor to see if the same people lived there, if plants were still hanging, and if the untidy arrangements of books, magazines, and coffee mugs were still on the wooden sills.

I'd always thought it was inevitable that I'd live like that, sunk in coziness that could be detected a block away. My place in Boston, though, was spare. Josh liked writing songs in the extra bedroom off the kitchen; he said the echo made him sound like a bigger singer than he was. The scarcity of my possessions, my lack of souvenirs, was hard won, fought for against the family tendency to preserve and collect. Now I was beginning to regret the success of my efforts. I went into a little shop and bought a candy bar, then walked down to the river, stopping by the Soldiers' and Sailors' monument, where I ate the chocolate. It was the poisonous quality of my imagination, I thought, that I would feel such regret, that I bothered to imagine one place when I was in another.

Across Riverside Drive was the enormous apartment building where Josh grew up. One Saturday when I was still in high school, he invited me to come to the city, and he met me at the Port Authority and brought me uptown to the Soldiers' and Sailors' Monument. Around the base, where I now sat, he'd painted in shining red letters: Josh loves Louise. It might have been sandblasted off or eaten away by strong acid, for not a trace of the letters was to be seen or a particle of paint to be detected as I pushed my hand along the rough surface.

Later, I walked back up Broadway. I stopped outside Marilyn's luncheonette and looked through the plate-glass window to see if she was still back in the kitchen and we could walk home together. The only customer, a man who wore mirrored glasses and a worn dungaree jacket, sat at the counter with a plate of chicken, brown rice, and the house salad. He was cutting up the chicken with the patience and precision of a surgeon, separating skin from meat, meat from bone, setting the skin and bones on the counter near his plate. He was stalling, I thought, postponing the moment when he'd have to leave. It looked peaceful inside, the counters wiped, menus waiting for the next customers. The waiter, a friend of Marilyn's, was doing the crossword puzzle. Now the man was combining the meat with the salad and rice. I looked again toward the kitchen for Marilyn; when I looked back a second later, he'd eaten everything and was signaling impatiently for the check. He had somewhere to go after all.

Near Marilyn's, I stopped at a florist's and bought two bouquets of rosebuds from the chilly buckets outside the shop. As I came up the block, I saw a tall, pale figure by the garbage cans. It was Madame Lansky, standing in the twilight, wearing a shapeless blue robe. She looked more fragile than I remembered. She should have been inside, I thought, where it was warm.

"Good evening," I said, and I smiled, holding up the flowers in their bright-green florist paper, thinking she'd understand that I was only a dinner guest, bearing a small gift. She looked at me, glum-faced, and said, "Good evening," then turned her head as if she'd said too much and stared down the street.

In the vestibule, I rang the bell on Marilyn's mailbox, hoping she was home. She'd given me the key, but I didn't want to use it, in case Madame Lansky was looking through the glass of the door. As I waited for Marilyn to buzz me in, I turned slowly, trying to catch the landlady watching, but when I came around there was only my reflection and the empty street.

In the kitchen, Marilyn was cutting green beans into tiny pieces. Scrubbed new potatoes dripped onto the counter. Buddy appeared from nowhere and, racing me, dashed into the kitchen and came to a halt at Marilyn's feet.

"Budsy-boysy," she said.

She looked more tired than she had the day before, but she brightened when she saw the package I carried. "Flowers!" she said. "Oh, Louise. I never buy flowers."

"Any calls?" I asked, regretting my question immediately.

"No, Weasel," she said. "But I haven't been in very long. Here, I'll put them in water."

Marilyn undid the wrapping, revealing the tight buds in their blankets of cellophane and tissue. They were perfect, she said; she liked blushing pink best for little roses. She found a small round vase, in which she arranged the flowers, thanking me over and over, so pleased by the small gift that I felt stingy for not bringing more.

"I went by the luncheonette," I said when she asked what I'd done with my day. I told her about Chicken Man, and she laughed.

"He comes by every Thursday and does that with the special."

"It would drive me crazy," I said. "Haven't you ever thought of working someplace decent, where they'd pay you enough money?"

"I get paid enough, Louise. I'm not hurting for anything. All my friends are there, and I can't think of a more decent place, if you want to know. I don't have to cook food I don't believe in."

"Maybe when the baby's old enough you'll be able to open a restaurant of your own," I said.

"For God's sake, Louise," she said. "What are you talking about? Here. Take these."

She handed me the flowers and I carried the vase to the living room.

Marilyn sat on the couch after dinner, her feet up on the hassock. I did the dishes and then sat drinking tea and watching her from the armchair. She was working on a needlepoint design, using fat thread in shades of pink and blue. Buddy came in from the kitchen, where he'd been eating his dry food. He picked up a wad of pink yarn that had fallen to the floor and began batting it furiously across the room, the wool picking up dust and hair as Buddy brought it under furniture and out again. When he tired of his game, Buddy settled on the couch next to Marilyn, where he made himself comfortable, looking smug and proprietary.

"One of Alan's fans came up with a nice offer," Marilyn said, holding her needle still and looking over at me. "A house in New Hampshire for next summer. It's an old farm, away from everything. But maybe things will be so different then we won't want to go. It sounds perfect now, but it's hard to know whether to accept the offer. To know in advance how we'll feel."

"Why not accept it," I asked, "and if you change your mind tell him then?"

She looked at me steadily and I felt summed up and unworthy.

"I wish it were happening right now," she said. "We could give you this apartment and you'd have a chance to sort things out, to rest for a while. And there might be room for you in New Hampshire. You could come up there, too."

"Maybe," I said. "I've only seen New Hampshire from a car. Or maybe Josh took me there and we stayed for a weekend. I can't remember exactly."

"He called me," Marilyn said. "Last month. He wanted to tell me about the girl. It must have been just awful for you, Louise. You should have said something to me about it."

"Don't look at me like that," I said. "For heaven's sake. Don't worry, I'm fine. You forget have an apartment of my own to live in, a perfectly good life."

"All right," she said. "I'm sorry. But maybe I was thinking how nice it would be for me if you were here—"

"And you were off in New Hampshire? That would be nice for me to move here and wave goodbye to you. Why should I move here, to feel like the fifth wheel?"

"You know you'll find someone," she said, "sooner or later. Don't feel so sorry for yourself." Marilyn lay back against the arm of the couch and put her feet up, as if she were giving in and her exhaustion was overwhelming her at last.

"I don't know that at all," I said. "And I don't want to find someone ever again."

"It's too soon," she said. "You'll feel differently in a while."

"No, I won't," I said, but something moved in me and I saw that Marilyn might be right.

"Weasel," she said. "I have the feeling that everything will be fine for us both, don't you?"

I thought of her baby and felt the way I had when she told me she was marrying Alan, the way I had in school when Marilyn, pudgy and smaller than I, passed me in a race. I had feared for Marilyn and watched out for her all my life.

"It'll be fine," I said. "Don't worry. I'll help you with the baby. If you like, I'll come for the last part. Or when the baby's born."

"I knew you would," Marilyn said. "You always come through for me in the end."

"Yes," I said. "No matter what. Just rest awhile now."

"I get so tired," she said. Marilyn tucked the needle into her work and laid the needlepoint on the table, with the wads of yarn. I got an afghan and covered her feet, which she said were a little cold. Gradually, Marilyn relaxed and fell into a sleep so profound that she looked like a stranger. On the bus once, going to Boston, I'd watched Josh as he slept. In sleep, he was unusually beautiful, his features carved in pale, freckled skin, like someone I didn't know, and I stared at him so long that when he opened his eyes and caught me looking at him he frightened me. I'd looked away, pretending I hadn't been staring. Buddy slept against Marilyn. I reached to pet him, but withdrew my hand before I touched his white fur.

Marilyn's baby would be smooth and pink, beautiful as any fawn or rosebud, as anything new and untried. It didn't matter if I moved there or not. Never again would my sister shake her head over me. Nothing of mine, no mistake, decision, action, would equal the touch of the baby's skin, the smallest gesture the baby made. Our mother had it all wrong; Sadie should have welcomed the deer and planted the garden for them. They would get it all anyway.

The rosebuds were not enough, I decided. I needed to go out and find something for Marilyn. I should get lilies and tulips to cover the table, Valencia oranges to stack in a pyramid. I left my chair and quietly moved around the apartment, gathering my coat and purse, writing a short note and propping it against my teacup. I hesitated at the door, searching in my purse for the key. I looked back at Marilyn and Buddy sleeping together on the couch, then opened the door to the landing.

His emerald eyes wide open, Buddy sprang noiselessly from the couch and raced toward the door. I reached for him, but he was past me in no time and out on the stairs, his whiteness startling against the murky carpet. I heard, flights below, Madame Lansky calling to a tenant, "Not so fast, you." Her voice was loud, angry, and magnetic. His legs a blur of white, Buddy headed for the sound.

I dropped my purse and coat and I slammed the door shut. This will disturb Marilyn, I thought, and I stood very still. This will wake her, I thought. But I turned and ran down the stairs as fast as I could after Buddy. When the landlady saw him, when Madame Lansky screamed at the sight of him, I would capture him, I would lift him up and hold him tight in my arms, and I would tell her he's mine, he's mine.

*Beautiful Baby*

$\mathcal{M}$y baby slept in his carrier, serene. He was a deep sleeper, one talent among many, balancing what might look so far like a life full of deficits. A plain blue curtain defined the waiting room, no receptionist and no sign-in sheet, and the place was full, with half the crowd under three months old. I stood holding his carrier at the door to the hallway, hesitating, when a tired woman said, "There won't be room to swing a cat in a few minutes. You'd better sit while you can."

I settled us onto a folding chair next to the curtain. The tired woman's baby was an obvious girl with her pink coverall and white blanket. The pink ribbon in her pale hair was edged with delicate loops that made me think of princesses in garments sewn by good witches. In a room of tired women, the mother looked especially drawn, though she'd taken as much care with herself as with her baby, her hair permed into the tight curls that were popular then, her jeans and cowboy shirt with pearl snaps ironed neatly. Her Western boots were reptile, dyed red, and her feet were so small that the boots looked cute, not dangerous.

"Her name's Tina Marie," she said. "Mine's Cissy."

"I'm Lynda," I said. "He's Eli."

The other mothers, who had stopped talking or dreaming or fussing over their babies to listen to our brief exchange, returned to what they were doing, and I settled in for the wait.

Eli had what would might be called an ethnic look, caused by the mixture of his father and me. I gave him his dark skin and thick black hair, much improved on him. My family had brought these with them from several Slavic countries, along with broad faces, heavy foreheads, and a tendency to be stubborn. His father's people were from Wales and Scotland, with their own oddities, to be sure, but Eli got the best—green eyes and the shape of his pretty skull. The green eyes and the delicacy of my son's face would keep his father with me always.

A heavy woman settled into a chair saved for her by a tiny mother in a very short skirt and clunky shoes.

"Have you seen the restroom? I can't believe they'd advertise a beautiful baby contest and not have a place to change a baby," the heavy woman said.

"There's never good conditions at this type of thing."

I wondered if the women knew each other already or if they'd chummed up on the spot, like me and Cissy.

Cool air touched my neck. The curtain had parted and a woman stood surveying the room. She was older than any of the mothers, maybe fifty, maybe mid-forties on a bad day, her gray hair naturally curly in the way Cissy had forced hers to be. She was glowingly pretty with deepsunk eyes that would look great made-up. In her long black skirt and white shirt, she resembled a schoolteacher or a church worker, and her stubby, broad feet were in Birkenstocks. A little gold cross hung around her neck on a gold chain that winked when she turned to me.

"Newcomer?" she asked. She smiled and I decided church worker, a missionary out among the savages.

"Yes," I said, and I gave her my name. This was why there wasn't a number to take or a sign-in sheet. The woman must check every so often and put us all straight in her mind.

She glanced at my chubby dark baby and smiled as if she couldn't help herself, then let her eyes stray around the waiting babies. Once you look, babies are as individual as anyone else despite the uniformity of their postures and wardrobe. Most adults would look the same if you wrapped them in pastel blankets and laid them in plastic carriers. There was a red-headed boy playing with his toes, a gorgeous Mexican baby—boy or girl, I couldn't tell—sucking on a pacifier, an African American girl with soft hair crowning her high forehead, a set of identical twins, blonde and cute but not what I would call beautiful.

The woman's eyes rested on Tina Marie who at that moment happened to smile. The baby's smile made a lightness around her like a halo. Eli was sunk. I started to think what else we would do that day.

"You're next," the woman said to Cissy. "Try to be patient."

"Oh, I am," Cissy said.

The woman disappeared back behind the curtain, like the Wizard of Oz.

Cissy, beaming, looked eager, less tired momentarily, and stupid? That would be reading things into the situation that I didn't know then. She didn't look, wasn't, more stupid than the rest of us.

Eli woke up, and I thought he smiled at Tina Marie and Cissy, but maybe it was at the movement of the curtain. You never know what babies see. Their eyesight is developing and of course goes uncorrected. Maybe they're living their first months in a myopic haze. Eli turned out to have perfect vision, along with straight teeth, more gifts from his father.

A baby dressed in overalls and a checked shirt appeared from be-hind the curtain in a carrier with a checked cover. His mother was dressed to match. I thought I heard a man's voice, but then Cissy got the nod and I forgot about it. Cissy gathered up the baby and diaper bag, fussing that she was keeping the lady waiting, but she took the time to give me a bright glance as she passed. She wasn't out for a lark on a Tuesday morning, she was on a quest.

I tried to hear what was going, but the footsteps and sound of Cissy's one-way conversation with Miss Birkenstock soon faded. I had imagined that the studio was small and cramped, like the would-be reception room, but when I edged the curtain to one side, I saw that it took a sharp turn down a hallway, then passed beyond sight or sound. Cissy, Tina Marie, and the woman went into another dimension, and Eli took a look around. I asked the heavy woman if she'd been to many of these, and she told me that Baby Allison had won two contests and was up for a movie being shot in Houston.

Before long, I heard Cissy on the other side of the curtain, giving the woman her address and phone number, Tina Marie's date of birth and vital statistics, and a man's voice, calling something out in the background.

Cissy was transformed when she reappeared, full of energy. "I think we might have some luck!" she said, and then realized that all the other mothers were looking at her in a not friendly way, and she said, "Oh, it's getting late," pausing only long enough to exchange phone numbers with me. She wrote hers on a grocery store receipt, which I stuffed back in my purse and wondered why. Cissy and I had nothing in common but our babies, though at the time Eli was my occupation, vocation, and companion all in one. I wasn't working. I didn't see many friends, and my mother and brothers lived too far away to visit often.

By the time we were called, Eli and I were ready to get out of there. The hallway beyond the curtain took a sharp turn, went on for longer than you'd think it could, and ended in an open studio. Miss Birkenstock turned out to be Helen Joseph, Photographer, just like the sign outside the hall door, and there was a man in the studio who looked like something out of an earlier age, trim, a pencil-mustache that was turning gray, starched shirt, and a bow tie. His name was Don. Helen Joseph said he was the publicity agent for the contest.

Photographs of babies, all kinds of babies, were pinned to the wall behind the camera. Helen Joseph really appreciated babies. Her pictures showed their unguardedness and bright attention, their cleverness at letting their wishes, affections, and feelings be known without a word. In Eli's first month of life, I watched him sleep, and even though I knew precisely how he was made and born, I was sure that he was an unearthly creature. Solid as he was and fleshly, I wondered in those moments if he would stay with me or choose to return to his baby planet. Helen Joseph captured that quality in her gallery of babies also.

I set Eli down on a draped platform she'd rigged so that the baby wouldn't be flat and get upset but was tilted up where he could see everything. There's nothing a baby hates more than being treated like a package. Eli looked around, checking out the new place.

"The lights won't hurt his eyes," she said before I could ask. She turned her attention to Eli. "There's a boy, a really terrific boy," and she went on cooing in a way that seemed to fascinate Eli, but it might have been her moving around him, snapping Polaroids, that charmed him, kept his eyes following her.

"You're really good," I said. "Most baby pictures look alike."

"Thanks," she said, working.

The man had a clipboard in front of him and acted businesslike, asking me our last name, contact numbers. I started to recite my office number, then I remembered I didn't go to work anymore.

"Something wrong?" he asked.

"I'm on maternity leave from my law firm," I said, "but you can have that number anyway. My home phone's unlisted."

"You're a lawyer?" he asked. The word came out *liar*. He had a strong East Texas accent which made him sound suspicious, like I was trying to sell him something.

"Tax law," I said.

"Your baby's a dream," the woman said. She was looking at the Polaroids of Eli spread out on a table, and I watched the images of Eli's face appear out of a yellowish blur.

The man coughed in a fake way.

"Would you like these?" she asked, and I accepted the Polaroids and retrieved Eli before I realized that we had flunked the pop quiz.

On the other side of the curtain, I looked around at the new crop of mothers in the reception area. One of them spotted the photos in my hand and gave me a sympathetic look. I felt foolish for having come to the contest.

I drove home along Allen Parkway, enjoying the curves that snaked along the bayou. The contest had been in the Esperson Building, one of Houston's early office towers, and I could see its little spire as we passed. While all waiting rooms have a touch of the afterlife to them, there was exceptional health in the one we'd just left. Not one hopeful at the beautiful baby contest had so much as a runny nose. No ear infections, no colic, not even much moodiness.

We hauled ourselves upstairs and Eli napped in his crib. I covered him with the blanket my mother had sent him, pale blue and white, hand-woven. It became his favorite and, in future years, would disappear and reappear, dominating our lives. Now it was protecting him from the spring breeze coming through the window.

I should have slept while he did, all the best baby books counseled me to, but it was wonderful to be free even if I was washing the breakfast dishes, putting away the newspaper and tidying the living room so that it didn't look like we'd spent the small hours on the couch, nursing and watching an interview with the former wife of a politician. I wanted the place to look as if an easy life was being led there, the kind of waltz Eli's father would want to join.

Each month since I left work in my eighth month of pregnancy, an envelope had arrived from Will's bookkeeper with a check for our support. I used the first to outfit Eli because by then I really believed in the baby. Will came over when he could and helped me assemble the crib and changing table. I was feeling fine, going to a water exercise class for pregnant women, taking long walks in the bright Houston winter, and waiting every minute for my baby. When I found out I was pregnant, there was a moment when Will might have asked me to abort the baby, but he didn't, and I had a moment alone when I might have decided that I couldn't alter the course of my life by having this baby, but I didn't. I knew there was a very good chance that the baby would have to grow up with me alone, fatherless, and that seemed unfair, a potential strike, but I couldn't part with the baby, not then, not ever. My decision had to do with what I wanted above everything else, so it was selfish. Besides, I had the strong feeling that it would be bad luck to turn down an opportunity to alter everything I knew about living in the world.

Will had been through it all before, though he was not happy then, he said, not like he felt now. When they were eighteen, his girl friend got pregnant and they married. Their daughter was now twenty-five, finished with college, engaged to a solid citizen. As for Will and Susan, they were as unhappy as a couple could be. He was a quiet man who kept his anger to himself, a natural tendency reinforced by years with a woman who spared him and the world nothing of her misery. She was smart enough and had her own kind of guts. She'd gone to college when their daughter was in middle school, had gotten a Master's in Education and now was an elementary school principal. She won awards. She was asked to speak on educating the young and got her picture in the paper every once in a while, but no matter what glory she earned, she felt cheated of the early years when she should have been in college, when she shouldn't have been forced (her word) to marry Will. She was still trying to catch up to her lost time like it was a runaway train. A wise poet once said that there is no bond stronger than mutual unhappiness. That was Will and Susan all over.

I met them because I was a lawyer in Will's firm, new to the city. It was my third law job and I had lost what interest I had in tax law though I was resigned to it as a temporary way of life, trying to catch my own runaway train. I was saving my money hard, living in a garage apartment near Rice University, modest by any standard, much less that of a lawyer billing lots of hours. When I got home at night from ten or more hours of work, I heard the family in the big house across the swimming pool and back yard calling to one another, *Come watch this show. Is your homework done? Bedtime!* I was piling up capital so that one day I could leave the law.

My freedom came in the form of Eli and a new life as a single mother. Once he accepted the idea, Will was happy about his new baby, in a way he hadn't been when he was not much more than a boy himself, caught. I loved to see him with Eli, as open and generous in his love as the babies in the waiting room were with their vitality, but it didn't necessarily mean anything for our future with him. Sometimes after Will left, I fell into a fury of cleaning and sorting through my books and clothing, getting ready to leave at a moment's notice.

Will arrived mid-afternoon, the time we used to have our trysts. We'd agreed not to make love anymore, not until we were sure of what was going on between us, but I fell into his arms. I found him, I can't say why, irresistible. He was not much taller than I, under six feet, so we just fit together. We stood listening to the sound of the trees, then separated.

While Will watched Eli sleep, I told him about the beautiful baby contest. At first he thought I must be joking, that I'd entered such a contest.

"What if Eli had won, what then?" Will did divorce law and it made him more cautious than his nature dictated. He had the wit to do something out of character though he wouldn't carry through without long thought and preparation, except, of course, doing his part to get me pregnant.

"The end of his private life. We couldn't go anywhere," I said.

"I don't mean that," Will said, and then I saw that Eli's brief comet of publicity might have shed light on Will and embarrassed him or worse. But he didn't mean that either. What I'd done was more irresponsible than risking embarrassment, he said, what I'd done was risk Eli.

"Those contests are mostly scams," he said, "traps for the innocent. What were you thinking of bringing the baby there?"

He looked at me, looked around my little apartment, as if he weren't sure it was good enough for Eli, and for a split second I saw him trying to take my baby from me. I didn't like it when he asked me questions in a slow distant way like I was a client and he had to figure out some way to make things come out right, no matter what I'd done. I was in charge of the baby, right or wrong, though this was wrong, I knew it now that Will was there, now that I could see him. Sometimes it seemed that he didn't exist, that he was already out of our lives (though I didn't say this), and perhaps that's why I had gone impulsively to a smalltime contest in a makeshift studio and put us all at risk.

"Those contests prey on the hopes of poor dumb women," he said. "How could you put Eli in the hands of criminals, even for a minute?"

"But what could they get out of us? What do we have? They didn't ask for money. I didn't give them my home number. They couldn't find me again, try to sell me something—"

"No," Will said, "because you're too smart, no matter how you act now and then, but the other women there maybe weren't so gifted."

I heard Cissy's voice, giving her address and phone, and wished I could warn her to have nothing more to do with the contest. Then I remembered I had her number in my purse. I'd call her later, I resolved, once Will left.

Will looked at the Polaroids spread out on the kitchen table and changed the subject to our favorite, Eli's beauty.

"I was an ugly baby," he said. "I must have pictures around somewhere. I looked like something out of the Dust Bowl—"

"Which you were!"

"Well, yes, historically. But by the time I came along, we were all right. I've wondered if my grandparents thought I was ugly. Maybe I looked to them like hard times."

"Oh, Will," I said, "they adored you." I'd heard his stories about fishing trips and special treats and his grandmother saying, *You're my baby boy,* and playing gin with him as soon as his hands were big enough to hold cards. Will was lovable, a quality that often left opposing counsel at a disadvantage.

"I suppose they did," he said. He'd disappointed his family, getting into the situation he had with Susan and, no way around it, here he was again. We looked at each other, thinking the same thought.

Eli opened his eyes at the sound of our voices and smiled his toothless best at Will who changed him and cuddled him and played around with him while I fell asleep, knowing that Eli was in good hands. I slept so deeply that when I awakened I didn't know where I was or who I was with, as if I still might be in the curtained waiting room and it felt like a terrible exile. I'd missed the better part of

Will's visit and my shame came back to me, though not so raw now, something to let pass.

Over mint tea, fresh from the window-box, we had our weekly check-up. We'd agreed not to talk every visit about the future because it would have spoiled Will's time with Eli and made me feel like a shrew, but we knew we had to talk. I had given Will an ultimatum: by the time Eli was six months old, Will had to be living with us, or I would move to another city where Will could visit Eli when he liked. Like the lawyers we were, we'd already come up with documents for Eli's custody and Will had set up a trust for him, committed to the costs of his upbringing and education. He was doing everything right but the main thing, and I was trying to be kind, which didn't come naturally. I knew from what had already passed between us that Will and I were capable of relying on love and letting time drift, and I could do that dangerous thing to myself but not to the baby. Besides, once I was getting a full night's sleep, not living in this infant dream day in and out, I knew I'd start to hate Will.

"I can't come Friday," he said. "Susan's cousin's coming to dinner, but how would it be if I spent the weekend?" I could hardly look at his face. He didn't ask for much from me, I realized, and I wondered how these visits were for him, especially this moment of parting.

We rarely had the chance to fall asleep and wake up together. It seemed like a paradise, of course, a weekend with a daddy in the place with us, and I with a chance to sleep, to wash my hair, to talk to someone who could answer in sentences, but I told him I'd have to think it over and he left disappointed. Motherhood had made me calculating, shrewd, I imagined him saying to himself, *No spontaneity.* If he had thought those things of me, I wouldn't have blamed him. I wanted to call him back and do anything I could to keep him with us.

I tried to give us an outing a day, and that week we ventured to the zoo and to the library, where Eli kicked his feet in the stroller while I looked for a book without a demanding plot. I called Cissy one time to warn her about the contest, but there was no answer and I let it leave my mind. We met a friend for lunch, and Eli slept until dessert.

Late in the week, on a rainy morning when I was trying to decide what we'd do that day, the phone rang.

"It's Cissy! From the contest. We met there, remember?"

"Of course," I said. "How's Tina Marie?"

"She's a doll. A beautiful baby," and she laughed giddily.

"Did something happen?"

"We got the call back! We won!"

"Oh, my God." I laughed too and shrieked a little, echoing her. Eli looked up at the new noise. "Tell me all about it."

"Helen called just this minute! The photographer. You remember." Cissy paused, maybe regretting that she'd called me. "She wants us to meet her Saturday morning. Tomorrow! We're going to Louisiana, to the headquarters of the contest, to take some formal shots and fill out paperwork and get things going."

"Why Louisiana?"

"It's the headquarters," Cissy said, slowly, as if I were being dense. "She explained it to me. The contest is regional. Then there's nationals, I guess. Like golf. Cissy's won for the Gulf Coast, so now she's in the running for Texas and the whole South.

"Helen's driving us, which is a good thing. She said Lafayette's not easy to fly to, and I'm just as glad. I was scared we'd have to get there ourselves and we hardly have bus fare. Well, maybe we'll have more than bus fare now. My husband thought I was crazy to go to that contest."

"What does he think now?" I asked.

"He says it's all vanity. He doesn't approve. But I told him it's a chance for us and he agreed not to stand in our way."

Now I felt worse than ever. "You know, Cissy, you should be careful with these people. What do you know about them? About this contest? Lots of them are scams—" Eli started fussing, and Cissy heard him and said a little too quickly, "We'd better get off the phone."

She was a stranger, someone I'd known for under thirty minutes, what was I to do, force her to listen to my free and unwanted advice?

"Take care. Call me when you get back," I said. "Tell me all about it."

We used to listen to a tape by a singer named Rafi. "Rise and Shine" was my favorite song and, I fancied, Eli's too. Rising with the blue-birds, shining and shining, often we listened to the tape all the way through, with Eli on the bed next to me reaching for his toes, me ad-miring him, before I got up and dressed. I didn't play Rafi that week-end, for Will had more refined taste in music and we were on good behavior, rehearsing for a life that might never come. Even Eli seemed especially easy, waking only once in the night. I was pre-tending to be a serene, competent mother, so that all would go well, and it did.

Who was Will pretending to be? A free man, of course. He jogged in my neighborhood, risking being seen by friends, acquaintances, or clients just as if it didn't matter. He took us out for lunch at his favor-ite barbecue where the meat cutter and cashier knew him and, while Eli finished the nap that began on the drive back, we made love. Later, as we walked Eli around the familiar streets, Will wondered aloud what it would be like to live there, not in a garage apartment but in one of the houses that lined North Boulevard.

"Too big for us," I said. "We don't need so much." I wanted us to seem possible, not too expensive, not too demanding.

"It's not *need*," he said, "it's what I want for us. That house," point-ing to a house that would have fit nicely in acres of English lawn. "Not too grand for us."

It was then that I figured it wouldn't work out. That was how Will saw what he would have to do for us, three stories tall, ornamental shrubbery, curving driveway out front, oh, no, too complicated, too large.

By Sunday afternoon, when Will went back home, I yearned for the ease of being alone with the baby whose demands were simple ones, although it made me sad after Will left and I saw that he had mashed my toothpaste out of any recognizable shape and that he probably would never do so again. I had it decided. When he visited throughout Eli's life (if he visited Eli), Will would have to stay in a hotel so that never again would I feel this splitting love and grief. My head hurt with the arguments for and against Will divorcing Susan and coming over to our side. I thought of it from Susan's angle and from Will's, from Eli's and my own, and the square of difficulty pulled me into a terrible crankiness.

"At some point, you know," I said, "you just have to make a leap. Like, who was it? John? Faith in things unseen?"

We were saying goodbye, standing right outside the apartment door, elevated above the evening, breathing in the heavy air that was scented by chlorine from the bobbing bright jewel below us and the Confederate jasmine creeping up the wall of the garage.

"That proscription is easier when it involves only yourself. I have other people to think of. This has been my habit for years, to think of the others. If it were just you and Eli, I'd be with you like a shot."

"I wonder," I said, feeling like the snake in Eden. "I wonder if you would come to us."

"I'm not the only one who needs faith," he said.

My college roommate called from Nashville a few days later. Her husband was a partner in a big firm and they needed someone in the tax department. If I wanted it, I had the job. Without thinking, I accepted the job, the city and state, sight unseen. Once I was off the phone, I wondered if my friend had been working on her husband or if everything had simply come together, like coins landing in a circle.

I remembered that one of my mother's grandmothers came from Tennessee.

I had been waiting for Will so long, throughout our affair waiting for him to find the time for me, then to decide in our favor, but I had waited too long and asked too much, of him and of me. It's one thing for an adult to wait and wait but I couldn't do that to Eli. He needed to see that he was sufficient unto himself to lead his life, whatever it might be, and not spend his childhood in suspense.

Will might have said, *You can't go,* or, *I'll stop you.* I might have answered, *How? How can you stop me?* We didn't shout or scream or threaten and our tears were shed together. I knew how unhappy I was making Will but I could not stay. Will reminded me that the six-month deadline wasn't up yet. I was being unfair. I was depriving Eli of the company of his father. Will switched tactics; he would visit us as soon as he could, I was right and we had to leave Houston and start over somewhere else, Nashville wasn't a bad place and other people had given up prosperous partnerships and the city they'd known all their lives, and they'd done fine. Didn't I see? I was depriving Eli of more than Will's company, for if he joined us in Tennessee, what kind of life could we promise Eli? I was being irresponsible and impetuous, risking everything the three of us had, singly and together. He went one way and then the other, but I was heading in one direction only.

My mind was on packing when I saw Cissy's picture in the paper. I was, in fact, using the newspaper to wrap bowls, when I saw a Sears studio portrait of Tina Marie and a blurry photo of Cissy leaving a police station in Lafayette, Louisiana. According to the paper, Cissy had allowed Helen Joseph (not her real name) to take Tina Marie off to be photographed, and when they didn't return after eight hours, when she discovered that Helen had checked out of the motel, Cissy went to the police. The studio in Houston, the curtained waiting room, the gallery of baby portraits, it was all gone, a stage set to convince a bunch of women who already believed. False names, bad checks, a cold trail. Tina Marie was gone.

Because of our peculiar circumstance, because of me, I had not been more than a hundred yards from Eli since he was born, and I couldn't imagine not knowing where he was, how he was feeling, what he needed that only I could give him. I cried for Cissy, amputated now and incomplete. I called Cissy's number but no one answered. I called the police and both newspapers, but no one would tell me where she was. I waited for the phone to ring, though I dreaded her voice and the world of trouble it would speak.

One afternoon before we left Houston, I drove us downtown to the office building where Helen Joseph had tricked us all. I held Eli in my arms, and he was grumpy and restless from the minute I parked the car. The name plate that had been next to the door—Helen Joseph, Photographer—was gone, slipped out perhaps as she fled. Before the door were two bouquets of flowers, one real and one plastic, the kind you see in cemeteries after holidays.

I retreated down the hall to the elevator, afraid that harm might come to Eli just from our being there, and he twisted in my arms. I thought of the baby photos in the studio and decided that anyone who loved babies enough to capture their individuality, would care for Tina Marie, then I told myself I was getting soft. I wondered if in some way that she would never understand, Tina Marie would remember Cissy as Cissy in every minute of her life would remember Tina Marie.

As I drove us back to our dismantled garage apartment, I saw that because I had Eli I had everything. I loved Will and wanted a life with him but if that wasn't to be, as I was so sure it wouldn't, then something else would happen. You can't change human beings, not even babies. Faith is belief in things unseen and so is love.

I understood that as we packed and said goodbye to Houston and to Will. During that time of tears and farewells, I was all right except when I thought of Cissy, for how would she live without her baby? It was worse than death, waiting, not knowing. How could Cissy wake up in the morning? I kept the Polaroids of Eli in an envelope separate from my other pictures of him, as if they might bring harm to us. I couldn't throw them away but I wouldn't let them touch the other photographs.

In Nashville, while I worked, Eli stayed in a church day care right next to the law firm. I had lunch with him every day and was able to visit him morning and afternoon. He thrived there and I checked each little girl baby to see if she could be Tina Marie. I searched out copies of the Houston newspaper but they yielded no mention of Tina Marie or her disappearance. It became my habit not to give up hope.

We rented a plain little house in a pretty suburb, and made friends with our neighbors who had a baby too. I began to see a life there for us, though, as it happened, we returned to Houston after all.

Will and Susan divorced, and Eli and I moved back, just as if it had all been planned to give Susan a chance to decide that she wanted a divorce. It happened more smoothly than I could have imagined, before Eli could be bothered by much of anything. Will didn't buy us the big house on the boulevard but another like it and I didn't object. The only thing I minded was that we had to go and come, and that only happened when I was tired or discouraged, for I was fortunate and so were Eli and Will. My desire for Will to have been with us sooner was unworthy, though it persisted.

I didn't give up even through the years. I looked for Tina Marie at Eli's elementary school and at soccer games, at Disneyland, Bingo nights and the Rodeo, I searched for her in the throng of kids changing classes at middle school, and I scanned the cheerleaders at high-school football games. Do I need to say that I never saw her?

We have tried for another baby, tried for years, but had no luck. It was my occupation and my sorrow, and then I gave up hope. Now, when I tire of contemplating the mystery of why I could get pregnant when I shouldn't have and couldn't when everything waited for the next baby, I turn my thoughts to the beautiful baby contest.

All the babies are beautiful in the blue-curtained waiting room, all healthy, and all with their mothers. The babies are still unearthly, hesitating between heaven and earth to determine if we are worthy and if they should stay with us. If the babies wait too long, they become just like us, trapped forever in earthly love and complications.

## The Woods

*O*ne winter Sunday while Ben was out west, Carlotta took Josh
for pizza. It was a melancholy night, and raining so that it was hard to
see. They crossed the Colorado River, drove toward downtown, and
they were lucky. The juggler was performing at their favorite pizza
parlor. While Josh ate stuffed-crust pepperoni pizza and she had a
big salad and the crusts Josh didn't want, the juggler worked with
three balls and then four and balanced a bar stool on his chin.

They had seen him before, one night in late spring. He was a small
boy who lived in their neighborhood and went to the high school
Josh would someday. The juggler worked for tips and to force himself to practice. He could do everything but he had no showmanship,
which Carlotta liked. After he finished one bit, he'd pause and think
what to do next. When the pizza eaters applauded or called out asking him if he could balance this or juggle that, he looked a little startled, then nodded and responded to the challenge.

While they ate and watched, Carlotta wondered if the juggler
drove himself to the pizza parlor or if his parents brought him. He

was twice Josh's age. He could drive legally in Texas and that put him out alone at night. Was he in danger less than five miles from the woods in which they lived? Of course he was in danger. They were in a city that was growing every day. People were moving in from everywhere around the world, strangers who knew nothing about the state much less the city, and some of these people were criminals for sure. Even if they were a band of angels, they'd be driving cars and cars were dangerous. It was dangerous altogether being a boy, a young man. As the juggler threw a fork, a shaker of grated parmesan, one bottle of chili sauce, and an empty coffee mug around his head, she thought of drugs, sex, cars, and the normal accidents of living, the diseases that struck the young, Hodgkin's Lymphoma.

When they were finished eating, she gave Josh a five dollar bill to put into the paper coffee cup labeled *Juggler's Tips*.

On the way home, Carlotta told Josh that before he went to bed he would have to read his chapter in *A Paradise Called Texas*, his social studies textbook that weighed about twenty pounds and had on its cover a head shot of a monstrous bronze mustang. He told her he would read it in the morning; he'd read most of it at school and he knew it already. She differed. As they argued back and forth in a tired way, Josh stared out the car window at the married student housing. The streetlights diffused on his watery window. The car turned down the hill. Josh looked up into the trees high above the river. He saw a man who stood as tall as a tree and as still as a tree. Then the car moved onto the bridge and they were crossing the river.

For a long time after the Comanches had been driven out, not many people lived in the woods or the limestone hills. There was no easy way to get there from the rest of the city until, forty years ago, a man who owned some of the hills persuaded the city to build a bridge across the river. The chosen site was at a dam, and the cliffs on both banks were blasted through to make a place for the new road. When the bridge was completed, a new road wound upward to the hills and valleys, and people moved out, building houses for themselves. New trees grew and maidenhair ferns covered the scars on the cliffs.

Just below the dam was a turbulent pool where kayakers practiced for bigger whitewater. Down river, at the opposite bank, fly fishermen cast where smoother water flowed. Between the banks was an isle covered with scrub trees and rocks. Often people fished or drank beer there, throwing sticks into the river for their dogs to retrieve. When the floodgates were opened, the isle disappeared, all but the tops of the trees.

The neighborhood in the woods was zoned so that the woods would be preserved, though the zoning and preservation were compromised by shifting times—trees did come down, houses did go up above the treeline, small and large infringements—still the woods were protected. Overprotected, some said, for what was the use of protecting the cedar trees that took the water and light from the oaks and sycamores? Beyond the city, on the ranches, the cedars were cut on a regular basis but here they were allowed to take over and become a hazard. If the neighborhood ever caught on fire, the cedars would fuel the flames beyond control.

In addition to the plague of cedars there were the deer.

Trapped between the river and the new highway to the west, herds of deer wandered through the woods, browsing, standing still and blink-eyed, close to the people who soon got used to them. Between the cedars and the deer, the neighborhood in the woods had grown barren. Get ambitious, grab a shovel, ram it into the ground with all your might, and you hit bone crushing, spine rattling limestone. There was no soil, just a deceptive layer of rotted leaves. Even native plants that deer were supposed to despise disappeared. The serious gardeners fenced their lots, acres to a half-acre, brought in truckloads of topsoil, threw in their old vegetables and fruit composted to richness, and made a garden and a lawn so that, driving along, you saw the brown of the deer territory, the green claimed by the people.

Most people lived with the devastation or tried to establish shrubs and plants the deer would ignore. Deer families crossed the roads in their perambulations, and the people who lived in the woods soon learned that when a fawn crossed, the doe wouldn't be far behind. The does were cautious and the fawns were not, so you had to wait and wait to be sure you could drive on. Somewhere, watching over the enterprise, might be the buck who crossed even more slowly, bearing the weight of his antlers. Strangers to the roads or impatient residents hit deer; sometimes the careful drivers did as well. The deer flung themselves suddenly out of the woods onto the path of the car or stood waiting to be killed. The worst was when one limped off, for the deer would die if lame and unable to browse.

When they first moved to the neighborhood, Josh liked to play in the woods with his friends. Carlotta would sit on the deck, reading and listening for their voices. Once, the boys came running back to the house, excited. They'd found an arrow! It was a deer arrow, a rigid steel shaft with razor blades embedded at the tip. Carlotta reached for it but Josh wouldn't let go and for a terrible second it seemed that his hand was grasping the razor blades. He finally relinquished it and she promised to keep it in a safe place. She talked to other mothers, and they too worried about letting the children loose, for other children had found cruel arrows. It was illegal to hunt there but that didn't seem to stop anyone. A few women also confirmed what Carlotta thought she'd mistaken: the report of guns.

Josh had spotted the arrow first, so it was his, and he wanted to keep it in his room, which his mother wouldn't allow. He thought of taking the arrow to school for sharing time, but Carlotta wouldn't let him carry it on the bus. She drove him to school herself and insisted on carrying the arrow to the classroom. She stood at the door and watched as Josh held the arrow above his head so everyone could see and told the class where he'd found it. All the kids wanted to touch it.

When she moved to the woods, Carlotta left fruit for the deer but a neighbor convinced her that she would only attract opossums and raccoons who would invade her house, so she stopped. She grew used to the sight of fawns staring at her as she got the mail in the afternoon, the mothers looking protective and fearful. The same neighbor told her that once in the spring a rutting buck had attacked a woman, but Carlotta and Ben decided that was ridiculous. They heard that a buck had gored a dog, a yellow Lab, and they couldn't decide if that was true or not.

Their house was anchored to the side of a valley, and their steep half-circle of a driveway led down to their carport and climbed back up to the road. One night when Carlotta, Ben, and Josh first moved there, before she was used to the sharp incline, she left her car parked up by the mailbox. In the morning, when she went up to get the newspaper, she saw that her left passenger window was shattered. The police came, took pictures for the insurance company, and told her the window had been shot out. The back seat and floor were riddled with glass. There were tiny pieces everywhere, even up front on the driver's seat and in the sun roof. The estimator at the body shop didn't ask Carlotta what had happened, but when he gave her the bill a week later he said that all the guys in back wanted to know what she looked like.

Carlotta figured that the person who shot her car was after the deer but then there was a rash of mailbox tippings. During a morning walk when Josh was safely in school, she saw a rugged stone column with a regulation U.S. postal box embedded, lying on the ground like a one-eyed giant with rigor mortis. High school kids, her neighbors said. It was a fad. Carlotta didn't believe it. Who had the strength to pull over something so heavy? It was possible with a pick-up truck, she was told, and she wondered again who had shot her car.

———

"I saw him," Josh said.

"Who?"

"Turn around, Mom. Look."

"I'm driving across the bridge, I can't turn around. Who did you see?"

"I don't know who he is," he said as if he were talking to the stupidest person in the world. "He's standing there."

"It's raining so hard, sweetie. Who would stand there? Maybe you thought you saw a man but it was really a tree."

The boy had quick eyes and often saw things the parents couldn't: a clown in the middle of an oilfield, tiny birds against the sky.

Josh wished she would turn the car around so he could look again but he knew she wouldn't.

"Do you want to read the book aloud to me?" she offered. And when he didn't answer, she asked, not in a friendly voice, "Well, do you?" Her voice startled her. When they quarreled Josh told her she was mean and now she recognized that he was right.

When Carlotta was a child, younger than Josh, she lived in the country, ten miles from the nearest town, in a state where lawns grew easily and the deer stayed away from people. One summer day, family friends threw a party, and just below the house, tables were set up with five-gallon tubs of ice cream, and drinks. There were hot dogs and hamburgers, and a bar for the grown-ups. The gathering was larger than most of the parties her parents went to and there were people, grown-ups and children, whom she didn't recognize. Maybe it was the Fourth of July.

At some point, she walked down the sloping green lawn. When she got to the pond, she saw her father standing by the wooden shack where people changed for swimming, a dark place with its own musty smell. At the entrance was another man, the father of the girls

248

she played with most often, the host of the party. He was drying himself with a towel. Her father didn't notice her but the other man did.

"Get out of here," he yelled. "Go away!"

Her father turned and saw her for the first time.

"Go on, sweetie," he said. "Go find your mother."

She ran back up the hill as fast as she could. Her heart was pounding. She had done something wrong but she didn't know what.

The man had been naked, drying himself, and he thought she'd seen him. But if he didn't want to be seen, why was he standing out in the daylight? It reminded her of something in the Bible.

Why had she gone down the hill? Had her mother asked her to find her father? She couldn't remember and her mother was dead, so was her father, for that matter. The only one left was the man and he was too mean to ask, even if she thought he would remember the moment.

Why hadn't her father defended her? He could have said, *Don't yell at Carlotta,* or *No need to shout,* but he hadn't. *Go find your mother. Go on, sweetie.*

The endearment didn't matter because he used it all the time and she barely heard it. She recalled the other man's voice, harsh and unfriendly all the way back up the sloping lawn.

Carlotta tried to stand again among the party-goers, near the tables with the abundance of the sweet ice cream she loved. Everyone was taller than she. All she could see were their legs. Why had she gone down the hill? Why was she looking for her father?

"It wasn't a tree, Mom, it was a man."

"I can't turn around now, Josh. We're almost home, it's dark, it's raining. Your father's away." Then, "Tomorrow, we'll go back and look."

She promised him things all the time to put him off, to quiet him, to try to forestall his disappointment or disagreement. She didn't like the idea that he was seeing a man in the woods. It might be real, it might not. Homeless people lived in the woods on that side of the river (on their side, too, she suspected), or so she'd heard. The police patrolled all the time, and strangers, homeless or not, certainly strangers on foot, would be questioned and, probably, escorted back to the other side of the river.

Josh didn't argue with Carlotta, though he knew that, even if she remembered her promise, it would be useless to return the next day. Tomorrow the man wouldn't be standing there. Who would stand in the woods all day and all night?

At home, in bed, Josh read what he had to in his book about Texas. They were studying Quanah Parker's mother and the Comanches who'd kidnapped her and kept her for twenty-four years. When Josh finished his homework, Carlotta read him *Chicken Little*, a picture book with wild, extravagant drawings. Lately, Josh asked for books he'd liked years before. Ben tried to persuade him to read to himself, but Josh refused. He liked being read to before sleep, and Carlotta indulged him because she also clung to the comfort.

Carlotta sang to Josh, then fell asleep by his side. She awoke with a start and went to her own bed in the adjoining room. When Ben was away, Josh sometimes asked to sleep in her bed but he hadn't that night.

Carlotta tried to read her mystery but soon turned

out the light. Sleep was slow in coming, so she listened to the rain on the metal roof and wondered why her son was so fanciful. He was an only child, and he might imagine seeing things because he needed companionship. She had brothers and sisters and so did Ben, and they'd always wanted to be only children. She thought again of the party, the crowded lawn, going down the hill to find her father. She turned the light back on and tiptoed past Josh's door to the little room where they shelved their dictionaries and atlases, and returned with the Bible, but when she settled back into bed, she realized that there was no index to look up seeing someone naked. She read the Twenty-third Psalm. *My cup runneth over.* She turned out the light, and, still listening to the rain, fell into a dreamless sleep.

By the time Ben came home, the weather had cleared and a series of high blue days replaced the gray rainy ones. He and Josh went off quarreling for a walk every evening. The boy never wanted to leave the house but liked it once he got going. They visited a cat up the road whose name they knew from the tag around its neck. Carlotta was allergic to cats but she liked looking at them. She would have liked an outdoor cat. Ben was sure the cat would be run over or would disappear in the woods. Josh was content for the moment with his pet mouse. He didn't want a cat unless it could be everywhere in the house, curled up on every soft piece of furniture, and that would never happen.

While Ben and Josh walked, Carlotta finished cooking their dinner, chicken for them, chick pea soup for her. She didn't eat meat but Ben and Josh did. Josh wouldn't eat any green vegetables but he'd tolerate a carrot every day. Ben would eat green vegetables and meat, or no meat. He was glad someone else was cooking dinner.

On the way home, Ben and Josh met a neighbor who'd retired from the state insurance board and was now the Republican precinct chairman. He told them that mountain lion droppings had been spotted in the woods near their house. Yes, it was true. He said that mountain lions were strong enough to haul off small children and then he looked at Josh who was big for his age and said, "This is what the neighbors are saying. There's probably no danger."

"It would be natural if there was a mountain lion," Ben said. Out West there were mountain lions that came down to the town when they were hungry enough. "There's all this food walking around. Not you, Josh."

When they got home, they told Carlotta about the mountain lion and she told Josh not to play outside for a few days.

"Yes," said Ben, "until the rumors die down."

Carlotta had trouble sleeping again and, in the nature of things, she began wondering if they were giving Josh the childhood he deserved. He might be happier in a flat place where he could ride his bike and visit neighbor kids and develop autonomy. The kids who lived in the woods depended on their parents for rides and couldn't wait until they could drive. This made the roads even more dangerous than the natural curves and inclines did, because you never knew when a sixteen-year-old in an SUV was going to come hurtling at you.

But the school district was so good. They might move to a house in a flatter part of the neighborhood but that would entail doing everything to their house that needed to be done before it could be sold and then doing the same to the next house, and who was to say that they would like it? The noise of the highway could be heard over there. Where they were now, you heard cars from the road below but mostly birdsong and kids calling from across their little valley.

She found her robe at the foot of the bed and pulled it on, draped the comforter over Ben who had kicked it off and she felt around and found the Bible on the floor where she'd left it. She hesitated at the door of Josh's room which glowed like an aquarium with the green of his favorite nightlights, small wafers he plugged into the wall, three of them so far. He too had kicked off his covers but he held them pinned beneath him so she unfolded a nap blanket and covered him with that.

Downstairs in the kitchen, she emptied the dishwasher and heated up a cup of milk in the microwave, then stirred in a spoonful of honey. She liked dark crude honey and this was refined and pale amber, and reminded her of the round jars of orange blossom honey her grandparents had sent from Florida every December in a crate of grapefruit. Every year she had tried it, hoping it would taste like oranges.

She looked up Genesis 9:22 as Ben, who had won a prize at Bible camp when he was Josh's age, had suggested. She read the whole chapter because the one verse didn't make sense. The first part was complicated and fearsome: the Lord told Noah to be fruitful and multiply and gave Noah and his descendants the Earth, pronouncing (truthfully) that the dread of man would be upon every beast of the earth, every fowl of the air, every fish in the sea. Everything moving on the earth would be food for man, and every green thing too. Man was made in God's image and human life was sacred except if killers were being killed, and that left a world of latitude. No more deadly flood but a covenant between God and man. Noah took up farming, planted a vineyard, got drunk on his wine, and lay naked in his tent. Ham entered the tent, looking for him innocently, Carlotta thought, some domestic errand, a question for his father, and saw Noah naked and asleep. Ham left the tent and told his brothers what he'd seen. They, savvy, put a cloak over their shoulders, entered the tent backwards, covered their father without seeing his nakedness, and left the tent, but when Noah woke up he somehow knew that Ham had seen him and cursed him and his descendants.

She wondered why she had remembered that verse: seeing his father's nakedness. Reading the Bible always gave her more than she'd sought and not exactly what she wanted. How had Noah known that Ham had seen him naked?

It seemed accurate that Noah was furious, waking up befuddled from the stupor of a drunken afternoon nap. It wasn't his nakedness, perhaps, but being seen unconscious and vulnerable, that made him so furious. The naked man had frightened her, and her father said, *Go find your mother.*

What had Ham wanted? What had she?

Carlotta took the sweet hot milk and went outside on the deck that hung over the valley. She saw the three radio towers on the farthest ridge, their red lights blinking, and the lights of the sports court across the way. The neighbors with the sports court always forgot to turn out their lights and once a year Carlotta called the city inspector and he went over and explained about the light ordinance. For a few nights they remembered and then they forgot again.

When she finished the milk she climbed back upstairs and waited again for sleep.

The next Saturday night, Ben and Carlotta went to dinner across the river while Josh played with the boy next door.

Their dinner hosts had moved to Texas from the Midwest, knowing only Carlotta and Ben, but they'd been here so long that they no longer asked for advice. They were invited everywhere. Carlotta wasn't sure if she was envious or not, which probably meant that she was. There was another couple at dinner, a droll woman who had once cut off the tip of her finger and since then kept only dull knives in her house. Her husband was a lobbyist. Toward the end of dinner he told a funny story about the governor, and then Ben and Carlotta went home. They drove through the quiet streets near the river, silent after the talk of the little party.

Carlotta asked Ben if he thought Josh was all right.

"Yes, he's all right," Ben said. "He's certainly sure of what he wants to do and doesn't. What do you mean, is he all right?"

"He sees things," she said.

"He's always seeing things," Ben said. "Remember—"

"I was wondering if he sees things because he's lonely. If he saw someone in the woods because he wants someone else there." She wanted to ask Ben if she'd been right to insist that they have a child so late. Not every life had everything it yearned for, she could have survived.

"There's no reason, Carlotta. Or no reason we'll ever know. He's a boy with great eyesight and an imagination. Just leave it alone. He's fine. He's a kid. That was pleasant tonight. I miss them when we don't see them. Why don't we see them more often?"

"We won't see them at all if we move all the way out west."

"We'll see them more. They'll visit. Everyone visits out there. We'll have to take numbers."

"They'll visit once," Carlotta said.

"The drive's not bad."

"Once you give yourself over to it, the drive's not bad. There are hours when you wonder, but eventually you relax. But most people, even Texans, consider driving eight hours each way for a weekend a bad drive."

"I haven't been offered the job, Carlotta. They only approached me about it. I don't have to take it if they offer it. There's a long way to go."

Mercury vapor lights cast an orange glow over the water. As Ben made the turn down to the bridge, Carlotta glanced up and saw a tree with something odd about it, a double trunk but the second trunk was a strange shape for a trunk, almost like a man but too still to be a man. Standing funny.

But then a car behind them passed illegally, in a big hurry to be over the bridge first, and she forgot what she'd seen.

Carlotta worked two days a week at a private school, teaching art to the oldest children who were beyond the age when they concentrated easily. They were more interested in each other, which Carlotta found restful. The school wanted her there every day but she wouldn't do that, and they wanted her to talk to the children about the creative process and she wouldn't do that either. She believed that the important thing she did for the children was to provide them with a large clean airy room, paper in interesting colors and patterns, scissors and glue, pencils and paint, and then set them a task that would engage their minds enough for them to start working. She loved the moment when one by one the children fell silent, looked at the paper, and recognized that it was a vast desert. The moment didn't last long.

After work, she rushed to her yoga class which met in a karate dojo at the edge of downtown. Sometimes during class they heard the rhythmic pounding and screams of practice sessions from the next room.

Her teacher started with the tree pose which Carlotta was sorry about because she wasn't any good at balancing poses. The tree required simultaneous groundedness, relaxation, and uprightness. The more effort she made, the worse she got. She had to have an awareness of her right foot on the ground, her right thigh working and flexed, not hyper-extending her knee as she wanted to. Her left foot was planted in her right groin, though it slipped and she had to lower her hands to correct it. She'd once asked her teacher why her foot slipped and he told her it was because she didn't have enough strength in her thigh to hold her foot up, which hurt her feelings. Now, years later, she saw that he was right because she could hold her leg up a little better. She backed up and used the wall so that her legs would get work even if she couldn't balance. From here she could see the class, each student standing upright on one leg, arms in front of the sternum, palms resting against one another, like dancers frozen in place. But were they like trees, she wondered, and tried to see them as a sparse forest. The tree part of the pose came from the foot rooted to the ground. Now her teacher was bending forward, his left foot still firm in the opposite groin. His nose was touching his standing calf. His hands were flat on the ground. He instructed them to stick their sit bones up in the air. She tried not to fall over. Once she succeeded in bending forward, then straightening her leg, she wondered how she would ever get up, which was fatal in yoga. To look ahead was to jinx yourself. Coming up, her hands still pressing together, she bent her knee and was able to rise with only a little help from the wall.

Repeating the pose on the left leg, the class looked more like trees, an esplanade of one-legged trees. This leg was easier. The whole enterprise felt easier to Carlotta. She lifted her body out of her hips. She balanced.

At the end of the class they lay on their mats and the teacher took them through a relaxation and as Carlotta sank into the floor, she remembered a trip with her parents to a large party somewhere by a lake in Pennsylvania. It had seemed like a terribly long way but it was probably only a few hours. Compared to the drive to West Texas, it was nothing.

The house was full of people and behind it a lawn sloped sharply down to a string of picnic tables by the lakeshore. She stuck with her mother who gravitated to the kitchen to offer help, but her mother struck up a conversation with another woman and Carlotta was handed a tray of glass dishes of red Jell-O. Alone among strangers she carried the tray across the flat part of the lawn, and then she started down, the Jell-O wobbling and glinting in the sun. The tray was heavy and when she reached the downward slope—Always in this part of her memory she told herself that her foot had slipped on the slick green grass, but this wasn't so. Her knees had trembled and the tray grew too heavy. She put one foot before the other carefully, carefully, until she came down too heavily on one foot and the rest was a disaster of glass bowls and glistening mounds of Jell-O.

On the way home there was a storm that was the beginning of a hurricane. A giant maple, as tall as the house, right outside her bedroom window, had been uprooted. When she lay on her bed, reading in the summer afternoons, she'd missed the particular green the tree cast into her room.

"That's it," her teacher said. "Clean up your mess. Go home."

257

———

Carlotta had to go to a dentist appointment, and after school Ben took Josh with him to the office where Josh drew pictures and Xeroxed them, colored them in, Xeroxed them again, and then played Math Blaster on a spare computer. On the way home, they picked up pizza for dinner. It was Wednesday evening so the juggler wasn't there.

Josh looked up again at the scruffy trees high above the river. The man was standing without moving, as tall as a tree.

"He's still there," Josh said.

"Who?"

"The man I saw. He's still standing there."

"What are you talking about?"

Ben didn't like the bridge. There were no guardrails on his right, only a barrier about a foot high. He wondered why no one drove off into the water. Ben had heard of boys diving from the bridge into the water thinking it was deep.

"I saw him standing there when Mommy and I got pizza. She wouldn't stop. She never stops."

Ben waited for Josh to say that Mommy was mean, ringing the triangle of their family. Carlotta was like a horse nearing the stable when she was heading home.

"Well," said Ben, meaning to say that he wouldn't stop either because the pizza would get cold, and then, no cars behind him, he pulled over between the bridges and parked.

They had often seen people walking across the bridge and spectators who came to watch when the floodgates were open, but they'd never walked on the narrow pathway that led over the bridge, inches from the passing cars. The cars weren't speeding, Ben thought, but they were so big and powerful that it would take only an instant of forgetfulness for one of them to hit Josh or him. He made Josh walk in front of him and they both tried not to look down into the churning water.

On the other side of the river, Josh pointed up. From below, the man was easy to see. He wasn't standing. He was hanging by his neck from the tree.

The man was in the woods, the way a deer was when pretending not to be there, still as the air, blending in, wishing itself away. If thoughts could cause invisibility, then he was invisible.

He hung quietly, hidden at first by the leaves, dressed in cloth the color of the winter trees, gray and brown, his skin long ago losing its living redness and turning the same parchment color as the trunks when the sun hit them toward sunset. Even the rope, plain rope from the hardware store, soon blended in, and if the boy had not seen him, then the rope would eventually have grown moss and rotted and become part of the woods. The animals had been at him, of course.

"You stay here," Ben said. "Don't cross the road. I'm going up to look. Don't move, do you understand?"

"Yes, sir," Josh said.

When there was a break in the traffic, Ben ran across and stood for a moment, figuring how to get up the sharp bank. Then a path seemed to appear, rocks for him to step on, roots that he could grasp, and he made his way up, hand over hand.

There was a lot of noise, water and cars like two great herds crossing paths, but it was peaceful on this high lookout. Ben saw the water, the woods across the river, and the darkening sky.

The tree from which the man hung was near a chain link fence and the parking lot of a building housing the river commission. People used to design low buildings along the river.

Ben fought down nausea and listened to the ringing in his ears. When he could, he made his way back down to Josh.

The water had just come to a boil and Carlotta was looking in the refrigerator for the chunk of parmesan she'd bought last week and for the tomato sauce she'd made on Sunday but she couldn't find either. She was wishing she'd asked Ben to pick up some spinach pizza for her when the phone rang.

The police didn't want Ben and Josh to leave even though Ben pointed out that they knew nothing. Traffic was stopped on both sides of the bridge, backed up into the city.

Carlotta was allowed to walk across the bridge when she insisted, "That's my son, I need to get over to him," pointing to Josh who looked very small behind the police barricade. Josh flung himself at her and hugged her as he hadn't in a long time, but then he stood away from her and said, "I told you."

"You were right, honey," she said. "But it was raining so hard."

"It's getting dark," Josh said.

"They'll let us go soon," Carlotta said. "Won't they?"

"Don't look," Ben said.

Standing here, below the cliff, she could see the hanged man clearly now, surrounded by the policemen in their bright rubber jackets and the EMS men. She had ignored him the first time she saw him, she had decided she hadn't seen him, but he had been there all along.

"Don't look, Josh," she said.

"There's nothing to look at," he said. "I saw him first, remember?" but he held her hand until a policeman came to them and said, "You folks still here?"

She watched over Josh night after night, as she hadn't since he was an infant, waiting for a sign that the whole adventure was bothering him. And why shouldn't it—a hanged man by the river? She was proud of him of course and that was what she and Ben emphasized, that Josh had been sharp-eyed to see him in the first place and correct to tell about what he'd seen. If Josh hadn't told, then the poor man would still be there.

The man's obituary appeared a few days later in the paper and they searched it for a clue. He had been missing since autumn. He had a child of his own and a wife. His parents lived in a neighborhood at the northern edge of the city. The obituary didn't mention where he'd worked. Obituaries in the local paper were written and paid for by the families of the dead and contained few revelations. There was no news story. Ben said that he must have been crazy, although they'd never know. He'd been missing for ten weeks. Carlotta and Ben figured that he'd been there about six weeks when Josh first saw him.

Ben was furious with the man for showing himself to Josh and doing God only knew what to the kid and to him, to Ben, who would never forget the sight.

"Why did I have to see that?" Ben asked. "Why did Josh? Someone was going to find him sooner or later, and I guess he just didn't care who it was."

The next morning, while they waited for the school bus up by the mailbox, Carlotta asked Josh if he was going to tell his friends about finding the man. He said that he didn't know, he hadn't thought about it, and she wondered if that was true. Usually he liked to tell his news but maybe this was too big or gruesome. Maybe Josh just wanted to forget it. The bus came and she told Josh, as she always did, "I'll be here when you come home." She waved to the driver and the big yellow school bus lumbered off down the road.

She was sorry for Josh and Ben and for herself, that, as Ben said, they'd seen what they had, and she felt the horror of the man's family that they had slept all the nights he was missing, that they had gone on living when he hadn't. All along he had been waiting for them to come and cut him down, and they hadn't been the ones to find him.

Still, these sensations were the privilege of the living and no lon-

261

ger his to feel. Thinking of him alone, as a man who'd lived and now was dead, Carlotta felt glad for the man, and she considered that he'd chosen well for himself, the high bank over the river, the beautiful view of the woods.

Laura Furman
is the author of a
memoir, *Ordinary
Paradise*; two novels,
*Tuxedo Park* and
*The Shadow Line*;
two short story
collections, *The
Glass House* and
*Watch Time Fly*. She is co-editor, with
Elinore Standard, of *Bookworms: Great
Writers and Readers Celebrate Reading*.

Her fiction and essays have appeared
in *The New Yorker*, *Mirabella*, *House & Garden*,
*GQ*, *Ploughshares*, *Southwest Review*, *Threepenny
Review*, *Yale Review*, *Glamor* and others.
She was the founding editor of *American
Short Fiction*, and has been awarded a
Guggenheim Fellowship and a Dobie-
Paisano Fellowship. She has received the
Jesse H. Jones Award for fiction from the
Texas Institute of Letters. She and her
husband, Joel Warren Barna, and their
son make their home in Austin, Texas.